JOHN L. MONK

FOOL'S RIDE

BOOK TWO OF THE JENKINS CYCLE

This is a work of fiction. Names, characters, businesses, places, events and incidents are either the products of the author's imagination or used in a fictitious manner. Any resemblance to actual persons, living or dead, or actual events is purely coincidental.

FOOL'S RIDE

Copyright © 2014 by *John L. Monk*
All rights reserved.

Cover Design by Yocla Designs

This book may not be reproduced in whole or part, by mimeograph or any other means, without permission. Making or distributing electronic copies of this book constitutes copyright infringement and could subject the infringer to criminal and civil liability.

ISBN-13: 978-1530502653
ISBN-10: 1530502659

For Dorothy

ACKNOWLEDGMENTS

I'd like to thank my wife, my beta readers, my editors, and all you wonderful readers for making *Fool's Ride* possible. Special thanks to Rob for weathering that lightning storm in the shrimp boat with me while I shook my fist at the sky. Also, thanks to T in Carolina for digging me. I dig you too.

JLM

ONE

Sitting in a chair in a glassed-off room, newly arrived from my exile in the Great Wherever, I contemplated the patio party going on outside. Not a wild party. No drinking games or Jell-O wrestling. No togas or double secret probation. This was one of those hold your drink and chat parties.

There were two large men in the room with me: one white, one black, both dressed in suits. A slender blonde in a tight red dress stood nearby, alternating between watching me, the two men, and a skinny man in jeans and a checkered shirt standing by the door to the patio. The man had a book tucked under his arm, and he watched me as if waiting for something.

I smiled.

He smiled.

Behind him, on the other side of the door, a line of people stretched about twenty feet.

"You ready, Ernest?" the black guy said. He had a friendly voice and a patient expression.

The white guy didn't look at me—he was watching the man with the book. The woman cocked her head at me but didn't speak. Her face was triangular, like a praying mantis. Thin lips, and a spiky Tinkerbelle haircut.

Looking from her to the guy who'd asked if I was ready,

I shrugged and said, "Sure."

"Okay," he said to the skinny man. "You're first."

The man whipped out his book and sprang forward as if jerked by invisible strings.

"Mr. Prescott, sir," he said when he got to me, his voice shaking. "What an honor. I've read all your books. Oh my god, I can't believe this is real. Sir, I'm a writer too—not like you—you're so good, inspiring, I just want to thank you. I read *Terror Calls* before *Terror Stalks,* but it was fine. Everyone said to read *Terror Calls* second, but I remember what you said in that *New York Times* interview about how you thought *Terror Calls* made more sense to read first, even though it was the second in the series, so I waited and then ... Wow, it's just so nice to meet you."

He placed the book he was carrying onto the table with the cover facing up.

The book had a picture of a skull taped with electrodes. A translucent image of a woman's face was molded over the skull, her expression a mask of agony and terror. Across the top, in jagged blue-and-white lightning letters, blazed the title: *Electro-Cute*. Some kind of horror book.

I swept my gaze from the breathless man with so much to say, to the book, and back again.

"Good," I said. "That sounds great."

When he just stood there and didn't go away or start talking again I said, "Thank you?"

The man nodded, still smiling, gazing at me in adoration, and that's when I noticed the pens on the table. There was also a big stack of *Electro-Cute* books off to my right.

"Ah," I said, finally getting it.

The Great Whomever was getting bored again.

Knowing I was lucky to be alive, I picked up one of the pens, opened the book to the title page, and then paused. I couldn't sign my ride's name, not believably.

The name on the book was "Ernest Prescott." I checked in the back to see if he'd inserted an afterword or something that would show me his signature. It had an afterword, but no signature. Only initials.

"One second," I said, and fished out my ride's wallet.

Using Ernest's New York driver's license as a guide, I did my best to scrawl his signature onto the title page of the man's book.

"What's your name?" I said to him.

He'd given me a funny look when I pulled out the license, but here I was ready to sign and everything was okay again.

"Richard," he said, beaming at me.

Keep writing, Richard! I wrote underneath the signature, then slid the book back across the table to him.

"Thank you so much, sir," he said. "I'm just so honored. Wow. Thank you!"

Richard trundled off, clutching his signed copy like a treasure chest overflowing with chocolate bunnies.

A young woman, all in black, wearing black lipstick and black eyeliner made up to look like she was weeping, approached and said, "Sign my books please?"

She looked like something from one of the *Hellraiser* movies, with cleavage. I happen to be a fan of cleavage. I wondered how long it took to get her hair, makeup, and cleavage to the perfect balance of cadaver and Elvira sexy, and if she ever went out normal or was she always like that.

"Uh ... whom shall I make it out to?"

"Nobody," she said in a bored tone. "Selling it on Ebay."

I had to smile. "A capitalist goth girl?"

Rolling her eyes, she said, "I'm not *goth*, I'm a *rivethead*. And I'm a woman, not a *girl*." She pushed her two books over to me. "They said we could bring two, so..."

Most of my rides over the years had been losers of one stripe or another. So it was interesting to me that I was in the body of an author—with rivethead fans, no less. I peered beyond her, outside to where the party was. An outdoor bar or restaurant, judging from the red exit signs over two of the doors, the built-in bar, and the open sky above. She was the only rivethead.

Pity.

"Can we hurry it up?" she said. "I'm sorry—my mom's waiting for me."

"Sure," I said, and signed both books.

She didn't say thanks when I closed the second book.

She scooped them both up and hurried out. Her mom was waiting, so that was okay. Considering how awful my signature must have been, I wondered how she'd pass them off as real.

Someone new stepped in to fill her place, also with two books. Another young woman, though quite normal looking.

"I'm Rachael," she said, bouncing a little and hugging herself. "You're amazing."

And that's how it went for the next three hours. There were people who wanted personalized inscriptions and those who only wanted my name. One guy tried to push his own writing on me, hoping I'd read it and make him famous, but the two guys in suits rushed him out after a whispered word from the slinky blonde mantis lady standing nearby. I wondered who she was. She watched everyone who came in, though mostly she watched me.

When I smiled at her to see if she'd smile back, she raised her hands, palms up, in the universal expression for, *What now?*

At one point, just when I began thinking about food, she showed up with a sandwich and fries and told the guard at the door, "Hold everyone for ten minutes."

I heard grumbling from outside, and a few people left. Which was fine—Ernest Prescott didn't need those kinds of fans. The fewer fans the better, because all that signing was tiring my hand out, especially the personalized stuff. One kindly old lady had me write, "We only slice the ones we love." It seemed important to her. She even misted up over it, like it had sentimental meaning.

I contemplated my sandwich—a BLT with fries, crinkle cut, and no ketchup. And a bottle of water. Domestic.

The sandwich was so good I chewed it slowly, savoring it—then quickly, when the slinky blonde who must have had a name looked pointedly at her watch and said, "Five minutes, Ernest."

After finishing it with time to spare, I realized to my chagrin I needed to visit the little author's room.

"Uh, hey," I said. "Where's the bathroom?"

She frowned at me like I was hopeless, then said to the

guard near my table, "Brian, be a dear and show Ernest where the bathroom is."

"Will do," he said, and took me through a door at the back of the room, then down a hall to another door with the word *MEN* on it.

"Be right out," I said, then went in and shut the door.

Electro-Cute had Ernest's picture inside the dust jacket, but I'd been so inundated with fans I hadn't gotten more than a few seconds to look at my new face. Now I did, up close in the mirror. Dressed all in black, Ernest looked to be in his early fifties. He had thinning, flowing silver hair, a pointy ducktail beard, and a flourish around his mustache that gave him a Faustian sort of appearance. For an author, he appeared highly recognizable, which I'm sure was intentional.

"What the hell did you do?" I said to the reflection.

I found his phone and checked the date—March 5, 2008.

"You're kidding me," I said.

I'd been away a long time. Almost six months since my last ride.

The most I'd ever been away from the world was about three months, and that was because I'd been going through a pouty period and let every portal go unanswered. Eventually the lure of doughnuts and television had gotten too tempting and I'd broken down and taken the next portal that came along. That first trip back had been a particularly good ride, with season tickets to the Orioles—almost like the Great Whomever was apologizing.

I wondered if the passage of half a year meant I'd get another cakewalk ride. And then I wondered if I'd get cake.

TWO

When I got back to the glassed-off signing room, the line hadn't shrunk any like I'd hoped. In fact it had grown. I noticed most of my fans were women and wondered what that meant. And the men I met seemed a little ... intense. Some of the women, too, but mostly the men.

Ah well. If I ever got to meet J.K. Rowling, I suppose I'd be intense too.

Ernest Prescott was clearly a major player in the horror field. I'd heard of him, seen a few of his books, but that was it. Considering my bizarre lifestyle—returning from death in the bodies of horrific people—I normally steered clear of the gruesome genre. Give me a heroic tale with a warrior and a spunky unicorn, throw in a beautiful princess and a daring quest, and I'd pay money for it. Then I'd giggle my way to the nearest cushy chair to read it.

Not for the first time, I wished my ride came with an instruction manual or residual memories I could draw upon. How did famous people act? I didn't know if I was supposed to smile or look around the room or stare straight ahead or wave at people.

Soon I discovered it didn't matter what I did. As each of Prescott's fans came up, I learned more about my ride. He was original and unique. He was different and interesting and amazing. He changed people's lives by showing them how bad the world was. All his jokes were funny. When he asked how they were doing, his fans seemed flattered that *the Ernest Prescott* cared how they were. I felt like shaking my own hand to see what it was like.

A creepy guy with facial tattoos said, "You opened my eyes to the truth."

The tattoos were designed to look like surgical stitches, and I wondered who would do something like that to his own face.

When I went to sign his book, he pulled a knife and lunged at me. I hadn't actually taken my eyes off him, and at the shine of the knife I pushed backwards to get out of the way. And because I wasn't afraid of dying and stuff, I also grabbed his wrist and jerked him hard into the table, slamming him against the edge and making him go, "*Oof!*"

Almost immediately, one of the guards tackled him.

The blonde woman who hadn't said much since I'd arrived yelled, "Don't hurt him, Brian! Be careful!"

Brian threw her an irritated glance, turned the man over on his stomach and materialized a set of handcuffs, which he used to restrain him.

"Not too tightly." she said. "If you hurt him he could sue."

"Yeah," I said, feeling left out.

"And you!" she yelled. "What the hell were you doing grabbing him like that? Trying to get cut? What if he'd hurt your hands?"

Nodding like I was following along, I said, "Then I'd sue *him*."

She stared hard at me for several seconds and then smiled, showing glittery white teeth. I could tell the smile wasn't for me, but for the crowd of people pressed up against the glass staring alternately between the subdued man and me. I raised a hand and waved at them—and they erupted in cheers and clapping!

I was a hit.

"I need to get out there," she said. "Don't do anything else if you can help it. Christ..."

She went through the door shouting for people to calm down.

One of the guards—the white guy whose name I hadn't caught—glanced at me, half smirking, and then turned away. The other one, Brian, held the knife guy down and watched the door. Five minutes later, a swarthy-looking man in nice clothes came in with two police officers behind him.

"What happened here?" one of the cops said. He had that air about him cops get: in-charge, powerful, indefatigable. He was a little husky too, and his bulletproof vest added to the effect.

"He attacked me," I said. "With a knife."

"Where's the knife?"

The smirky guard showed him where the knife was—resting on the floor where it had fallen after I'd done my cool move on the guy.

The other officer, a bit younger, said, "Someone said you grabbed him. Why'd you grab him for?"

"Instinct," I said. "I'm like a jungle cat sometimes. A tightly wound spring waiting to snap. You know how it is."

A brief smile flittered across his face. "Jungle cat?"

"Deadly when riled," I said.

While the blonde lady got rid of the crowd and shut down the party, the police asked the guards and me more questions. There wasn't much to tell them.

After the police left with the crazy guy, the woman told the guards, "Good work Brian, Sean. Bonuses for both of you. I'll let Jacob know."

They thanked her and left.

When we were the only ones in the room, she said, "You fucking idiot. What the hell was that ridiculous display? That's what those two are for. What if that man had a gun?"

She was sort of grumpy and presumptuous, almost like we were...

I examined my hands—no rings on these fingers. She had on rings, but I could never tell if a woman was married or engaged or simply liked jewelry. Not fair, but there you had it. If she was Ernest's wife ... well, I'd come up with something.

She stood there patiently, glowering at me, waiting for

me to explain myself like I was a child and not fascinating and amazing and interesting and wonderful like all my fans told me I was.

"Well, dammit?" she said.

It's an incredible feeling, sometimes, being so free I could do anything I wanted without fear of divorce or getting fired or whatever it was this woman thought she had over me. That's why I said, "Who do you think you are?"

Which was a good way to find out who she thought she was, as well as defend myself a little. There's something psychologically taxing about taking crap from strangers.

"I'm everything as far as you're concerned," she said. "Jacob and I dragged you out of that vanity-press shithole and we can put you back just as easily. Now pick up those fucking books and *let's go.*"

Who knew the publishing business was so tough? I couldn't imagine Stephen King or Dean Koontz putting up with this. But there was something about her attitude, the confidence with which she delivered her threats, which made me think she could back them up. I mean those fans were practically drooling over me. Ernest Prescott was clearly a big deal. Which meant I still had some power here no matter what she thought. Sure, she'd pulled Ernest out of his *vanity press shithole,* but it took work to build someone up, didn't it? Much easier to keep the talent happy than to irritate them.

There was way more going on here than what it appeared on the surface. So for now, I'd play it safe.

Nodding like she was right and I was wrong, I picked up the books and followed her out.

* * *

We exited the building at a messy intersection with roads slivering into each other to form a triangle: Vernon Street, Florida Street, 18th Street. I knew if I kept walking to my right I'd run into California Street. Sort of a happening area in Washington, DC, with restaurants and bars and people everywhere I looked.

This bugged me a little. My ex-girlfriend, Sandra, was way too close for comfort.

I'd gotten about as much resolution as I could hope for after learning Sandra was all right and living a normal life in Virginia—with Peter Collins. A jerk, sure, but he was her jerk, and it was none of my business. But now I had a problem. In addition to being my rival in college, Peter was also a former ride. Almost eight months ago, when I'd looked at his phone to check the date, his number was at the top of the display, and my spooky-perfect memory had captured every digit. So it was within my power to call him and find out how he was doing with his little drug problem. If he hung up on me, I knew where he lived. Being so close, I could go there easily and...

And that's what I was afraid of. That I'd show up and try to fix her life by scaring him away. Or maybe I'd screw up and wouldn't just scare him. Though I had no burning desire to harm Peter, I might feel differently if I saw him again.

Sandra had occupied so much of my existence—from my college obsession to all that guilt for killing myself and leaving my stupid carcass in her room to find.

I shook my head. That part of my life was over.

"What the hell's wrong with you now?" the woman said.

I unclenched my fist, unbit my lip, slowed my breathing, and looked at her.

Somehow, I hadn't noticed that she was good-looking in an older, platinum blonde, blue-eyed, slender sort of way. All the bases were covered: good bone structure, decent profile and all that ... But she wasn't doing it for me. All those checkmarks right down the list, and if she stood too close I'd hold my breath for fear of breathing in whatever was wrong with her.

A young Middle Eastern gentleman driving a limousine pulled up to the curb. He got out, came around to our side, and opened the door for us.

"Mrs. Sandway," he said, courteously.

"Thank you," she said, with no warmth, and got in.

He smiled at me. When I got in beside her, he shut the door, walked back around, and off we went.

Mrs. Sandway was still making with the angry vibe, filling the space with its tiresome heaviness. To escape that and pass the time, I looked out the window. It was fun watching the different people going about their day-to-day. The tourists, the business types with their building badges, the homeless people everywhere being deliberately ignored.

Out of nowhere she said, "When the story breaks, you'll seem more interesting than ever. You might even make CNN. If that happens, our sales will skyrocket. But Ernest." She gave me a withering look. "Don't do that again. And seriously, what the hell? Since when do you go hands-on like that?"

I shrugged. "You only live once."

She frowned. "That's another thing. Don't challenge me in front of the boys. Stick to the script and everyone's happy. I'll tell Jacob ... something." She barked a harsh, scornful laugh. "He'll probably congratulate you. You need to be the grownup. Another of those lunatics tries something, move away."

"Will do," I said.

The car stopped. We'd arrived outside a big Marriott hotel.

"We're here," she said. "I didn't want to be there all day, anyway. Those events are worse than useless. Soon we won't need them."

I nodded.

"I trust you can get on your plane by yourself without fighting anyone, right?"

"I'm a big boy now," I said. "No worries."

She smiled. "Jacob and I are working on something big for you. For your next book. Until then, keep to yourself, and when you're at the airport tomorrow and you're photographed: *be mysterious.* It's expected."

The driver went around and opened the door for me. I got out and stepped back. When I peered through the tinted window she was on her phone, head high, talking-talking-talking, not listening, somehow turning even ordinary activities into something dismissive. A black hole of relentless will.

She saw me looking and tilted her head.

Before I could wave goodbye, they drove off. And with

her departure, it was like this weirdly oppressive weight had been lifted from me.

The first thing I did when I entered the lobby was visit the front desk. I got out my ID and put it on the counter.

"I forgot what room I'm in," I said when a lady came over.

"I'll check for you," she said in a sweet, pleasant voice.

It was such a pleasure to be spoken to like a human being I almost asked her if she'd seen any good movies lately, or was there somewhere good to eat in the nation's capital, or did she think people on other planets looked at our tiny light in the sky and wonder if someone was looking back.

"You're in 512," she said.

"Thank you very much."

I took the elevator to my floor and followed the arrows to my room. There was a room key in Ernest's wallet and it worked when I tried it. On entering, I found the bed tightly sealed in sheets and blankets. A laptop case and a suitcase were stacked on a sofa chair in the corner.

Someone had delivered a huge bouquet of flowers and four bottles of champagne on ice. I didn't care about the champagne, but the flowers helped banish the hotel smell of air conditioning and chemical freshness. A card was tucked into the bouquet, thanking me for choosing Marriott.

I searched Ernest's bags but didn't find an airline ticket. I felt a brief moment of panic and then forced myself to relax. I wasn't Ernest Prescott—I was Dan Jenkins. Dan Jenkins liked hotels and was afraid of airplanes. Not the whole dying part—the *about to die* part. All that screaming, having my fate taken so completely away from me for a short ride down to Earth in a giant hunk of metal. No thank you. If I needed to go somewhere, I'd rent a car.

I grabbed the hotel phone and called the front desk. A man picked up on the first ring.

"Guest services, how may I help you?"

"This is Ernest Prescott," I said. "Would you please confirm my checkout date?"

"Certainly, sir," he said, and the sound of a keyboard

carried over the phone. "Tomorrow morning, sir, but you don't need to check out. Just drop the pass in the box at the front desk and we'll take care of everything."

"Actually, I wanted to extend my stay a few days. Is that possible?"

"I'll check," he said, and I heard more clicking. "How long did you want to stay?"

"Two more days?"

"Thank you," he said, and subjected me to more clicking. "If you don't mind moving your room tomorrow, we can put you up for the remainder of your stay just down the hall. King-sized bed, non-smoking. How's that?"

"Sounds great," I said. "Thank you very much."

"Certainly, sir. Just call Guest Services before moving and we'll set you up with new room keys and help you with your luggage."

I thanked him again and hung up.

Rather than fly and risk dying in a fiery crash, I'd rent a car and drive to Ernest's address in New York in style. In two days. For now, I was in charge of my destiny and it felt great. But something told me Mrs. Sandway wasn't going to be happy with me.

THREE

I stayed in my room for the remainder of the late afternoon and evening, hoping to catch up on television. There were a lot of great movies to rent. But as I was scrolling through all the stuff I'd missed since my last ride, I felt a small, halfhearted tug from my conscience. I'd made a gentleman's agreement with the Great Whomever that I'd work a little harder when I was back in the world—me being the gentleman. Now I was extending my stay in DC, when whatever Ernest had done was likely buried in his garden at his New York address.

I remembered my disastrous ride as Nate Cantrell, who lived not twenty miles away. I'd been so busy spending Nate's fortune and fornicating with his fiancée I'd gotten the poor guy shot. I partially blamed the Great Whomever for that one—none of my other rides had been good people, only Nate. Well, Peter after that—barely (drug habit, stole my girlfriend)—but Nate had been a major departure from the rinse-and-repeat cycle of life and death I'd become accustomed to.

With a feeling of dejection and a sense I should do something, I flipped through Prescott's book. What could be so great that it had capitalist rivetheads mingling with strange old ladies and knife-wielding maniacs? Despite my aversion to horror, I turned to page one and began to read.

It opened like an eighties slasher movie: college cheerleading squad en route to a competition, forced to detour through a creepy town filled with religious fanatics. Then suddenly, out of nowhere, shockingly, surprisingly, their bus breaks down in the middle of town, and the only mechanic in a hundred miles is a limping leering inbreedy guy. He offers to fix it if they're willing to "pay the price." Which, of course, they agree to pay—anything to get them back on the road the next day so they could make it in time for the competition.

I saw it coming a mile away. I wanted to shout at Rhonda, the head cheerleader who was secretly a lesbian, to stay out of the shower, but she wouldn't have listened. When it comes to taking showers alone in strange old hotels, cheerleaders are like moths to a bug zapper. Rhonda got in the shower, blood shot out of the showerhead, she screamed, and then she ran out. Or she tried to—the door wouldn't open.

The same thing happened to the rest of the showering, weed-smoking, boy-crazy cheerleading team, and all of them got locked in their rooms just like poor blood-soaked Rhonda.

By around the third naked cheerleader, I was getting into the story. Prescott, for all the clichés he was tossing around, had an engaging way with words, and his characters were funny or sad or human in all the right ways.

The story took an even darker turn when the doors to each room proceeded to open, one at a time, and that's when I got my first taste of what made Prescott such a popular horror novelist.

* * *

Veronica entered the dimly lit ballroom gripping the knife in front of her, desperately trying to remember she was the co-Captain and not some spineless freshman flinching through basket tosses and hurting people.

Suddenly the overhead lights came on, momentarily blinding her. When her vision cleared, she saw them. Unlike the other rooms she'd tried on that floor, hoping to find the girls so they could escape, this one had been unlocked. Now she knew why: the ballroom was filled with people.

There was a woman with red hair wearing a nurse's outfit, standing stiffly with her arms at her sides. Veronica's eyes widened and she stifled a scream. The woman's face looked to have been removed and then stitched back onto her skull. Except ... no, that didn't make sense. The photograph displayed on the easel next to her had the same red hair, but the face was different. A caption under the photograph read, "Vice."

A few feet away, the mystery of the missing face was cleared up when Veronica saw it stitched on another woman. Beside that corpse was a portrait captioned, "Versa."

Two women with their faces removed and switched. Vice Versa.

Veronica began to cry. She couldn't go back the way she'd come. The manager was out there with his suped-up cattle prod and electrified body armor. She needed to keep moving, but he'd strung a twisting pathway of razor wire through the room. From each jagged steel blade, a sinister unknown substance glistened, daring her to try and slip past.

Corralled by the deadly barrier and unable to turn back, Veronica moved forward through a parade of people preserved through taxidermy. They were all female, their faces masks of the terror they'd experienced before death.

Each woman was propped and positioned to awful effect:

A young woman with her musculature removed, turning her into a human stick figure with a normal-sized head. Her title read, "Bug."

An older woman suspended by a wire, her legs and arms sewn to her stomach so that they hung down. This one was titled, "Florero."

Another woman had been literally turned inside out in a red, gory display of viscera. Next to her was a photograph of an old black lady shopping in the produce section of a grocery store. Her caption read, "Healthy."

As Veronica went through the makeshift gallery, the razor wire narrowed to less than three feet wide, forcing her progress to a crawl and pushing her closer to the gruesome things.

It soon became apparent the manager had gone through a transformation over the course of his career. Near the back of the room, closer to the exit, the corpses were better preserved. Unlike Vice Versa, these had no accompanying portraits. Each had cardstock signs hung from their necks with names like "Audry" or "Waitress" or "Bookworm."

Sometime later, having reached the far exit, Veronica blinked dazedly. She'd come upon the last corpse in the collection.

"No," she said, shaking her head.

She sank to her knees, paralyzed with fear, revulsion, and pity for the doll-like figure of a young girl with platinum blond tresses. The manager had posed her daintily in a frilly white chiffon dress. Unlike the bodies of the women, there wasn't a mark on her. No hideous stitches or anatomical modifications. Her skin was white like porcelain, preserved through the awful alchemy of a master at the height of his talent.

The girl's sign read, simply, "Missing."

* * *

Despite my dislike of literature where children were hurt, I kept reading. The author focused his attention primarily on the college-aged cheerleaders. To my shame, he kept me reading throughout the night and into the early morning, when I eventually closed the book a little more than halfway through.

Sick to my stomach.

The manager turned out to be an insane taxidermy hobbyist with a plan to add the cheerleading squad to his collection, posing them with their severed heads and teased-out hair as pompoms. Awful stuff, but that wasn't the worst. The girls were electrocuted before they were stuffed—the voltage calibrated to kill slowly without setting them on fire. As the manager said, "The better to preserve your peppy beauty, my dears." In a special twist of psychological torment, he offered to spare anyone who volunteered to throw the switch.

Prescott's descriptions of the eventual torture of the switch-throwers, and the cutting and stuffing of the manager's "electro-cuties," were incredibly real—right down to the rainbow sheen of fried human skin floating in puddles of blood and urine. In my mind's eye, I saw each girl snuffed out while her friends watched in horror, awaiting their turns.

"Man," I said, getting up.

I put the book over on the table next to the TV and wiped my hands. Then I went and brushed my teeth again, feeling tainted and somehow used. I regretted having stuck with the book so long, because now that nasty stuff was in my head forever.

How anyone could write such books, let alone read them—avidly, adoringly, and then say they were "amazing"—was beyond me. Whoever read *Electro-Cute* wasn't doing so for the contrived cheerleader story, either. When Daphne told the girls she broke up with her boyfriend because "it just wasn't working out," nobody would confuse that with high literature. Ernest's stock and trade was snuff, pure and simple. Blood, gore, and humiliation. Terror, torture, and despair. And death. Up close, macroscopic, eyeball to skin.

Mrs. Sandway said she and Jacob had discovered Ernest—built him up, made him successful. I wondered what kind of people would willingly set loose something so awful into the world, and if I was expected to do something about it.

These weren't 3 a.m. questions. Besides, it was 4 a.m. I was tired and wanted to sleep, but I needed to get all the icky out of my head or I'd have nightmares.

I turned on the TV and flipped around for a while. Pundits arguing, infomercials, reality TV, music videos—I barely registered any of it, and the TV was still on in the morning when I woke up.

Yawning and feeling achy, I rooted through Ernest's suitcase and discovered he didn't have much in the way of variable attire. Black socks, black pants, black shirts, and nary a polo in sight. I supposed it went with the whole death and torment vibe, but it seemed a bit dull. After careful consideration, I chose a black shirt and some black pants, then went downstairs to the hotel restaurant and enjoyed four eggs, six strips of bacon, two Belgian waffles, and four tiny glasses of orange juice.

Halfway through my meal, a boy of about thirteen walked up and said, "Excuse me, sir, can I have your autograph?"

Mingled feelings of flattery and disgust warred within me as I contemplated the sandy-haired boy. He had a mesmerizing mohawk haircut. I'd always wanted a mohawk, but Mom hadn't wanted me to be cool so I never got one.

"You read my book?" I said.

"Well no, not actually," he said, then seemed to realize the potential for insult. "Sorry. But I totally saw *Sliced*. Way cool special effects. Don't worry, though—my mom made me close my eyes for the naked scenes. It's R-rated, so..."

"Is that right?" I said.

A woman in her forties came up behind the boy and said, "Hi, I'm Trish—it's so wonderful to meet you. Everyone at the office is reading your books. I hope Bobby's not bothering you?"

I shook my head.

Bobby held out a piece of paper and a pen—which I took, because that's what you do when people hand you pens and paper and stare at you with hopeful eyes. I signed it and handed it back to him.

Trish's voice grew stern and responsible. "What do you say, Bobby?"

"Thanks a lot, sir," he said.

"Anytime," I said.

When they left, I glanced around and saw everyone in the hotel restaurant staring at me. Some obliquely, some openly, but all of them collectively. It was a feeling quite unlike any I'd ever had before. In high school, I'd wandered the student-packed halls, unseen—a chubby ghost in no-name shoes. Every morning, before the bell, I'd arrive at class with moments to spare—as if hanging out with my friends had nearly made me late again.

Being the center of everyone's attention was a heady experience, and I liked it. Even if it was in the body of someone I might have to kill in the next few weeks.

FOUR

I'd almost forgotten I was supposed to switch rooms today. If the hotel made me wait until the afternoon, it'd mess up the exciting day I had planned.

A quick call to Guest Services set my mind at ease.

"They had you staying on five," the man said. "But if you don't mind going down a floor, you can move now."

"Wonderful," I said, and looked around at Ernest's luggage and books, his flowers and champagne. "I have a lot of stuff. The guy yesterday said I could get some help."

"Certainly, Mr. Prescott," the man said. "Anything for you. I'll send somebody up right away."

The way he said it, I was sure he knew what a big deal I was.

"Why thank you, my good man," I said.

"No problem at all, sir."

"Indubitably," I added before hanging up.

The move was quick and painless, and I tipped my bellhop a twenty. I had a rep to protect. I said *indubitably* to him, too.

After he left, I got out Ernest's laptop. Just my luck, the thing was password protected and wouldn't let me in no matter how many gross things I entered.

Undaunted, I went to the hotel Business Center, accessible with my room key, and sat down at one of the public computers. I searched online for any information about my ride, and it didn't take long to find something.

Prescott's admirers had whole websites devoted to his grisly horror novels. Numerous sites had fan fiction forums dedicated to his work. I clicked around and learned his latest movie, *Sliced*, was the impetus for a wildly popular fan fiction game called "What if she lived?" These were stories written about the characters in his books, particularly *Sliced*, where the reader got to imagine what life would be like if the main character had somehow lived past the ending. I skimmed some of the stories—lots of fantasizing from the victim's armless/legless/faceless/fleshless perspective, begging people to kill her (always female), hating humanity, turning into a monster herself, and a lot of hopelessness and sorrow and shame.

The forums covered every conceivable piece of trivia or Prescott-related news. It was there I figured out why that old woman at the book signing had wanted that macabre dedication, "We only slice the ones we love." It was a catchphrase from *Sliced*, the movie. Fans in the forum raged back and forth about its appropriateness because the line hadn't been in the book.

I abandoned the fan sites and searched for Ernest on Wikipedia, where I learned he'd gotten a B.A. in psychology and a minor in English literature. He'd then leveraged that into a marketing position at a non-profit association. In the evenings and on weekends, he wrote his first book, *Clench*, which he published through a vanity press that, in his words, "Made me pay for dinner and then dry humped me behind some dumpsters."

Things turned around for Ernest after he met Lana Sandway—fashion model turned soft-core porn star turned reality TV dominatrix. When her husband, an aging millionaire businessman, died amidst a flurry of tabloid speculation about his heart attack, she fed the frenzy by hooking up with Ernest, an unknown writer at the time. Claiming to love his work on an "intensely personal level," she purchased the rights to *Clench* and spent a fortune running full-page advertisements in newspapers around the world.

After a while, I browsed news sites and ran searches for other things I wanted to know, like who'd won the last World Series, random celebrity news, and searches on various people I'd ridden over the years. Not a lot of news there, mostly stuff I'd already read.

I hadn't checked my free email account in over six months. A lot of spam had accumulated in my time away. There was also a reply to the email I'd sent the minister, the ex-priest who knew about my strange afterlife:

Hello Dan. Your story was fascinating, if a bit tedious in places. What's this fixation of yours with food?

I'm disappointed in your treatment of Peter—and most of the things you've done, if I'm being honest. The more I consider your tale, the more I think you should stop coming into the world until you're ready to be responsible. Make no mistake: this tendency of yours to murder your "rides" is an evil. There's always another way.

I snorted quietly and typed a reply:

Easy for you to say, padre. I could recite your Bible back to you in reverse, so please don't lecture me about evil. Anyway, how's Nate doing?

Then I sent it.

There were three more emails from the minister, spaced months apart. The first one asked where I was. The second one *also* asked where I was, but he'd added more question marks on the end like he was shouting at me. The third one included a phone number and instructions to call him on my next ride.

Still smarting from being called *evil* and *tedious* in the first email, I decided I didn't want to talk to him. Also, I had a big day ahead of me: the Air & Space Museum, the Natural History Museum, probably not the Holocaust Museum, and oh yeah, walking up and down the National Mall staring at people. Because one can never get enough of that.

* * *

Though my feet were killing me, it had been a great day. I'd gone through the gem room at the Smithsonian twice. They had the Hope Diamond. Sort of interesting, seeing something cursed that didn't look like me. I'd half expected it to pulse with a ghostly light only I could see, but all it did was sit there. Big for a diamond, yet small for something so famous.

Later, while I was sitting on a bench wondering what those big plops of metal were out in front of the Modern Art Building, Ernest's cell phone kicked in with Chopin's funeral march.

Smiling, I hit the green button and said, "Hello?"

"You didn't get on your plane."

It was Mrs. Sandway—*Lana* Sandway.

"Hi, Lana," I said, trying it on for size and thinking I liked Mrs. Sandway better.

"This is a very important time for us. You need to stay reclusive, out of the public eye—except for book signings, of course, and anything else we come up with."

"Because of the movie?"

Talking over me, she said, "Jacob and the boys really did good by you this time. Just the thing to jumpstart your next book. You don't want them to think you're ungrateful, do you?"

This was the second time she'd brought up the mysterious Jacob. I hadn't found anything about him on either Ernest's or Lana's Wikipedia page.

"What's the surprise?" I said.

Lana chuckled quietly. "Now, Ernest: we *do not* talk shop over the phone. Be a dear and catch the next plane out. If you do as you're told, I might allow you to ... do what you want with me again ... and again..." Her voice lowered to a breathy purr. "And *again*."

"I was thinking of driving."

"You can't be serious?"

"Can too," I said.

"Are you feeling all right?"

I opened my mouth to answer but she cut me off.

"What's wrong with taking a plane?" she said. "Your driving record is atrocious, frankly. I'll be damned if I let you kill yourself out there. Do you *want* to be a bum again? We can arrange it. We—"

"Yeah, yeah," I said. "You pulled me out of that hole and

can put me back, totally got it. I'll go home when I'm ready. Say hi to Jacob for me—maybe let him beat you up or something?"

I hung up without saying goodbye and wondered if she'd call me back. She didn't. Probably be too submissive for a pro-dominatrix.

In retrospect, I knew I'd gone too far with that last crack. But for once, I really did feel in charge of this thing. The ride. I had the power here, not her. Whatever she had over the real Ernest didn't apply to me.

And yet, I knew I needed to check out Ernest's house, and maybe meet this Jacob character—if for no reason other than Mrs. Sandway held him in high enough regard to mention him again.

* * *

The next day, body aching from walking through all those museums, I slept late. When I got up, rather than going out, I forced myself to finish Ernest's book—hideous and predictable, pompoms and blood all over the place.

I wouldn't have minded more museums, but my feet hurt too much. Instead, I asked the lady at the front desk to call me a cab.

"Where's a good movie theater?" I said to the man who picked me up.

"What kind of theater?" he said in an accent I could have sworn was Nigerian.

"A big one," I said. "You know—lots of screens, stadium seats that recline, cup holders, clean carpets, ushers that tell people to shut up. Nothing but the best."

He smiled knowingly. "Ah yes, the Hoffman Center. But there is a small problem."

"What's the problem?"

"It is in Alexandria!" he said, laughing like he'd told a funny joke. "Old Town. I can take you there, but it will be thirty dollars. You want to go? You should! I love that place."

"Sounds like a plan," I said, smiling despite myself. He was sort of upbeat.

The ride out of the city was a blast. Most of the memorials had been too far to walk to on yesterday's hike, but my cabbie drove by the Lincoln and the Jefferson, and of course the Washington was visible the closer we got to the river.

I paid by credit card and tipped him my last twenty.

"When you want to come home," he said, "give me a call. I'll pick you up—no problem."

He wrote his phone number on the receipt and handed it to me.

"Thanks a lot ... Sam," I said, reading it.

He smiled cheerfully. "Don't forget."

The theater Sam had taken me to was enormous, with twenty-two screens spanning two levels. The polished granite floor was inlaid with famous quotes from movies like *The Godfather* and *Casablanca*. A pair of glass-walled escalators ascended to cinematic heaven, providing visitors a close-up look at the huge movie panels of James Dean, Marilyn Monroe, and other iconic stars from movie history. Easily the coolest theater I'd ever seen.

If Sam kept his promise and picked me up, I'd write him a bigger tip.

Despite having read one of Ernest's books and finding it appalling, I was curious about his movie. Maybe it wasn't as sick as *Electro-Cute*. Maybe the producers had tamed it some. After all, hadn't that woman at the restaurant let her son see it? And weren't some of my favorite movies pretty violent?

Giddy like a kid staying up to watch Creature Feature, I bought my ticket to *Sliced* and sat five rows from the front with a big bag of popcorn—butter in the middle and on top—chocolate-covered raisins, and an enormous Coke.

No napkins.

The previews were for more horror movies. None of them seemed particularly scary, though the crowd gasped in all the right places. The audience was a little noisy at first, lots of talking and inappropriate laughter, but when the movie began they quieted down.

The basic plot was: an interrogation specialist for the US government, working overseas, returns home after the War on Terror has been retired as a foreign policy. But something's happened to him—he can't quite let go of the things he's seen and done. Sort of like Rambo, but with a government torturer instead of a Green Beret with amazing pecs.

The interrogation guy returns home to his surprisingly large family, and he's happy to be there—at first. Over the course of a few days, he begins snapping at his wife and kids, accusing them of things. Deep down, he suspects they're all involved in a terror conspiracy. He abducts them, one by one, secreting them to an abandoned government warehousing facility.

Then came scene after scene of cutting, agony, and cruel depravity, carefully orchestrated to wring the maximum emotional effect from the audience. No slice was too deep, no rip too excruciating, no desecration too degrading.

Other than that little bit near the front about the government guy coming home and going crazy, there was no movie. Just torture scenes, back to back, endlessly. And the daughter we sort of liked in the beginning because she was sweet and pretty and kind to animals—she has her jaw surgically removed. Then she's given a razor blade and a mirror and told she can live if she wants to.

Spoiler alert: she doesn't want to.

I sat through the whole thing, waiting for a plot that never happened. When the credits stopped rolling, I noticed my popcorn and candy remained untouched. I flinched a little at the sound of clapping—from the audience. I wanted to stand up and yell at them or something, but held off. It wouldn't do any good, and when it got out that *the* Ernest Prescott had gone to his own movie and made a scene, all I would have done was bring the film more publicity.

As I made my way to the aisle to dump all my uneaten junk food, I saw a curious sight: the audience was still sitting down. Mystified, I watched them watching the credits. Perhaps four minutes later, after the world's most boring credits ever, the screen changed.

The killer's son from the beginning—the one who'd been too busy in the big city to see his dad—called and left a message: he'd finished his project early and was coming home on the next flight. Family was too important, he said.

Cut to the goose bumps and rueful laughter from the breathless audience, and ready the sequel for more of the same. Even the red glowing eyes from the Terminator's robot skull had been a better sequel teaser, and nobody had to wait four minutes to see it.

Somewhat surprised at how awful the experience had been, I left the theater. For the life of me I didn't know what the Great Whomever wanted. So far, there wasn't anyone for me to kill. He couldn't want me to kill the guy for being a depraved writer, could he?

I wouldn't kill someone for that. Shun him, maybe. Talk bad about him. Point him out in public and hurl insults and boycott his movie merchandise, sure. But kill him? I saved stuff like that for rapists and murderers and the monsters who hurt children.

Ernest's movie and books were dumb and sad and they weren't real. Maybe a copycat would get inspired and try to hurt someone, like that idiot at the book signing with the face tattoos and the knife. But if such meanness could inspire a person to violent acts, they'd find a way to hurt people anyway.

Until I learned more, Ernest Prescott was safe from the likes of me.

FIVE

All right, fine, I wasn't completely dense, or new to the game. I fully expected to show up at Ernest's house in a few days and find lampshades made from human skin, severed heads in the freezer, piles of corpses buried in the back yard, and basic cable television. But my adventures as Nate Cantrell had taught me the wisdom of not jumping to conclusions. Maybe the Great Whomever was getting creative again and Ernest was innocent, just like Nate had been.

For now, I'd keep my conclusions under control and my eyes sharp for clues.

It was almost dark when I left the theater.

Sam the cabbie answered on the first ring. "I'm at my friend's house. I will be there in ten minutes, not to worry."

Though I loved how sincere and willing he seemed, I hated interrupting the poor guy on his time off. True to his word, he was outside the theater in almost exactly ten minutes. The mark of a professional.

When I sat down in the back seat, he looked in the rearview mirror and said, "You going back to your hotel?"

I pursed my lips in thought. "Well..."

Sam turned around and smiled at me from between the headrests. "You want to see the monuments? Go to Georgetown? All the clubs?"

"Nothing so strenuous," I said. "Tell me something—are you allowed to drive around Virginia? You know, anywhere?"

Sam laughed. "That's all I do on the weekend, back and forth to the city, with so many people drinking."

I gave him an address in Centreville I couldn't forget even if I wanted to.

"No problem," he said.

Along the way, we talked about the years he'd spent in France, his coming to the United States, and about his son, who was in the Marines. I'd been right—Sam was from Nigeria. It had me wondering what would happen if I ever left the country in a ride. So far, every ride had been within one of the fifty states. There was still so much about my condition I didn't understand. Maybe I'd cross over international waters and get kicked out?

When we got to Sandra's house the sky was dark. I asked Sam to wait over in the roundabout beneath some trees and keep the meter running.

"Take your time," he said pleasantly. "I have my music."

I thanked him and strolled to the front door like a good little stalker, wondering what the hell I was doing there—the last place I should be. Why not ring the doorbell? I rang the doorbell. A minute later, when nobody turned on the light and opened the door, I rang the bell again. An *insistent* stalker.

If Sandra answered, I'd say I was lost, hope I hadn't disturbed anyone, do you know where such-and-such street is? Is this even Centreville, or did I mess that up too? Whatever it took to keep the conversation going. If Peter answered, I wouldn't hit him. I wouldn't yell stuff about haunting him and burning little holes in his brain like I'd done before. I'd be polite, sophisticated, a credit to my upbringing.

But nobody answered.

I tiptoed to see through the glass over the door, but it was too dark inside. Leaning back, I saw the curtains were closed. They were the same ones from last time. If Sandra and Peter had sold the house, the new owners would change the curtains, wouldn't they?

The street was mostly dark but for the lampposts in front of the houses, only half of which had working bulbs. The one in front of Sandra's house had been lit last time, but now it was out. Almost like a sign.

A car drove past and parked over near Sam's cab. It wasn't facing my way, and no more cars came behind it.

The chances were slim Sandra and Peter had left a key under the doormat. Sure enough, when I looked, there wasn't one. I checked the little ledge above the door, but there wasn't one there, either.

I'd almost convinced myself this was crazy and I needed to go when I noticed the flowerpot. It was sitting on the top step leading to the front door. In addition to dried twigs from last year's flowers, there was a black rock about the size of a baseball sunk partially into the soil.

"You gotta be kidding me," I said, and plucked it out. Remarkably light for a rock that size, and it rattled when I shook it.

I opened the rubber seal in the bottom and took out a brass key. Peter's handiwork, I figured, endangering the family by hiding a house key in the third likeliest place a burglar would look. Lucky for him I didn't want to steal anything.

I slipped inside and shut the door.

There hadn't been an alarm last time I was there, and I didn't see a console on the wall. Even after my shenanigans at that coffee shop and my note left in his busted-up briefcase, Peter still hadn't thought to put in an alarm.

Peering around the familiar townhouse, another line crossed in a long list of transgressions, I noticed everything seemed in order. The same family pictures were on the wall, so Sandra and Peter clearly hadn't moved. There were a few changes since last time—a new dining table and a painting with horses running on a beach. If they were buying new tables and artwork they had to be happy, didn't they?

I thought about taking the picture with me when I left, or moving the furniture around like someone had been there. Maybe *then* they'd get an alarm—a good idea for a family with kids, living in a neighborhood with burned-out streetlamps. In that sense, my breaking-in wouldn't be so bad, now would it?

I left the painting alone and proceeded cautiously through the house like a ghost, hating myself for being there but unable to move on. Though I thought I'd come to terms with my feelings for Sandra, I was still the guy who couldn't forget anything, and those old obsessive feelings from college were as sharp as the day I'd first felt them.

"Poems are made by fools like me," I said.

I knew they had two kids, though I'd only met one of them: Danielle, who I thought of as my namesake, though I suppose it could have been a family name. Cute kid, looked exactly like her mother.

When I got to Danielle's room and peeked inside, I saw she had her own computer. I questioned the choice, what with online predators. Hopefully Sandra had installed all the proper software.

Sandra and Peter's bedroom looked the same as last time. The covers on the bed were neat on Peter's side, messy on Sandra's, and something about that made me smile—a human touch from my favorite human.

There was a book on Peter's nightstand.

Still unsure of what I was looking for, I went over and picked it up. Some kind of self-improvement book, written by a man with great hair who knew the power of positive thinking. A look at the back showed that in addition to curing gambling, infidelity, and overeating, the power of positive thinking would guide the reader down the path of a drug-free life.

More self-improvement books crowded the lower part of the nightstand, along with others I found particularly shocking: Peter was reading about angels. Not fiction, either, or not sold as such. This was testimonial stuff from people who'd had near death experiences, or people who'd gone through adversity and claimed an angel had flapped down and helped them.

I laughed. Peter the atheist was reading about angels. Did he think *I* was an angel?

Though I needed to get out of there as soon as possible, I ran back to the kitchen, grabbed a pen from a short ceramic jar on the counter, then hurried back to the room. I opened the only book with a bookmark and wrote in the empty space at the end of his current chapter:

Dear Pecker Colon,

Very proud of your progress, keep up the good work.

Pecker Colon was my nickname for Peter in college. Mean and silly, sure, but it'd reinforce the idea I'd been here and not some rogue book defacer.

I closed my eyes and thought carefully about my next words. I really was proud of him, and I felt guilty for the way I'd treated him in college, and again when I'd shown up and freaked him out so much he'd turned to Tony Robbins and Dr. Phil for help.

I wrote:

Just curious, but why does Danielle have a computer? At her age? Why not get rid of it? I mean you're her dad, I get it, but the world's a dangerous place. Did you know your lamppost is out? Anyway, the spirit world calls to me. Take care of Sandra.

I signed the note, *Dan the Man.*

My behavior last time had left me with this nagging worry he'd freak out, get deeper into drugs, and ruin Sandra's life. Clearly that wasn't the case. The house looked great and he was trying to improve himself. Happy tidings everywhere.

When I got to the living room, on an impulse, I went over and picked up their home phone, dialed an old number, and held it to my ear. When a lady picked up, I apologized for having gotten the wrong number.

"I pushed seven when I meant to push eight," I said.

She said that was perfectly fine, it could happen to anyone, and told me to have a good evening. She sounded happy and healthy.

I hung up, feeling immensely satisfied, and strolled through the front door as if I had every right to do so. After putting the key back where I'd found it, I proceeded to where Sam had parked. Then stopped.

The cab was gone.

I turned around to see if he'd moved down the road and saw the two bodyguards from the book signing standing in the gloom about five feet away.

"Hey, Ernest," Brian said.

"Surprise," Sean said, and zapped me in the chest with fifty thousand volts of searing, sizzling, agony.

I fell straight backwards and hit my head on the pavement, which was like falling into a tub of cotton candy compared to that thing he'd hit me with.

Sean stood over me and said, "Boss lady wants to see you, and you know how she gets."

He turned me over and I felt a sting in my butt. Then, together, they lifted me off the ground, dragged me over to a car, and tossed me into the back.

When the drug kicked in, I skipped right over drowsy into infinite, deathlike oblivion.

SIX

I woke up in the backseat of a car.
A moving car.
Their moving car.
I was groggy, could barely move ... No, my right hand moved fine, but my left hand was asleep. I rolled over, shaking it to get the blood flowing again.
"You awake, Prescott?" Brian said from the driver's seat.
"Yeah," I said and sat up, feeling faintly nauseous.
"Just stay quiet and enjoy the ride," Sean said. He sounded angry. "While you were sleeping, we picked up your shit from the hotel. Why'd you switch rooms? Thought you could hide from us?"
Brian said, "Man, leave him alone. You okay, Ernest?"
"What about Sam?" I said.
"Who?" Sean said.
"The cabbie."
"Told him to scram. Don't worry about him."
Time passed, and my wits slowly returned to me. We weren't in the city. We were on 95, heading north toward New York.
"No airplanes?" I said.
Brian chuckled. "You sure pissed Lana off. Never seen her so mad. I mean, she's crazy, you know? But damn. Told us to drive you. Said she wanted you back at the house."

"This is illegal," I said. "Kidnapping. That doesn't bother you?"

I saw Brian look sideways at Sean, who returned the look, his expression worried.

"Maybe we gave him too much of that shit," Sean said. "Prescott, you okay, man? You need some water or something?"

"Just lie back and relax," Brian told me. Then to Sean: "What's this *we* shit? You fuck up his brains, that's *your* ass."

"I gave him the right amount!"

"You better have," he said. "That's all I'm saying. Bitch is crazy..."

An hour and a half later, I shifted in the backseat and Brian said, "How you feeling?"

"I think I need to tinkle."

"*Tinkle?*" he said accusingly to Sean. "Why the fuck he talking like that?"

"Why you asking me?" Sean said, sounding panicked.

"Hey," I said, "just take the next exit or something. I won't run. I just need to, uh ... take a leak. Ok? And maybe something to eat."

"No problem," Brian said. "Feeling hungry myself."

"You sure you're okay?" Sean said.

"I'm fine."

We stopped at a big travel plaza somewhere in Delaware. Brian helped me out, seeming concerned, while Sean pretended everything was fine and I wasn't brain damaged or whatever they were worried about.

My first hesitant steps were weak and wobbly, and I had to reach out a hand to a nearby car for fear of falling over.

What the hell was in that needle?

"You need to lean on me?" Brian said.

"I think I'm fine," I said, and continued toward the entrance.

Brian hovered close with a worried expression, as if afraid I'd faint. At no point did I feel I was there against my will, just that I was deemed helpless, an invalid. Still on their team, it seemed. Just going through a rough patch.

Sean wanted to get our orders to go, but Brian overruled

him and we found a table by ourselves over near a pizza place. The food was great. And even though I knew it was crappy rest stop pizza, right then it seemed like the best I'd ever had.

A kid walked by with a soft serve cone, and now I wanted ice cream.

"Can we get ice cream?" I said.

Brian was shaking his head, staring hard at Sean. Despite that, I got my ice cream—a huge swirly chocolate and vanilla cone, dipped in chocolate that turned hard if you waited. But I didn't wait long enough, so the first part was too soft. I ate it quickly and got an ice cream headache, but I didn't care. I asked if we could get another.

Sean got up and stalked out of the building muttering curses under his breath.

"Sure, man," Brian said, as if talking to his dying grandmother. "You want more ice cream? No problem. They sure look good—I may get one too. But just so you know, you keep acting crazy like that, I don't think Sean's gonna be working for Lana much longer."

"Yeah?" I said.

"Doesn't bother me, so long as you back me up. Wasn't me who zapped you or gave you that shot."

And just like that, I had an ally.

"I got your back," I said.

A look of faint relief washed over Brian's dark features, and he smiled evilly. "Don't like that prick anyways. Always gotta be a smartass. Know what I mean?"

I nodded, was about to say *totally*, but settled for, "Yes I do."

"Gimme a second," he said.

He walked over near the wall, took out a cell phone, and made a call. He talked for about a minute, hung up, and came back.

"Time to go," he said.

* * *

Five minutes into the drive, I couldn't keep my eyes open ... and then Brian was shaking me awake, saying, "Hey, Ernest, we're here. You need to get up."

Now my *right* arm was asleep. My head hurt from

striking it on the ground, and now I wished I hadn't eaten so much. When I got out of the car, I threw up all the ice cream and pizza from the traveler's plaza.

"Jesus..." Sean said, jumping out of the way. "I thought he was better!"

When I raised my head, I saw we were on a circular stone-cut driveway in front of a big mansion, somewhere in the countryside. Depending on how long I'd been out, it could have been New Jersey or possibly New York. Ernest lived in New York, but my mental map had him in a more densely populated area.

After I wiped my mouth off, the palatial front doors opened and two figures walked out: Lana Sandway, dressed in simple jeans and a tight T-shirt, and a man, wearing shorts and a tank top with some kind of logo on it. As they approached, I saw he had short sandy-blond hair, and his well-muscled left arm was tattooed with spiky red and black razors.

The muscle guy spoke first. "Yo, Ernest, what's shaking, man?"

"My stomach," I said.

He made like he was going to punch me in the gut and follow up with a right hook, which caused me to flinch. Then he grabbed my still-tingling hand in a bone-crushing handshake.

To Lana he said, "Damn ... His hand's cold as ice. Limp as a dead fish."

"Limp," she said drily, staring hard at me from that triangle-shaped mantis face of hers. I could almost hear the clicking of mandibles.

"Heard how you took care of that crazy guy with the knife," the muscle guy said proudly, like I'd joined the same club as him. "You should train with me, I'll whip you in shape. Too much time alone staring at a computer."

"How you doing, Jacob?" Sean said.

The muscle guy smiled at him, a predatory gleam in his eyes. "Got a match coming up in Vegas. Lot of training."

"Oh yeah?" Sean said. "Who you fighting?"

Jacob opened his mouth to answer, but Lana stayed him with a touch.

"Now, boys," she said. "First we work, then we play. Sean, be a dear and give us your report."

Sean smiled thinly and said, "What, out here?"

"Where better?" she said.

Sean nodded, rolling with it, and said, "Ok. Well, the next day I waited for him in the lobby, eight o'clock. Like you said, remember? Only he didn't come down. A little later, I knocked on his door and he didn't answer." He shrugged. "So I figured he wanted to be left alone, you know?"

"You figured that?" Lana said.

Sean nodded. "Yeah. I called Brian to tell him, and then ol' Ernest here slipped out on me. Like on purpose, I think, otherwise I woulda seen him." He looked at me. "Sorry, man..." He turned back to her. "Later on, Brian says he's walking around in public for no reason. Then we see him going to museums and stuff. It was weird."

Lana nodded. "I know all that. Get to the part where you shot my Ernest with a fucking *taser* and then *drugged* him!"

And just like that, everything got really quiet. Jacob was still wearing the same smile he'd had since Sean started talking.

"Right," Sean said, licking his lips. "The next day, we figured out he switched rooms. You told us to follow him, so we did. He went to the movies. When you called and said to grab him, we figured we'd do it after. Only there were too many people around, so we waited. Then he hops in a cab, heads to the suburbs, and goes in some house."

Lana looked at Brian.

"That one threw me," he said, chuckling. "Almost like a whole different Ernest. Went in like he owned the place."

"You have the address?" she said.

"Yes ma'am."

Sean said, "So like I was saying ... he was acting crazy ... and we were in the suburbs ... and we needed to grab him without him yelling or whatever..."

To Brian, Lana gave a barely perceptible nod.

"...and I didn't want to ... but you said you wanted him home *now*, and..."

Brian took a silenced pistol from under his jacket and shot Sean in the head, dropping him where he stood. Like it was the easiest thing in the world, just another thing he had to do today. And here Brian had seemed like such a nice guy. But as shocking as all that was, the only thing I could think was, *I led them to Sandra. I led them right to her.*

Then, whether from being hit from fifty thousand volts or some lingering effect of the drug they'd used, I fell over and passed out.

SEVEN

When I woke up, my shirt was sticky from vomiting again sometime during the night. I was in a bed, and my arm was hooked to an IV drip. My head still hurt, but soon I fell back asleep.

Lana Sandway woke me up later when she came in with shorts, socks, and a clean shirt, which she helped me into. She grunted at me when I said good morning. Apparently she wasn't a morning person.

Then, as if sensing the delicate state of my emotions, she said, "How do you feel?"

"Hungry."

"I'll send something up later," she said. "Don't get out of bed."

Her manner was cold and oddly tense, as if affecting a nurturing bedside manner was pushing her to exhaustion. After she changed my IV bag, she left without so much as a smile.

For the first time, I got a good look at my surroundings. I was in a spacious room with geometrically textured ceilings, elegantly stenciled paneling in burgundy and green, and wall-to-wall marble floors. Beneath the bed was a thick rug done in a foxhunting motif. That and the recessed lightning, central air, and the decorative gas fireplace suggested new money trying to look like old money.

My chest felt sore from where I'd been zapped. But my nausea had passed, which was all the health I needed to get up and resume my place as the driver of this bus.

I pulled out the IV and held my hand over the tiny wound. When I was sure it wouldn't bleed everywhere, I got up to look for my shoes but couldn't find them.

Shuffling to one of the room's three windows, careful not to slip, I opened the curtains and confirmed I was still somewhere in the countryside. The view from my second story window was vast and green with grass, with a sky-blue pond in the distance. Stands of trees and thick tufts of brush grew where the land dipped and folded into natural seams. Off to my left, the house bent sharply, forming a wide V-shape.

Lana must have had Jacob or Brian put me on the other side of the mansion, because I didn't see the driveway.

There were several doors in the room. I poked my head out the one I'd seen Lana go through and saw a wide hallway going down about fifty feet. There were six more doorways spaced evenly along either side. From the outside, the place had seemed big and impressive, though it was harder to appreciate it now after Sean's murder. Kidnappers and killers, all of them, and they knew about Sandra.

I needed to find a phone and warn her—or better yet, warn Peter. I felt I could convince him he was in danger. Or maybe I'd call the minister. He could go over and keep watch. That night everything went to hell at Nate's house, he'd said he owned a gun.

I slipped down the hall and found a wide circular staircase with a marble banister. It led down to a grand foyer with an actual fountain in the center and little places around it to sit. When I got to the stairs, I slipped at the top and crashed down the first four steps, getting banged up a bit in the process.

Limping my way down, I listened for anything that sounded like people, but all I heard was my somewhat labored breathing. Ernest was in his fifties, a little overweight but not terribly so. After last night's zap and nap I needed to take it easy.

When I got to the front door, I didn't see my shoes or wallet or phone or any of the things I needed. If they had a closet somewhere nearby, it was camouflaged in the layers of molding and panels and all that rich stuff.

The mansion was basically four wings meeting in a four-way stop, with the entrance in the middle. At the end of each diagonal, the hall slanted off, like a foot.

I chose the closest hall on the left, passing a sitting room, and came to a set of French doors just after the bend.

Cracking one of the doors, I spied the strangest bed I'd ever seen. It was a sculpture of a gigantic, scaly, clawed hand with a wide circular mattress clutched in its palm like a platter. Nobody was sleeping on it, and I didn't blame them.

Just when I planned to backtrack, to try one of the other hallways, I heard Lana's voice from the foyer. She sounded cold and imperious, which was basically normal for her.

Quickly, before someone glanced down the hall and saw me standing there, I slipped into the room and shut the door.

The room was bigger than the one I'd woken up in, and more lavishly furnished. On closer inspection, each finger of the demon bed had ivory-colored rings carved into them, creating handholds. The claws themselves, which curled over the bed, had ropes hanging from them looped through some kind of pulley system.

One wall was a floor-to-ceiling stack of square-hewn logs with manacles bolted into them. From a hook at the top hung a coiled bullwhip. In front of the whipping wall, a ten-by-ten section of carpet had been cut out revealing the concrete subfloor, darkly discolored.

Out in the hall, Lana laughed. I'd been so preoccupied by the freaky furniture I'd lost a precious few seconds of focus. I ran across the room and through a door, entering a bathroom with a big empty tub in the middle right out of *Scarface*.

The shower didn't have a door, but rather an entrance constructed of stone, which took me around a corner to a spacious cave with showerheads and nozzles everywhere and a wide ledge for shampoo and soap. I sat down on the granite bench against the wall and tried to control my breathing. If the echoes gave me away, there was no way I could explain what I was doing there.

Minutes later, I left the shower-cave and tiptoed over to the door. I cracked it open and peeked out—and saw Lana and Jacob getting X-rated on the demon bed. Lana was face-up, a hand through each ivory ring, with the ropes from the claws looped around her ankles.

Kinky, disturbing, and complicated, but Jacob didn't look confused. He worked the ropes with both hands, leaning into it like he was hunting for something, and no way was he giving up without finding it.

Lana was talking.

"Tear me ... beat me ... fuck me ... kill me," she moaned. "Oh yes, right there ... do it ... harder ... stab me ... kill me ... *now!*"

Jacob did something tricky and athletic, and suddenly she was facing away from him. He proceeded to pummel her with a thick black rod. It made loud smacking sounds, and it had to have hurt. Lana seemed to love it though. She kept yelling, "Kill me! Kill me!" over and over again. And the look on Jacob's face while he hit her, with every scream, was positively feral—a contortion of desire, crazy starved eyes, his face beet-red from exertion. He grabbed her hair and snapped her head back ... and then he *really* began to whale on her.

The beating verged on serious, like he could really hurt her. And despite who Lana was, I reached to open the door—to save her, I guess—but stopped when she yelled for him to kill her some more. Then she gave up vocabulary altogether and screamed, screamed, *screamed* ... and then she was laughing. Exultantly, in triumph, and then a little scornfully, like she'd beaten *him* and wanted to rub it in.

Jacob, for his part, gave a huge sigh and rolled over onto his side, panting and spent from all the sexual homicide he'd been dishing out.

Under normal circumstances, I'm hardly the Peeping Thomas type. But I needed to know when they left the room or if someone wanted to use the bathroom so I could steal away to my hiding spot in the shower. Nevertheless, it had been fascinating to watch. Like two psychopaths at war on some twisted plane where Hate had murdered Love.

No cuddling afterward or cigarettes or any of that. They lay there getting their breath back, neither of them touching each other now that the act was over.

A minute later, Jacob said, "So what about the muse? We gonna wait and keep feeding her or stick to the schedule?"

"Ernest is fine," she said, like she'd said it a hundred times already. "After today, he'll be back to normal. That idiot, Sean. You said he was good, a professional. Then he half-kills our golden goose. And why on Earth did you give him that needle?"

"Why didn't Ernest come home like you told him?" he countered. "Because he's his own guy, that's why. Every guy's gotta be free. Pussy and freaky only go so far."

"It's good enough for us," she said, coyly.

"And *money*," he said. "That's great for us. We said we'd be honest, didn't we? And Ernest is money. He's got something in that fucked up head of his. Darker than you, even."

Lana laughed heartlessly. "You turning into a fan, my son?"

"Don't do that..."

"I married your daddy, that makes you *mine*. Why won't you call me mommy anymore?"

"I said shut up!" Jacob yelled, and got out of bed. He went over and picked up his clothes and started to put them on.

Lana hopped out and came around, then slipped her arms around Jacob's burly chest. He tried to pull away, but she dug in with her nails and said in a quiet voice, "Don't piss me off, okay?"

Jacob froze like he'd been splashed with water.

Lana said, "You knew the deal when you hooked up with me: who I am, what I do, who I do it to. That's what you liked about me—I gave you the power you never had. Daddy didn't understand you, but momma does."

And wonder of all, Jacob broke down and cried. He fell into her arms, hugging her around the waist while she gazed down on him with a superior smirk.

After about a minute of that, Momma Sandway said, "There's nothing that can stop us—no turning back. Ernest knows that, even if he's confused right now. Tonight we'll show him the muse, he'll get inspired, and then we cash more checks."

I wanted her to keep talking about this mysterious *muse*, but she took Jacob's hand and headed my way. I ducked back and hid in the shower and remained perfectly still, once again willing my out-of-shape self to breathe quietly.

The door outside opened. But rather than head for the toilet or fill up the big empty tub or go wash their hands, Jacob and Lana came right into the shower cave with me. I was so shocked I sat there staring at them, perched on the bench like that's just where I sat sometimes.

"Hello, Ernest," she said, looking confused and a little worried.

"What the fuck, man?" Jacob said.

I looked from naked Lana to naked Jacob, then Jacob to Lana, and then Lana to Jacob again.

Then, in a lost quavering voice, I said, "Where am I?"

EIGHT

Lana whispered something to Jacob. He nodded and left.
"Ernest," she said, "do you know who I am?"
I blinked at her. "You're Lana."
She smiled encouragingly and said, "What do you mean you don't know where you are, hmm? Does your head hurt?"
"A little?"
"Did you fall down?" she said.
I paused, thinking about it, giving it my absolute best and said, "When?"
The muscles in her jaw rippled like she was chewing her tongue. She wasn't smiling anymore, and she regarded me with an icy gaze.
From the bedroom, Jacob yelled, "Got it!"
"Come with me, Ernest," Lana said. "Watch your step."
I got up carefully, trying not to fall down, and followed her out of the shower cave. Interestingly, she hadn't blushed or shown anything like modesty where her nakedness was concerned. She had small, perky breasts that matched her slender figure. No tattoos or piercings, trimmed pubic hair, and her back was a red mess of welts from the beating she'd taken. Beneath those sketched a tracery of old scar tissue, as if she'd been whipped repeatedly over the years. And again, despite her face and

body measuring up to the definition of "beautiful" by anyone's standards, she stirred nothing inside me resembling desire.

When she reached for my hand to steady me, I pulled away and said, "I'm fine."

Lana's eyes narrowed, and she smiled a hard, tight smile. She didn't try to touch me again.

When we got into the room, Jacob had a wheelchair with him.

"I don't think that'll be necessary," I said, and edged around it toward the far door.

"Ernest," she said through gritted teeth. "Sit in the fucking chair or I'll have Jacob put you in it. Please?"

Because she'd said please, I nodded and sat down. Also, now that I'd started down this course, I couldn't very well announce I was okay again. Lana was already unstable, and I had zero desire to get chained to that whipping wall and beaten.

Increasingly, I wondered about the real Ernest and how he interacted with her. Did he also have a domineering personality? Or was he weak and needy and more like Jacob?

"Stay with Ernest," she said to him. "I need to get something."

Jacob said, "Sure. We'll be fine."

After she left, Jacob's face relaxed fractionally.

In a mocking tone he said, "She's a real bitch, huh? Great in the sack, though." He sighed longingly. "Sorry about Sean. That one's on me."

I nodded, unsure of what to say.

Jacob said, "After your muse, you'll snap back fine, you'll see. I'm not supposed to say nothing, but..." He peered around conspiratorially, then held his hands about two feet from his waist. "She's big, know what I mean?"

"That big?" I said.

"Keep that to yourself."

I nodded.

Apparently there was an overweight woman in the building. If they introduced me to her and expected me to get busy or whatever, I'd play cold fish, like I always did.

Heck, I had a rock-solid alibi this time—still messed up from the zapping and drugging I'd taken.

Jacob nudged me softly and gave me a knowing look.

In a low voice, he said, "So what were you doing in that house for, man? That's got everyone freaked out."

Desperately, I wracked my brains for something to explain my actions. Looking for drugs? Wanted to beat up a bad reviewer? Just because? I opened my mouth to say something, and then Lana came back carrying a box.

"Found them!" she said, happily. She pointed at me. "Hold his arms."

Jacob leaned down in front of me and grabbed my arms. He must have seen the alarm on my face because he winked at me, guy-to-guy, an us-against-them kind of thing.

Lana took out a leather strap with friction clips and lashed my left wrist tightly to the arm of the wheelchair. Her hands were strong, steady, and merciless, and I worried she'd cut off my circulation. I experienced a moment of panic and struggled to free myself, but Jacob held me easily. After the first wrist, she did the other one. When she was done, she checked her work and then loosened the first one, fractionally.

"Now his legs," she said.

Jacob bent down and said, "You kick me, Ernest, I'm beating the shit out of you. Got it?" He said it almost like he was joking around, but there was a hint of a threat in it. Jacob was some sort of pro fighter, and I'd just seen him beat up his girlfriend who he sometimes called *mommy*, so when it came to violence I took him at his word.

"Got it," I said.

After I was strapped in, Lana leaned down and kissed me on the cheek. I flinched, but she either didn't notice or she ignored it.

"Can't have you wandering around hurting yourself," she said. "You're just exhausted. You need good food. For the mind and your warrior heart. Now think, Ernest: do you know where you are now?"

I didn't like being restrained so I said, "In your bedroom. We were just in the shower. I was a little groggy when I woke up, but everything's much clearer now. If you'll undo these straps, I'm sure I can move around all right."

Lana shook her head. "Let's see how it goes after the fun later. Hopefully by tomorrow you'll be ready to write again. How does that sound?"

"I'm feeling great now," I said, and jerked my hands hard against the straps to prove it.

Frowning, she said, "Jacob, would you put him somewhere out of the way please?"

Jacob laughed good-naturedly, grabbed both handles, and pushed me toward the door.

Before we crossed the threshold, I turned back and said, "What happens tonight?"

Lana didn't answer and Jacob didn't either. He pushed me down the hall, past the foyer, and into a room with a large television hooked to a DVD player.

"Wait till you see this," he said, wheeling me into place. Then he turned on both the TV and the DVD player with a remote. "You'll love it."

NINE

Jacob had stood witness while Brian murdered a man, as if it were no big whoop. He fornicated (or whatever he called it) with the woman who had ordered it done. The same woman who, whilst fornicating (or whatever she called it) had yelled out crazy stuff like "kill me" and "stab me." Jacob had beaten her black and blue with a rubber club. They had a whipping wall in their room with an easy-to-clean concrete floor. And they were business associates (or whatever they called it) with Ernest Prescott, whose writing was so sadistic and hateful it turned my stomach in a way commonly reserved for Hallmark stores and vegetables. And now this same Jacob, willing participant to all that awfulness, wanted me to watch movies with him.

He slipped a DVD from a clear plastic case, confirming my worst fears.

"Home movies?" I said.

"Better," he said, and put in the disk.

Strapped down and trapped, unable to scratch my itchy nose and wondering what would happen when I needed to use the bathroom, I sat in my chair and wondered what a guy like Jacob thought Ernest Prescott would find enjoyable.

The scene opened to darkness, then the cheerful sound of Brother Bones whistling Sweet Georgia Brown. Very creepy. Just as I wondered if it was simply a bootleg Globe Trotters' video, the screen brightened and the camera zoomed in, leaving nothing to the imagination. What followed were depictions of torment and barbarism, savage and raw, exposing the limits of human endurance stretched to the breaking point. Unlike the events in *Sliced*, this was real. There was choking, there was pummeling and blood, there was violation and agony and humiliation and grief, each scene more shocking than the ones preceding it, building again and again to the same predictable climax where the victim was forced to hang his head while Jacob raised his fists in victory, howling like a maniac.

That's right: Jacob was playing me his extreme fighting videos. *His* videos, because he was in every one.

"Wow," I said at one point. "You sure hit *that* guy."

Jacob faced me with a condescending smile. "Oh yeah, Ernest the karate fighter. Just be glad I wasn't there when that asshole pulled his knife. I'd be in jail and he'd be dead, know what I mean?"

Coming from anyone else, I'd have figured it for bluster. With Jacob, it was probably the closest he came to modesty.

The video kept playing, fight after fight, and despite myself I was getting into it. It was something to do. Also, years ago, back when extreme fighting first got popular in the U.S., I'd rented the first five or so pay-per-view specials.

There's something about two people battling it out that triggers our survival instinct. And even though I'm technically dead most of the time, my survival instinct carries with me, such that two people duking it out on the mansion's big screen TV easily became the most interesting thing in the room.

In that respect it was a little like watching *Sliced*, and I wondered what that said about me, that I could enjoy the one while condemning the other.

Watching Jacob's videos, I found myself flinching and wanting to punch the air, despite my restraints. But after a while, it got tiresome watching Jacob win every fight. I kept hoping for the other guy to choke him out, like Royce

Gracie did over and over again in those early extreme fighting championships ... but no, Jacob kept knocking everybody out. He was a hitter, not a grappler. He had no style or finesse, only brute strength and aggression. Royce Gracie liked to grab his opponents around the middle and hold on for fifteen minutes while they tired themselves out, beating on him with short ineffectual punches. Then he'd flip his leg up around the guy's neck and do this weird jujitsu thing and the guy would give up, screaming in pain.

"Hey look at that," Brian said, coming into the room with a plate of sandwiches and a six-pack of beer. "Prescott's watching sports. How you liking it, man?"

"Fun fun," I said, flashing him a thumbs-up, one of the few gestures I could do that didn't require raising my arms.

Brian said, "Made them myself. You want roast beef or baloney?"

"Both," I said. "I'm starved. Thanks."

Then, despite being a big guy who liked to shoot people at the nod of my literary agent and captor, he proceeded to feed me. I'll give Brian one thing: he made a mean sandwich. I downed four total, taking little swishes of beer in-between, even though I didn't like beer.

"You sure you don't want more?" he said, casting an amused glance at the last two sandwiches.

As if sensing the very real danger of me saying *yes*, Jacob reached over and snagged one. There was one left. A baloney. But I could tell Brian wanted it, so...

"You go ahead," I said. "I'm full."

Brian smiled and said, "Don't mind if I do."

So there we were, three killers watching extreme fighting on TV, eating red meat and drinking beer. And out of nowhere, despite being lashed against my will to a wheelchair, I didn't feel so lonely.

When you're a dead guy, you make do.

After finishing his sandwich, Jacob hit pause and said, "Gimme a minute." Then he walked out.

Brian watched him go, then said, "Hey, man, I want you to know: I appreciate you being cool about what went down yesterday. Lana made me check on that house we found you at."

"That house?" I said, hoping against hope.

"Yeah," he said, giving me a significant look. "As far as I'm concerned, nobody lives there. Cuz you cool. Maybe someday you'll do *me* a favor. Know what I'm saying?"

Yeah I knew what he was saying: he was keeping Sandra and her family safe. My throat tightened and I'm sure my face flushed. Relieved beyond measure, I wanted to dance or cry.

"Thank you," I said, not pretending at anything for once. With every fiber in me, I meant it, and I wanted him to know that.

Brian nodded. Cuz I was cool.

Seconds later, Jacob returned.

"Yo, Brian," he said. "You and me in the gym, when Ernie and Lana are getting their freak-on, what do you say? Teach you a few moves."

Brian frowned at the mention of *freak-on*, but it passed quickly. He gave me a final significant look and said, "Sure, man. Maybe I'll teach you something, too?"

* * *

Hours later, after we'd sat through all of Jacob's victories, Lana walked in dressed in a dominatrix getup. She wore black high-heel boots strapped up to her calves, with glinting chrome spikes sticking out in every direction. She was a big one for spikes—her patent leather corset pushed her small breasts up impossibly high, spearing the room with razor tips where the nipples should be. Her lips were dark maroon, almost black. Her nails, about an inch long, were arterial in their redness.

Instead of a cat o' nine tails, she carried a bedpan.

Brian and Jacob threw each other knowing looks, like they had pressing business somewhere else, then cleared out.

"How's my poor little patient doing?" Lana said, stroking my face lovingly. Gone was the nervous tension she'd shown tending to me upstairs in the bedroom. She was in her element.

"Just watching TV."

"I have something far more entertaining in mind," she said. "But first, we need to get you out of those clothes."

"You think guys like me fall for lines like that?" I said.

Lana arched her neck, trying for seductive. Then she laughed, trying for throaty. But again, though beautiful in a technical sense, she didn't seem sexy to me. She seemed tired, burned out inside, all ends and no candle. Furious at something indefinable, and I wondered if even she knew what it was.

She flourished a knife and grabbed my shorts.

"Hey, what are you doing?" I said.

With her tongue poking out of her mouth, she proceeded to cut my shorts and underwear away, leaving me exposed and a little colder than I had been.

"You're going to have to raise yourself," she said, a hint of exasperation in her voice.

"Hey," I said. "Seriously, I'm fine. That thing with the shower was just ... you know, after effects from last night. I'm ready to get back to normal."

Lana threw me a curious look and said, "That's what we're doing, Ernest. Now lift!"

She flicked her knife near my nether regions, nicking my inner thigh and causing me to jump—then slipped in the bedpan.

"Hey!" I said. "Easy with the knife, okay?"

Lana stood up straight—posing for me, it seemed like, while leering at my nakedness. Then she frowned. "Do you want me to assist you?"

When it dawned on me what she meant, I shook my head and said, "I'd rather you get me a new pair of shorts."

Lana's eyes flashed dangerously. She stepped behind me, kicked the blockers open on the chair and jerked me angrily backwards, then forward, rolling me down one of the wings I hadn't explored.

This was it—she was going to torture me. That's what the bedpan was for, in case I messed myself. I'd never been systematically tortured by a psycho who got off on pain, and she could torture me until I got kicked—about three weeks from now—or until she screwed up and killed me, whichever came first.

My last ride had been a sick bastard who got off torturing dogs and posting videos of it on the Internet.

Vile, heartbreaking stuff, and even though I hadn't found any human victims in his computer files, I'd killed him for it anyway. Was this, now, my punishment? Because animals supposedly didn't have souls?

We came to a closed door on the right—single, not a French door like the bedrooms all seemed to have. About fifteen feet down was another single door, also on the right.

Lana pushed open the closest one and wheeled me in. The room was muted, with fabric on the walls like they have in movie theaters to muffle the sound. Scattered in the room were three sofa chairs—the reclining kind, judging by the little levers poking out the sides.

Along the left wall, where the movie screen would be, hung dark red curtains.

Lana left me where I was, went over to the nearest chair and tugged it out of the way. Then she got behind me and pushed me into the previously occupied spot, facing the curtains.

"Are you going to torture me?" I said at last, unable to bear it any longer.

"Only if you want me to," she breathed.

"I'd rather you let me go."

She laughed. "Now why would I do that? What's in it for me?"

"We could go have sex."

Any port in a storm...

"Come now, Ernest," she said. "Aren't you a little bit curious about your muse?"

Lana walked over to the wall and pulled a rope, drawing the curtains wide, revealing another room separated from this one by a plate glass window. There was someone inside, naked on a gurney, strapped down like me except on her back—pitiful and afraid, and very alone.

"I'm disappointed in you," Lana said. "All those demands: dark hair, big boobs, good teeth, young, and as requested—*pregnant*. Ready to burst. The boys worked very hard to find her. She's a pretty little sow. Pristine. It was all I could do to keep Sean off of her, but he's no longer a problem." She laughed harshly. "The news is obsessed with her disappearance, which is why we simply don't have time for you to get over whatever the hell's wrong with you." She walked up to the window. "We need *Sliced 2,* and soon, before they forget about us. And when we're done, the world will weep with the certainty they never had souls."

Still staring at the poor woman, feeling nothing but pity for her, I realized what was going on. She was the *muse* I'd been hearing about—the inspiration for Ernest's next sad little book. I wondered how many muses he'd had over the years.

I shook my head, for once at a loss for words.

"Jacob actually had a good idea for once," Lana said, eyes dancing. "If the baby lives, we could raise it ourselves, just the three of us. A new mind untainted by the world, fresh for us to mold. Our own little apex fiend." She laughed her real laugh, hoarse and desperate. "Think of the possibilities!"

"No," I croaked out, but she wasn't listening. Too lost in the possibilities.

"Sorry about the bedpan," she said, staring hungrily through the window at the woman. "I still don't trust you, and once I start cutting ... well, I have to control the bleeding. I can't be running in here if you have to pee. I'll make it up to you when it's over, I promise. All night, if you want. I'll even save some of her blood."

She flicked a switch I hadn't seen on the wall and suddenly I could hear the quiet sobs of the woman in the other room playing in surround-sound.

Shaking my head, I shouted, "Let her go! Don't do this! You don't need to do this!"

This couldn't happen. I couldn't let this happen. No way could this happen. If I could just get free...

Lana glanced back at me. "You're not yourself. I want my Ernest back."

Then she was out the door, shutting it firmly behind her, leaving me to stare helplessly through the window at that sad, lost woman and her doomed child.

Refusing to give up, angry and desperate and willing to try anything, I closed my eyes and bowed my head.

And made my case.

TEN

"Listen," I said, under my breath. "I know you're there. You're always there, and I know you can hear me. I can't see why you chose me or even what you want most of the time. But if you don't do something to stop this, right now, help me get out of this goddamned wheelchair, then we're *through*. I mean it—never again. I'll stay in my hole and rot for eternity, no matter how many portals you send for me."

When nobody said anything, I shouted, "Do you hear me? Help me now or it's over! Do you hear me? *Do you?*"

When the walls didn't reverberate with a ghostly voice saying help had arrived, when the straps on my arms didn't rot away like I needed them to, I hung my head in defeat, cursed with the knowledge that God or something like him existed and didn't actually care for us at all.

Fuming, I decided the Great Whomever could take a flying ... no, scratch that. I wasn't calling him that anymore. I had a new name for him.

"You hear that!" I shouted. "How do you like your new name, asshole? You're now the *Great Who Gives A Shit!*"

Because when you're sitting with your pants off perched on a bedpan, about to watch a crazy woman start cutting pieces off an innocent pregnant lady, and you can't do anything but shout insults, you shout insults.

Just when I'd nailed down my new name for the Great

Wherever, almost as if someone was tired of all the whining, my olfactory senses flooded with the smell you get after a hard punch in the nose, and everything turned upside down and sideways. Seconds later, I got kicked again, leaving me dizzy and blinking at thousands of little lights trailing everywhere.

"No," I said, shaking my head. "That's not what I meant. *Help* me, dammit! Don't kick me out!"

In the room with the sobbing woman, Lana flipped a switch on the wall and the plate glass pulsed with the sound of grinding death metal: chaotic, hellish, and loud. Shocked by the sudden cacophony, the woman began to scream.

Rocking to the almost non-existent tune, Lana wheeled over a tray of glittery surgical instruments and pushed it near the table with the screaming woman.

The third kick hit me so hard I thought I'd pass out, but didn't.

In all my rides, I'd never felt a fourth kick before, and I didn't this time. All I knew is I was sitting on a bedpan one moment and the next I wasn't.

* * *

Dan stands in the entrance to an apartment building. He hears a chuckle from behind him, then feels intense pain as a knife slams in under his ribs. He bends over, trying to breathe, but can't. No—he's breathing, it's just not helping. Pant pant pant, all for nothing. His chest seizes up on him, and then—

He's falling. The wind whips past his face in a roar of sound. The world is a spinning tube of black and white and black and white. His tumbling levels out enough that he catches sight of an enormous span, far above him. A suspension bridge. He hits the water, and then—

He looks up from his cell phone in time to see the back of a pickup truck rushing toward him, and then—

Bullets slam into him. He drops his gun, but the police keep firing. "Wait," he gasps, but the police choose not to, and then—

He's bouncing down a flight of stairs. His hands aren't where he needs them to be and he watches helplessly as

hard tiles hurtle up to meet him in a looming, life-ending faceplant, and then—
He dies in another car crash.
He slips on slick tiles and strikes his head.
Another crash.
Dan screams forever over the course of countless deaths, his voice changing with each successive ride: high, low, raspy, shrill, smooth. Sort of like in that "wazaaap" commercial everyone was imitating way back when.
He dies in an empty hospital room, choking on his own congestion.
His last breath exhales in a cloudy plume in a forest, cold and dark, his body numb and drowsy.
Something like glass stabs him in the chest again and again, and the last thing he sees is the comforting face of a child with enormous blue eyes. She's smiling at him like she knows him. She leans down as if to whisper something in his ear ... but he's gone before he can hear it.
Dan flails about, grabbing or dropping or leaping or twisting each time, hoping for anything to pull him out of the death cycle, but all he does is die, die, die.
Another heart attack and he dies.
Another car crash and he dies.
He dies.
He dies.
A slaughter of deaths later, Dan's hands close around something warm and meaty and he squeezes desperately for dear life. He knows he's fighting—not dying—and so he fights back with everything in him, and wonder of all: he lives.

* * *

I fought.

We were on the ground. Myself, a black guy with powerful arms, sweating and breathing heavily, and someone else, a white guy, also big. I had him around the neck from behind, with my legs wrapped around his waist. Though I held on tightly, I wondered if maybe I should let go and run off. Somehow I'd popped into another body, but I couldn't dwell on that astonishing fact.

"Let ... go ... man ... can't ... breathe..."

Though his voice was strained and raspy, I recognized him—it was Jacob!

Somehow, I'd come back as Brian, and we were sparring together like Jacob had suggested earlier. He'd offered to teach Brian a few moves. I remembered it perfectly, like all my rides after I'd been kicked out, with the perfect memory of the dead.

Rather than let him go, I held on tighter—and *squeezed*. With everything in me, I choked the sonofabitch. Because I also remembered what Lana had said about the woman on the gurney: *The boys worked so hard to find her.*

When Lana had entered the TV room, wearing her weird outfit with all the spikes, Jacob and Brian had cleared out quickly. Brian had pulled an unpleasant face at the mention of Lana and me getting our *freak on*. He'd known something of Lana's plans.

Jacob thrashed spastically while I continued to squeeze, both with my arms—like I'd seen in those videos years ago—and with my legs, to keep him from getting away. Maybe Brian was in the process of learning something, or teaching something, because he was in the exact place needed for me to take over. A good thing, because after seeing Jacob's victory videos, I knew there was no way I could go toe-to-toe with him in a fair fight.

Somewhere in the house, Lana was arranging her scalpels and saws, getting ready to do the unthinkable. Unless, of course, the Great Whomever (his name provisionally restored), had brought me back too late.

One of the peculiar perks of having a perfect memory is I can count things and events from various rides very quickly. Between one gasp from Jacob and a ragged pant from me, I knew exactly how many times I'd died in that terrifying smokestack of death.

My heart sank. Each death had lasted as many as a few seconds. Strung together, my time away had been close to thirty minutes. Long enough for Lana to have done anything she wanted to the woman on the gurney.

Jacob gave a last-ditch attempt to break free, and I responded by squeezing with all I had, throwing all my rage and disgust into it—at Ernest and his stupid writing, at Lana's ugly soul, and at myself, for watching TV with *the guys* and having fun like I belonged somewhere.

Moments later, Jacob was limp in my arms. I didn't know if I'd killed him or not, but he didn't appear to be breathing. With no time to check, I got up and scanned the room—a home gym with mirrors everywhere, workout machines in the far corner, and wall-to-wall wrestling mats.

I noticed a black lump over near the door, just to the side. Brian's gun, in a hip holster. I pulled it out and racked the slide back, sending a shell flying out. That was fine, I'd only need a few, and it had a high-capacity magazine.

Gun in hand, I rushed through the house hoping for that special moment when I saw something I recognized and stopped being lost. There were no windows in any of the rooms, so I began looking for staircases, figuring I was in a basement. After bursting into an indoor shooting range that smelled of frequent use, I turned back and pretended I'd gone right instead of left after leaving the gym. This took me to a lounge with an enormous bar and a dance floor. On the other side was an opening to a marble staircase leading up.

It struck me as funny that Lana would buy such an extravagant house. I wondered if it belonged to her dead husband.

When I got up the stairs, I was standing in the main hall. To the left, I knew I'd find the big foyer with the fountain in the middle. I took that in the direction of the TV room where Brian had fed me sandwiches, then followed the same path that Lana had wheeled me through, eventually arriving at the doors to the torture room and the viewing room. One of them, the closest, held Ernest. Loud death metal howled and screamed from the other.

I tried the door with the music and found it locked. It seemed solid and strong. Worse, it opened outward, into the hall, so I couldn't use Brian's big muscles to smash it in. Rather than doing all that, I knocked loudly and hoped to cut through the music. No reason for her not to open it.

Lana, however, didn't answer.

One thing I wouldn't do was shoot through the knob, for

fear of hitting the woman. So I knocked again, harder, more insistently. I needed that door open, but again nobody answered.

I ran back to Ernest's door and opened it up. The death metal intensified, blaring from the speakers Lana had turned on before leaving me trapped there.

"Brian!" Ernest shouted angrily, a confused expression on his face. "Get me out of this chair, dammit! What's going on?"

The woman in the other room was pleading, barely loud enough to make out: "No, please let me go. Please!"

Ignoring Ernest, I looked through the window and saw Lana consulting a thick book resting on a stainless steel table, her back turned toward me.

Somehow, the woman on the gurney was free from harm. But Lana had been busy in my time away. Across the woman's belly and breasts, and at various places along her arms, legs, and face, Lana had drawn surgical lines with a black magic marker.

Why would anyone...?

Lana shut the book, apparently satisfied with whatever she'd been looking at. Then she put the magic marker down and picked up a scalpel from a tray with a bunch of clamps and odd tools I didn't recognize. She smiled down at the sobbing woman and waved the scalpel dangerously close to her tear-streaked face. Then, with a sadistic smirk, she traced the scalpel down the woman's cheek and neck, languidly across her chest, then down and around her exposed belly.

Lana's face appeared almost ... not motherly, exactly, but enraptured. Fascinated by every scream or shudder or sign of terror she managed to elicit from her victim. She was savoring it, drawing it out like the world's most demented foreplay.

"No!" I shouted, but Lana didn't hear me.

I didn't know if the gun had been loaded with hollow-points or not. If not, they'd pass through the window mostly straight, even if I hit it from an angle. Though I could name every head-of-state in the last hundred years, I wasn't a ballistics expert, or even a ballistics novice. For all

I knew, hitting the window with a hollow-point would shoot pieces of metal everywhere, and possibly hit the woman on the gurney.

"Brian!" Ernest shouted. "What are you doing with that gun? Come help me!"

When Lana lowered the knife to a point just below the woman's bellybutton, along one of the black lines, I pointed the gun away from both of them and shot through the glass.

The glass cracked into a million little pieces. This would have worked out perfectly, but the glass stayed mostly in place except for a three-inch circle where the bullet had passed. Now my view through the window went from a clear view of Lana and the woman to a hazy, fractured view of something tall and black next to something white and horizontal.

With the window compromised, the death metal blared louder than ever, but not so loud as to occlude the woman's wails of terror ... wait, no, that was Ernest. I couldn't hear much else through the ringing in my ears from the gunshot.

Heedless of cutting myself, I bashed the gun hard into the broken glass, widening the hole. When I looked through it, the door was open and Lana was gone.

The woman's stomach was bloody.

No, please!

I ran into the hall and saw Lana stumbling as fast as her stupid dominatrix boots would carry her. I hesitated, locked between two decisions: try shooting at her or help the woman. Lana glanced back once, and the look on her face wasn't fearful or shocked. It was hateful, livid, unholy.

Lana turned the corner, and I went in to check the pregnant woman.

Her belly had a jagged cut along the side, as if Lana had been startled by the gunshot and jumped. She was bleeding, but not a lot. Trying not to panic, I felt along the cut with my fingers. The scalpel had sunk a quarter inch in one spot, but no farther. She'd need stitches to close it. The bleeding worried me because, slow as it was, I didn't know if it would stop.

The woman said something I couldn't hear over the music, which was driving me nuts. I found the switch on the wall Lana had flipped and turned it off.

"—don't kill me!" the woman shouted, too loudly in the now quiet room. "What did I do? Why am I here?"

I wanted to ask her who brought her here. But with a crazy dominatrix on the loose, I needed to stay focused.

It didn't help that Ernest kept yelling, "Jacob! Lana!" and *"Get me out of this fucking chair!"*

Ignoring Ernest and the crying woman, I glanced around for something to stop the bleeding. There weren't any bandages in Lana's surgical tray. From Lana's warped perspective, I figured, the more blood the better so long as the woman didn't bleed out and die too soon. Probably what those clamps were for. I didn't know how to use them without causing more damage, so I took off my shirt, bunched it up, and pressed it against the cut. After holstering the gun, I worked the leather strap holding her right arm until she could pull her hand free.

"Hold this until I get back," I said.

"Are you letting me go?" she said. "Who are you people?"

For the first time, I got a good look at her. About thirty years old, she had long brown hair, a generous mouth, and big brown eyes. Though scared to death, she was coherent. And there was something in her eyes ... A hidden strength. She'd do whatever it took to stay alive. She had a baby to protect, so of course she was brave.

"What's your name?" I said.

"Denise."

"Do you remember who took you? Was I one of them?"

"What do you mean?" she said, and then her eyes widened. She sort of drew back from me, straining against the straps, shaking her head. "It was dark, I didn't see anyone. Please, I won't tell anyone about you or the others. Let me go and I'll make something up. Nobody needs to know anything."

She thought I wanted to silence her.

"No, Denise," I said. "When you get out of here, I want you to tell everyone exactly what happened, just as it happened, and don't leave me out of it. Now, keep that wound under pressure and stay quiet while I take care of a few things, okay?"

I couldn't protect her and hunt down Lana, too.

After a brief hesitation, Denise nodded.

ELEVEN

I hadn't explored beyond the basement and the main floor, and I hadn't been outside since my arrival.

When Lana ran down the hall, she'd gone left. Though the trail was cold, I followed after her—cautiously. This was her lair, and all Brian's muscles and even his gun couldn't help shake the nagging feeling I was walking into a trap.

I peeked cautiously around the corner and saw the way was clear. A set of doors was open on the right, and another set stood closed on the left. The open doors led to a wide, ornate library with a circular couch in the middle and a few tables and chairs scattered around the room, but nobody was there. I turned to leave but then stopped. Wall-to-wall bookshelves in a library made sense, but one of the shelves was poking rudely my way.

After a quick look up and down the hall, I stepped inside, shut the doors behind me, and walked over for a closer look. The bookcase was pulled out about a foot from the wall.

"Wow," I said. "An actual secret door."

My first secret door ever.

Tentatively, I nudged it open. It moved slowly at first, then faster, as if counterbalanced. Beyond it, the way ahead was smooth and painted, which was somewhat of a letdown after all the movies I'd seen with stone-cut tunnels and spiral staircases delving deep into the earth. At the end of the passage, recessed lighting offered a dim view of the way ahead. Arguably gloomy.

With my gun out in front of me, fearing an ambush, I followed the gloomy secret passageway to a stairwell descending four feet into the very depths of the mysterious mansion. The walls switched from painted drywall to gray concrete at the bottom, then opened into a twenty-by-twenty foot room that had been turned into a jail. Thick steel bars ran wall-to-wall and floor-to-ceiling, and in the middle was a reinforced door. A large steel plate framed the lock, with a box around the mechanism to keep probing hands from tampering with it through the bars.

"Wow," I said, shaking my head. "An actual dungeon."

My first dungeon ever.

Other than a small pile of clothes on the floor, the cell was empty, and there were no other exits.

I needed to go after Lana, but I had reason to pause.

In addition to being a dungeon, the room doubled as an armory. One wall had an assortment of pistols hanging from hooks. The other wall had a rack of AR-15s and pump-action shotguns. Either they hadn't bought enough guns to fill the rack or one of them was missing. My problem was I couldn't tell if it was a shotgun or a rifle because they were all mixed together. Beneath the rack was a lower shelf with loaded magazines and boxes of ammo, also more or less jumbled together.

I thought about replacing my pistol with one of the rifles, but instead grabbed two additional magazines. Despite knowing what an AR-15 was, I'd never actually fired one, and I hadn't had much experience with shotguns. Maybe if I got through this without dying I'd go shooting in that indoor range.

One more thing to live for.

Taking the steps two at a time back to the secret entrance, it occurred to me a rifle might not be the best choice for slipping around a house. Too bulky, unless Lana was also in the SWAT team and trained to storm houses. The more I thought about it, the more it seemed a big scary military-looking weapon would appeal to someone like her, even though a shotgun made more sense in tight quarters.

I peeked through the bookcase into the library, but nobody was there. Outside the library, I saw the doors across the hall were open, and I was pretty sure they'd been closed before. When I'd come down the hall, Lana had probably been listening for me. To her I was still Brian, the trained security guy with a gun, so she hadn't risked opening the doors to take a shot.

A cursory look in the room showed another bedroom, empty of people. Lana must have doubled back on me.

"Denise," I said, then turned and ran back.

When I got to the corner, I popped my head quickly around and back again, then flinched when the wall behind me became perforated in a shatter of rifle fire. These weren't simple AR-15s—they'd been modified fully automatic.

That's right. First they try to torture a pregnant lady and raise her baby as some sort of uber-villain in their war on good taste, and now this: illegally modified weapons.

"Not on my watch," I said, diving around the corner, twisting and shooting through the air like I'd seen this one time in a movie. Lana must have left after the initial burst, because nobody fell down and died or shot back. I did bang my elbow and get the wind knocked out of me, but I'd never looked cooler, and that was something.

When I got to the torture room, I had a moment of panic: Denise was gone.

I moved to Ernest's room and saw her standing there naked, clutching my shirt to her stomach with one hand and jiggering with Ernest's restraints with the other. She'd almost gotten one of them off.

"Hey," I said. "Quit it. What are you doing?"

Denise threw her hands up and around and turned toward me, fingers hooked into claws, startled and frightened and ready to fight.

"Stay away from me!" she shouted, her initial fear now tinged with fury.

I peeked out the door, back to where Lana had run, but the hall was still empty.

Looking from Denise to Ernest, then back again, I said,

"You do know who he is, don't you?"

"That's the man I was telling you about!" Ernest said, pointing a finger at me. "He kidnapped me and brought me here. He brought *both* of us here. If he harms me, you're my witness!"

"Leave us alone!" Denise yelled, taking a step back.

Perhaps sensing his henchman had personal reasons for releasing Denise, Ernest had pressed the only advantage he had—he thought I wouldn't hurt the woman. In his mind, if he could get her on his side, he'd have something he didn't before. Maybe I fancied her, and if I hurt him I'd blow my chances.

"Yes, my dear," Ernest said to her, a devilish twinkle in his eyes. "This man knows we're worth much more to him alive than dead—especially me. So what happened, Brian? Did you want more money? It's yours—it was always yours, if you'd but come to me and asked. There's no reason we can't go our separate ways without butchering each other."

He smirked like he had me precisely where he wanted me.

After I shot Ernest in the head (wet, messy, loud), I waited for the woman to stop screaming. I suppose I could have kept him alive so I could ask where he'd gone after I'd taken over his body. But if I really wanted to know that, I could always visit Nate Cantrell and ask him.

My working theory was my rides went to a Great Wherever kind of place and waited in limbo, just like I did, and that was good enough for me. On some level, ignorance isn't just bliss, it's simply practical. Imagine if Ernest said he had *not* gone elsewhere after I'd taken over—that he'd been able to read my mind the whole time, or something awful like that? Then every future ride would be this weirdly self-conscious affair where I'd worry about being watched every time I went to the bathroom. No thank you.

When Denise stopped screaming, I said, "What's with you anyway? Ernest was the one who told me to bring you here."

"Who?" she said. "That man? Why did you shoot him?"

"It's complicated," I said. "Right now I need to get you

somewhere safe, okay? I'll tell you about it later, but we need to move."

"But you *shot him!*"

"Yes," I said, "because he was evil. Now let's go. Or do you want me to shoot you too?"

I checked the hall again—still empty—then turned back and said, "You coming? Or do we wait for Lana to come back with her knife?"

Reluctantly, Denise followed me out. When she saw we were heading to the library, she stopped in the hall, shook her head, and said, "I'm not going back in that cage. No way."

"Sure you are," I said, pointing my gun at her. "If I wanted you dead you'd be dead. See? So it must mean I don't want you dead. Your clothes are back there, there's guns, lots of books to read—now please, can we get out of this hallway?"

After we got to the dungeon/armory, Denise moved quickly to gather her clothes.

"Stop looking at me!" she yelled, holding them modestly around her lady bits.

Unbelievable.

"I wasn't looking at ... never mind," I said, and turned around.

Not like I hadn't seen everything already.

When I sensed she was dressed, I turned back and said, "You stay here while I go find Lana and shoot her, okay? She's a bad person, and I am too. Just because I saved you doesn't mean I'm the good guy."

Denise snorted. "That's pretty clear. Where's the other one?"

"Lana?"

"No, the other man—the white one? Did you kill him too?"

Wondering if she referred to Jacob or Sean, I said, "Did he have a big tattoo on his arm?"

"I don't remember," she said. "Why are we here?"

"What am I, a philosopher?"

"What?"

"Now listen," I said. "Lana's up there, and she's totally

nuts. Those two—the dead guy in the wheelchair and her—they do this thing where they take nice people like you, torture them, get all hot and bothered about it, and then write horror novels and make movies out of them. You following?"

She shook her head, *no*.

Sighing, I said, "They *torture* people like *you* and then they write *books* about them. They make lots of *money*. Please just nod."

Denise nodded. "It's messed up ... whatever. All I want is to get back to my husband. I promise not to say anything, I swear. Just let me go."

"Would you stop saying that? I *am* letting you go. But when you get out of here, tell people the truth. That's your job—tell them what happened here. Somewhere on this property, the police are going to find a bunch of corpses. You were this close"—I held my fingers an inch apart—"to being one of those corpses."

She looked like she might start crying again, but kept it together.

I grabbed one of the pistols, shoved in a loaded magazine, chambered a round, and put it on the floor where she could see it. Then I readied another pistol the same way and set that one down, too.

"You see those guns?" I said. "They're loaded, ready to fire. All you need to do is pick them up when I'm gone and keep them pointed the way we came from. Anyone comes in here you don't like, you get to shoot them, okay?"

Her demeanor changed subtly at the looming possibility of arming herself.

"What about one of those shotguns?"

"Just use these," I said. "If I'm not back in an hour it's because I'm dead and Lana is still alive. In that case, find a place to hide and shoot her when she walks by. Don't leave the house. Big and slow as you are, she'll cut you down with that rifle she has."

With new hope suddenly pulled away, her face tightened with premature grief.

"For what it's worth," I said, "I'm sorry. You seem like a nice lady. I need to get up there now. Remember the guns—just pull the triggers, that's all you have to do."

Without a backwards glance, I left her there and returned to the main floor.

TWELVE

When I got to the foyer, I took the stairs and started my search on the second floor. It made sense to me that Lana would be in an upper-story window covering the driveway with her rifle, ready to pick off anyone who tried to get away in a car. It was the logical choice, even if she didn't at times seem the most logical of women. Which isn't to say I thought women weren't logical, because that'd be sexist. Which I wasn't. I'd all but banished any qualms about killing evil women, which was basically proof I wasn't sexist.

Buoyed by enlightened thoughts like these, I spent the next five minutes creeping around the upper floor. I cleared the rooms like they did in the cop movies, pointing the gun one way and then switching quickly the other way. After the first few, I gave that up and just poked my head in for a looksee, then moved on to the next room. Way simpler.

I kept coming back to that bizarre smokestack of death following my kick from Ernest Prescott. I'd counted them, and what a morbid little surprise that was—a thousand and one deaths. As in, *A Thousand and One Soup Recipes*. Or more aptly, *A Thousand and One Nights,* the story of Scheherazade, the princess forced to tell a story every night to King Shahryar. Sentenced to death, she survived each reading by adding to the story and never reaching the end—thus staying her execution another day and inventing the cliffhanger at the same time. And if that wasn't a threat from the Great Whomever I didn't know what was. His meaning was clear: do not tempt me, I'm in charge, and you're just the help.

After I'd searched every room, I got a drink from the faucet in one of the four upstairs bathrooms. Then I padded back to the staircase and returned to the foyer. I still hadn't seen the kitchen yet, which was a shame. Another reason why this ride sucked so bad. If I lived through this, I'd make myself something good to eat.

When I got to the foyer, I considered checking on Denise, but decided it wasn't worth scaring her and getting shot. I still hadn't heard any new gunshots, so she must have been fine.

I'd almost decided to check out the basement again when I thought I heard a door open and shut down in the direction of the room with the whipping wall and demon-claw stirrups. After the gunplay in the viewing room with Ernest, it had gotten harder to hear, especially out of my right ear. Still, it was worth a look.

When I got to the doors, I noticed they were partially open, so I angled myself a little to the left—a good thing too, because a section of door the size of a softball vanished in a flurry of splinters and gunfire.

I peeked through the hole. Lana was on the bed, on her knees, with the gun raised to her shoulder.

"Missed me!" I shouted, and ducked back in time for the next volley. "Missed me again!"

Lana shouted, "What the *hell* is wrong with you?"

"I wanted more money," I said.

"Are you serious? You said you loved your salary! Why didn't you ask for a raise like a normal person?"

"I was tired of being pushed around," I said.

A second later, she said, "What are you talking about? Everyone liked you! Jacob had some kind of man crush on you, for Christ's sake. What's this about?"

"I wanted evil henchman training, but you made me shoot Sean and now I gotta cover his shift!"

It had to be the stress. I covered my mouth to keep from laughing.

"What the *hell* are you *talking* about?" she yelled. "Look, is this about that girl? You take a shine to her or something? Why didn't you say so?"

That was a damn good question.

"I didn't think Jacob would approve," I said, finally.

Let's see her get out of that one.

"That's ridicu ... Never mind. Where's Jacob now?"

"Jacob's dead," I said. "Ernest too."

I thought I heard her gasp, but again, my hearing wasn't so good.

"Perfectly fine," she said, moments later. "Actually, I'm glad. I always liked you, Brian. Bigger, stronger, better looking than either of them. I married Jacob in secret because I couldn't be sure Ernest would succeed. And when he did, I didn't need Jacob anymore. But now that you've killed them both..." She paused, as if choosing the right words. "I've always had a thing for you, Brian, and I've seen you looking at me when you thought I wasn't watching. We'd be good together. And anyway, Jacob was beginning to bore me."

Jacob may have been boring to *her*, but there was a .50 caliber Desert Eagle leveled about two inches from my nose, and it was very interesting to *me*. Likewise the tattooed arm straining to hold it up.

Jacob's face was puffy, and a vessel in his eye had burst from being strangled nearly to death in the gym. Now he had a bad case of Terminator-eye. I started to raise my gun, but he froze me with a look: *I'll shoot you if you move.* With his other hand, he raised a finger to his lips in the universal sign for *shush.*

"Ask her more about me," he whispered, nodding toward the room.

As long as he wasn't shooting me with that hand cannon, I felt obligated to try.

"Yeah, so Lana," I said. "Uh, could you tell me more about Jacob?"

"What for?" she said.

Jacob nudged me.

Shrugging, I said, "Turns me on?"

Lana laughed wickedly, like it was no surprise and was now reveling in my confession.

"Oh, so *that's* what you like," she said. "Let's see ... The little poodle would cry after he beat me. Like father like son. At first it was cute, but then it got tiresome. I don't do well with tiresome."

I remembered that Wikipedia article mentioning how Jacob's father died of heart failure. Given everything I'd seen from her, I wondered about that. And since she felt like talking...

"So about that dad of his—how did he die again? Heart condition, something like that? There was speculation in the tabloids..."

"He was old," she said. "Too old for the Spanish Fly he was taking."

Despite the tense situation, I laughed. "Spanish fly's just a myth."

"That's what he thought. But blister beetles are as real as the cantharadin they produce. They only work on men, however, and they kill you if you take too much."

Jacob nudged me with the gun and nodded, like he wanted me to ask her more about that.

"Did, uh, you ever give any to Jacob?"

Lana chuckled darkly. "After Vegas, we *had* planned a trip to Mexico..."

"And?" I said.

"And if you hadn't killed him, in a few months the tabloids would have gone crazy." She laughed again. "*Lana Sandway's pussy wipes out whole family!* Has a nice ring to it, don't you think?"

I stole a glance at Jacob. He looked like he'd been slapped in the face by an ugly truth. If she'd killed his father, which it was starting to look like, he obviously hadn't known about it. Now Jacob knew she wanted to poison him the same way.

Lana wasn't done. Proudly she said, "The coroner assigned to the case was a fan of my old movies. That's real power, Brian, and that should be a warning to you—be interesting, but don't get too clingy. Now, are you going to fuck me or do I call the police and tell them my disgruntled manservant went on a shooting spree? Between the cops and me, you won't stand a chance."

Jacob's eyes were raging, staring at me like ... no, not at me—through me—like I was in the way. Testing the theory, I edged back against the door. Yep, he wasn't looking at me.

For a moment there it seemed like he might ... no, he was biting his lip and frowning. Not good. He needed a push.

Through the door I said, "Ernest heard you two getting busy today. He told me he called you something weird after you finished, but I gotta hear it from you."

Lana didn't say anything for a second, and I wondered if maybe I'd pushed the act too far. Then, in a tone of suffering patience, she said, "When Jacob was feeling sorry for himself I made him call me *mommy*. Now come on, I'm putting the gun away. Get in here and slay me with that big bronze dick, I can't take it anymore."

To Jacob I whispered, "You're up."

He didn't look at me or register my existence in any way. He walked past, kicked open the doors and got shot to pieces for his trouble. Mostly through both legs and his pelvis area. I turned the corner, ready to unload—and then a backpack nuke went off.

Jacob had shot that .50 caliber gun, and it was *loud*.

I was watching Lana when it happened. The round tore through her neck, taking her head almost completely off but for a little flap of skin. She sat like that, leaning against the back of the demon bed in her bizarre dominatrix outfit, her head flopped upside down on her chest, the rifle still aiming our way.

Jacob hadn't finished dying yet, but he was close. He was leaning with his back against the doorjamb, staring into space and gasping for breath like a fish. His eyes found mine.

"Why ... man ... why?"

Staring down at him, I tried to come up with something to help when he got to the other side. He was bad, sure, but this was the end for him. A special moment. I wanted to say how evil always destroys itself in the end or some other cliché, but all I said was, "I wish I knew."

Jacob's eyes drifted beyond me, as if looking far away to an afterlife only he could see. He raised his gun, as if to shoot said afterlife. Then his face tore away with the sound of a thunderbolt—from *behind* me.

Through my mostly working ear, I heard the unmistakable sound of a shotgun being pumped.

Denise...

"I wish I knew too, asshole," she said, before shooting me next.

THIRTEEN

Back in the Great Wherever, with nothing but time on my hands, I counted my blessings: a few museums, aching feet, rest stop ice cream, cardboard pizza, foul beer, okay sandwiches, a twisted book, and a sick movie. And though I'm normally a fan of naked women, Denise and Lana didn't actually count—for a number of complicated reasons having to do with morality and my self-respect. Then, after all this *way cool stuff,* when I'd had the temerity to ask for a little help, the Great Whomever had flipped me some steam about it.

One good thing though: the world wouldn't be subjected to any more legalized snuff from Ernest and his agent. I knew it wouldn't last. Hollywood abhors a vacuum, and there'd be other writers ready to take up Ernest's bloody mantle. I hoped moviegoers and readers would be appalled when they learned the truth about where the stories came from, but my guess was they'd convince themselves *they* weren't the sick ones, and that everything was still ketchup and tapioca, just like before. In fact, when the story finally broke, my guess was Ernest's publishers would sell more books than ever.

But at least I'd saved Denise and her baby. Actually, that was only partly true. In her mind, she'd had a hand in saving herself—a good thing, psychologically. Thin gruel feeds the peasants and carries them to and from their labors.

Hello, I thought into the void, and waited.

There are no days or nights in the Great Wherever. There are seconds and minutes and hours, yet no clocks to track the time. If it had a clock, I wouldn't have been able to look at it because I didn't have a body. So I had to guess at time's passage without even a steady pulse to guide me.

After about five minutes of nothing happening, I tried again.

I was thinking, what with your powers and all, why can't I have a body when I come here? Maybe a couch and a TV and some video games? Anything except Atari would be a big improvement.

I waited for a moment. Nothing happened.

Also, the whole suicide-goes-to-hell business? Shouldn't I be burning or something if it's really a sin? What does killing myself have to do with all these bad guys?

These were things I'd thought before but had never deliberately articulated. Gift horse in the mouth kind of thing, but I was over that now. I couldn't imagine the Being credited with the creation of the universe could be the same Great Whomever who'd threatened me with that horrible smokestack of death. As signs from the heavens went, that one seemed more petty than divine.

I was about to ask more questions, interspersed with some great accusations when, out of nowhere, a portal opened within the no-dimensional nothingness. It waited patiently in the void, hunched near my consciousness like a coat on a chair in a dark room.

Normally I'd hope for a good ride and enter the world with both fingers hypothetically crossed. This time, I had a better idea.

That last ride sucked, I projected. *I'm not saying I don't want to help people, but you need to pepper in the good rides in-between the psychotic dominatrix snuff horrors and guns rides, that's all I'm saying.*

Seconds later, for the first time ever, a second portal appeared in the void. But unlike the first one, this portal had a strangeness about it. As if I'd somehow be limited if I went through it—like being a guest in someone's house with a responsibility to take care of things. Another one-off doorway, like I'd had with Nate Cantrell and later with Peter Collins. If I reached for it, I'd come into the world in the body of someone who wasn't a violent criminal. And though those other rides had turned out okay, I'd come close to getting them both killed.

I saw what he was doing. Rather than working with me, the *Great Who Gives a Shit* had thrown my very reasonable request for a little reprieve back in my face. This time by upping the ante and sticking all the responsibility on me. If I chose the bad guy portal, whatever happened to the good guy was *my* fault. And if I chose the good portal, I'd get the double whammy of having to keep him alive and unhurt, along with the guilt from whatever the bad guy did.

Sigh, I projected, because I couldn't actually sigh. *I get it. You have more information than I do and I should back off. A little old fashioned with the requirement for blind faith, but maybe that's your thing? I give up, okay? I'm not choosing between them—you win.*

Just like that, the second portal faded from my awareness like it had never even been there, leaving the first portal alone with me in a frustrating place I called "square one."

This time, I kept my imaginary mouth shut, crossed my nonexistent fingers, and reached for the metaphorical portal.

* * *

I was sitting naked on the edge of a king-sized bed. A television was on, playing a commercial for a product guaranteed to enhance my natural virility or my money back.

The room had a coffee table, a thin blue rug, no paintings, a padded wingback chair, a small desk with a phone and a lamp, and heavy hotel curtains. Not a fancy room, and it smelled faintly of lighter fluid and sour milk.

I stood up and looked in the big mirror next to the television and saw a man spilling over with fat, late sixties or early seventies. About six feet tall, he had short white hair and an unimportant face.

A large suitcase lay sprawled open on the floor. I walked over and poked through it: men's clothing, a shaving kit, nearly half a bottle of bourbon, and a rolled-up sleeping bag.

I looked in the mirror and grinned experimentally at my reflection.

"Hello," I said, letting each syllable roll around my mouth. "This is my voice. I'm talking with my voice and it's loud, loud, *loud*. I'm *loud* in my room with my voice."

"Are you crazy or what?" came a raspy reply from the bathroom.

I tensed in surprise and said, "Who's there?"

"What do you mean who's there?" it said.

I fell back a step, preparing for whatever belonged to that horrible voice. But when it stepped around the corner...

"Jesus!" I shouted.

"Oh screw you," it grated from behind cracked lips and a mouthful of rotting teeth. Four teeth, and they were attached loosely to a scantily clad female figure draped in leathery hanging skin. From the neck down, she looked somewhere in her thirties, but her meth-ravaged face was positively Jurassic.

The woman shambled forward and lay back on the bed with her legs spread and a Halloween smile on her face.

"I'm bored," she said. "We gonna do it or what?"

My flabby stomach tightened in a dry heave.

"What's wrong with you now?" she said, glaring at me.

"Nothing, I ... *Oomuai* ... Just my ... Something I ate. Sorry."

She laughed.

"You ain't eat nothing yet, sugar," she said. "And you better pay me. If you don't, my ol' man's gonna cut you open."

"Just a minute," I said.

I went to the bathroom, turned on the sink, and washed my face with a tiny little bar of hotel soap. It went in my eyes but I didn't care. I needed time—and I felt skeevy.

"Don't think you're getting out of paying me!" she yelled

from the other room.

After drying off, I returned to find her perched on the bed with her back against the wall smoking a bent cigarette and watching me through angry bloodshot eyes.

"Where's my drink?" she said, breathing smoke out with each word.

"Your drink?"

"You said you would. I don't like liars."

"Sorry, what drink?"

She rolled her eyes. "You gonna gimme it? You're supposed to act like a gentleman."

Then it dawned on me what she was talking about.

"Hold on."

I stepped over to the suitcase and found the whisky bottle. When I turned back, she was pointing at something. I followed her bony arm to the television and saw it on the stand: a glass of something the same shade of amber as the liquid in the bottle.

"Right," I said, and put the bottle down beside it.

I picked up the glass and handed it to her. She took her drink—touching me in the process—and then swallowed it down quickly. The glass had been filled almost to the top, but she finished it between a drag from her cigarette and her next exhale of smoke.

"Tastes funny," she said, making a face.

There was a wallet on the nightstand. I opened it and pulled out some bills: a few tens and twenties. Biting my lip, I tried to figure out how much she charged and hoped it wasn't too high. I held out hope for a box of doughnuts sometime in the coming days, because I'd earned it.

"Here you go," I said, and handed her two twenties.

She accepted the money without looking at it, as if anything I gave her would be acceptable.

Rats.

"You sure you don't wanna take a stab?" she said, arching an eyebrow. "You can close your eyes. I won't mind."

I shook my head like it was the hardest decision ever.

"Nope," I said. "Too tired. So uh, guess you should, you know, *get going* now. Good seeing you, though."

I stepped back and glanced pointedly at the door. Kind of bopping my head that way and looking at it, then back at her. Just kind of bopping my head that way again.

"I ain't going nowhere!" she shouted, beginning to cry. "It's raining! Wouldn't have come with you if I knew you was gonna toss me so fast. I ain't leaving, I don't care what you do!"

She seemed the type that could fly off the handle at any moment, start throwing things and cause a scene. The last thing I wanted was someone calling the police and learning my ride had warrants out on him.

"I'm sorry," I said. "What's your name again?"

"Sally," she said, wiping her eyes.

"Okay, Sally. Do you need me to help you find your clothes?" Helpful. Polite.

"It's raining!" she said, pointing at the window.

I walked over and pulled the curtains partially open. Rain pelted the window, blurring my view of the nearly empty parking lot. The closest vehicle was a large minivan. I felt the glass with my hand—too cold to send anyone out in the rain.

When I turned around, Sally was standing with the bottle of whisky, pouring another drink for herself.

She blinked at me and said, "You want some?"

"No, thanks," I said, shaking my head. "You go ahead."

She didn't nod or smile or say thank you back. She drank it down fast and poured another, grimacing as she did it. I hoped it'd knock her out. She probably did too.

I got the sleeping bag from the suitcase and flattened it, then looked for an extra pillow in the closet and smiled when I found one.

"What are you doing?" Sally said, eyeing me suspiciously. Her voice had changed. Deeper now, more careful.

"I think I'll sleep down here tonight," I said.

"For what?"

"I'm being a gentleman."

She didn't say anything at first. Then she started to laugh.

"You do that," Sally said, and didn't bother with the

glass as she finished off the rest of the bottle in a single, long pull. She steadied herself briefly against the wall and sat back down on the bed. Her cigarette lay smoldering on the rug, so I took it and flushed it. When I came back, Sally's eyes were closed in peaceful slumber. The poor thing. In sleep she looked almost ghastly.

Ever the gentleman, I covered her with the blanket.

I found clean underwear in the suitcase and put it on. Then I sat back on the chair and flipped through the channels on the TV.

The hotel had cable, but it didn't have good cable. My eternal curse. There was a rerun of the Brady Bunch on—one of the Cousin Oliver episodes from season five, after the show had officially jumped the shark.

"How fitting," I said.

When I got tired, I turned on the light by the door, shut off the TV and the light in the main room, then crawled into the sleeping bag and closed my eyes. It took me a while to fall asleep, and it felt like no time had passed when my eyes opened again in response to my full bladder. Eventually I got up, checked the clock and saw it was a little after two in the morning.

When I finished my business and tried to fall back asleep, I wondered: *Why does he have a sleeping bag?*

After that, I couldn't fall asleep no matter how much I tossed and turned. Also, the ground was a little too hard for comfort. I considered slipping up onto the bed, but only for a moment. Instead, I went and sat in the soft chair.

Listening.

Other than my breathing, the room was very quiet.

I got up, walked over, and leaned down over Sally, straining to hear something.

"Sally," I said, shaking her gently. "Hey, wake up."

She didn't wake up like I wanted. Her scrawny arm was as cold as the surrounding room, and she wasn't breathing. Whatever was in the whisky had been in the bottle first and not slipped into the glass. By finishing the bottle, Sally had sealed her fate.

FOURTEEN

I found five bottles of Zolpidem Tartrate zipped in an inside pocket of the suitcase. Though invented to treat insomnia, it was also a popular date rape drug. Strong stuff. Each bottle was prescribed to a woman named Harriet Evans, of New Haven, Connecticut.

Though I felt sad for Sally, I was realistic about my part in her death. Nobody could have known what was in that bottle. But for once, the Great Whomever had come through: I'd finally caught an easy ride. There wouldn't be any evil henchmen this time around, or leather-clad literary agents wielding machine guns. Sally would be alive if this guy hadn't tried to drug her, and that's all I needed to know.

I rooted through the suitcase for a cell phone but didn't find one. Sally had a pink-covered phone in her purse. If the date was correct, it was early April 2008. Almost a month had passed since Denise had shot me, though it only felt like a couple of hours.

"Thanks for that," I said to the Great Whomever. He could have made me wait out every boring second of it in real-time, or made it seem longer, but it only felt like a few hours had passed.

I worried about Sally's phone. Everyone had friends, and someone was bound to miss her. Maybe her *ol' man.*

So I turned it off. Whatever happened, I silently promised Sally her death wouldn't go unsolved.

I found my ride's license in a green nylon wallet: Fredrick Evans of New Haven, Connecticut. Same address as Harriet Evans.

Provided the rules for occupying scumbags hadn't changed in a month, I had a good three weeks—my arbitrary lease on life—in Fred's skin before those telltale kicks threatened to let him walk free. It was my job to make sure that didn't happen—within reason, and not necessarily right away. No more book signings, extreme sports, or drinking beer. I planned to have fun this trip.

I dressed myself in jeans and a red T-shirt with faded writing on it, then packed everything except for the sleeping bag into Fred's suitcase.

"Sorry, Sally," I said, and laid the bag next to her.

The next few minutes reflected poorly on me. Through a series of tugs and pulls, I managed to get Sally's lifeless body into the sleeping bag and then zipped it up. I felt lightheaded, and noticed I'd been holding my breath.

Stepping quickly away from the bed, I forced myself to breathe deeply. My ride was old and overweight, and I didn't want to faint.

I checked the covers and the nightstand for the money I'd given her but didn't find it. And it wasn't on the floor or under the bed. Frowning, I unzipped the bag again and found both twenty-dollar bills clenched tightly in her fist, now stiffening through the early stages of rigor mortis. After I got her zipped back up, I washed my hands to banish the lingering memory of her icy fingers.

Looking at my reflection in the mirror, I wondered what had gone so terribly wrong with this guy that he enjoyed drugging women more than romantic dinners, fresh flowers, and quiet conversation.

I smiled at my reflection and saw my unfamiliar face smile back. Normal smile, nothing sinister. Fred could have been a retired mailman or an executive or just some guy at the grocery store. What he needed was a thin black mustache to match his inner monster to his outer coupon clipper.

I stepped outside for a quick recon. It was a cloudy moonless night, the landscape rural and quiet. A Motel 8 sign and a few evenly spaced safety lights warded the gloom from the civilized world.

Directly outside my room was a shiny blue minivan. It had been backed into the space hatch-first to the room. A click from Fred's keys confirmed it was *his* shiny blue minivan. As luck had it, the nearest cars were way down at the other end of a long stretch of rooms. Likely my ride had requested something far away from anyone else so he could slip out easily with Sally's body, unconscious or dead, hidden inside the sleeping bag. It was a good idea.

So that's what I did.

Sally was light, and she tended to slide around in the bag as I labored her into the back of the van. After she was tucked away, I shut the hatch and checked to see if anyone had seen me—probably not—then went back inside to get Fred's suitcase. After stowing it between the back seats, I got in behind the wheel. The CD player came on with the engine, breaking the silence with the soulful harmonizing of a gospel jubilee quartet. Old stuff, like maybe from the thirties. That was too creepy for words, so I hit random buttons until the radio kicked in. Then I flipped around until I found a boring and predictable classic rock channel.

Pulling up to a deserted two-lane road, I considered my options. To the left, the unlined road stretched into darkness. If I went right, I'd pick up a ramp to what looked like an interstate. It was cold out, still raining, so I could have been nearly anywhere in the lower forty-eight, subject to the vagaries of April weather. I'd purposely driven past a few cars to check license plates, and of course they were from a bunch of different states.

I went right.

As soon as I got onto the interstate, it became quickly apparent I was in Fred's home state heading north on I-95 toward New Haven.

Though I hadn't memorized the street maps of every big city, I'd gotten most of them, including this one. Still, it didn't mean I knew how the house numbers were laid out.

I took Fred's exit and found his neighborhood a few

minutes later, then drove around squinting at faded numbers on mailboxes until I found one that matched his license: a large Tudor-style house with a double garage and no neighbors in sight, unless you counted the porch lights winking through the trees.

Earlier in the drive, I'd found Fred's phone in the dash. When I opened it, it had a full charge. Probably only used it for emergencies or he would have carried it with him everywhere like most people. Or maybe he hadn't wanted to be interrupted while he did what he'd planned with Sally. Now I had two phones. Still no one to call, but that was fine.

The clock on the phone showed 3:52 a.m., while the clock in the dash showed 4:55 a.m.

"Typical," I said.

I stopped the van and got out, my breath steaming faintly in front of me through the cold relentless rain. With the thick cloud cover and lack of streetlights, the world had never been so black.

For now, I left Sally's corpse in the back of the van. The cool temperature would slow the rate of her decomposition, and the van would keep the animals from getting at her.

Fred's front door was a longer walk than the side entrance next to the garage, so I opened the storm door and tried the keys until I found one that worked. On entering the house, I gave the air an experimental sniff. No tobacco, no decomposing bodies.

I wondered who Harriet was. His wife? A daughter, maybe? Whoever she was, I didn't feel like dealing with her at such a late hour, so I stayed quiet and kept the lights off.

I used Fred's phone to light the way, occasionally hitting a number on the keypad to keep it lit. By the dim light, I crept down a short hallway, past a staircase, and into the living room. Nobody was there. I found an office with books and papers and filing cabinets, but it was equally empty.

Suppressing a small shiver at the odd normalcy staring me in the face from everywhere, I stepped from a sparsely furnished bedroom back to the central hallway of the main floor.

I shuddered at the inexplicable feeling of something in the darkness reaching to snatch me away. As a child, I'd gotten that feeling at least several times a month. As if something were standing right behind me, and if I looked back, a corpse with red glowing eyes would smile at me with a mouthful of needle-sharp teeth. After that, I wouldn't exist anymore. I'd either be eaten or possessed by the Devil. Or, when my family found me, I'd be stark raving mad, and parents everywhere would use me as an example of what happened to children who never finished their vegetables.

The moment passed, and my sanity remained unscathed. But Brussels sprouts still sucked.

The upstairs had three furnished bedrooms, each of them unoccupied. The last bedroom, the master, was surprisingly Spartan for a room so big. Like the other rooms, it had a bureau and a bed, though Fred's was a king-sized bed. I opened a few of the drawers and found socks and underwear. In his closet were shirts and pants and nothing else.

Not a Harriet in sight.

I went back downstairs and searched more carefully. Just off the kitchen was a second set of stairs leading down to the basement. At the bottom was a heavy wooden door with throw bolts set into a steel frame.

"Now we're talking," I said.

After pulling back the bolts, I opened the door and stepped into an expansive basement, pitch black. I reached over and felt around until my fingers brushed a light switch. On flipping the switch, track lights flared to life from about ten locations, momentarily blinding my dark-adjusted eyes. Squinting, I saw a pole in the middle of the room with a chain looped around it, the end lying coiled on a ratty old mattress.

Approaching the mattress, I noticed the chain ended in a steel collar. I picked up the chain, lifted the collar to eye level, and examined it: about half an inch thick, locked and closed with a key sticking out of it. I turned the key and it came right out. I put it in and turned it the other direction and the collar popped open. I closed it again and locked it with the key, then put the ugly thing back on the mattress.

It's a harsh thing to say someone's better off dead, but if I'd picked the other portal and Sally had made it this far...

A quick check of Fred's phone showed it close to four in the morning. His old, heavy body was tired, which meant I was tired. None of what I'd seen required me to do anything right now, so I huffed up the stairs back to the main floor, then the next flight to where the master bedroom was. By the time I got to the top, I was gasping and out of breath.

Fred's bed was neatly made, the linen smelled clean, and I didn't see any villainous dominatrices anywhere, which was great.

I took off my clothes and settled in to sleep.

FIFTEEN

Morning arrived with the promise of good food, movies, walks in the park, shopping sprees, driving around listening to music, fishing trips, indoor public pools, one or two naps a day, and my all-time favorite thing to do: sitting around reading in coffee shops.

But I couldn't do any of that until I'd done something about Sally, still out there in the minivan. It was a little cold for April, but she'd start cooking from the inside if left for too long. When that happened, I wouldn't be able to drive the minivan in the comfort I was accustomed to.

I still had a little time before that happened, so I went back through the house looking for anything I'd missed in my first sweep. The upstairs rooms were as empty as last night, but the light streaming through the blinds showed everything covered in a thick coat of dust.

I returned to the little office I'd seen last night and thumbed through the papers and boxes of opened mail. It became quickly apparent that Harriet relied heavily on Medicare to treat her various ailments, one of which was chronic insomnia. A minute later, I also learned she was dead.

Up on the wall, in a gilded frame, Fred had set Harriet's death certificate proudly on display.

"Alcoholic poisoning," I read. She'd died more than

three years ago.

The date of birth on the certificate had Harriet older than Fred by two years. It also showed her as unmarried. I figured she was his sister, though she could have been a cousin.

With nothing more to look at, I left the room, shut the door, and resumed my tour.

The rest of the house had tables and chairs and things of that sort, but there was something about it all that didn't look completely lived in. Take the dining room, for example. The table was loaded with fine china, crystal, and actual silverware. The lace tablecloth was now yellowed with age, and each setting had the forks and spoons in the proper locations. Yet the silverware was coated in a rainbow of colorful tarnish, and the china and crystal were grimy with fossilized dust. The whole thing appeared to have been set and left that way for years.

There was nothing physically wrong with the structure of the house, and with Harriet out of the way, I planned to stay there. I didn't know enough about Fred's finances, other than he had a few credit cards and a tiny amount of cash left in his wallet. So moving to a fancy hotel didn't make much sense.

The house had an attached garage packed front to back with boxes, tools, and old furniture. Also, it had a freezer. I couldn't believe my luck. It was almost like someone upstairs was looking down and saying, "Dan needs a freezer, he's getting a freezer." It was a big one, too. Large enough to hold three more prostitutes if needed.

Anxious to start my day, I went outside to get Sally.

The light of the new day revealed something I'd missed last night: the property was sort of a mess. The lawn hadn't been mowed—ever. The hedges under the windows were like Chia Pets who'd let themselves go, and a branch from the tree out front threatened to bash in two of the second story windows under the press of a light breeze. The house wasn't falling down or damaged or anything. More like it was slouching around with the intent of one day crumbling and blowing away.

Fred's minivan, however, was brand new. And clean—

like he'd recently washed and waxed it. I wondered if he called it his *baby*.

After checking the perimeter, where Fred's suburban savannah met overgrown steppes ending in a tree line, I concluded no children or nosey neighbors were hovering in wait for me to drag Sally into the light so they could call the cops.

Even through the sleeping bag, Sally's body grossed me out all the way from the minivan to the side door. The garage would have been quicker, but it was too packed. Along the way, the hardness of her elbows and knees, and the wobbly weight of her head, were a constant reminder there was a human body in there. When I got to the freezer, I became seized with sudden terror at the thought she might still be alive, like Jacob back at that weirdo mansion.

I unzipped the bag and checked to make sure. Yep, still dead.

The freezer contained some packaged meat and bags of veggies, crusted with frost, but it was mostly empty. I set her gently inside it and used a bag of peas for a pillow. Then I pushed down on the lid along the edges in case one of the seams was loose or the door hadn't been squarely placed. Working with as many freezers as I had, I knew what to look for.

One time, I'd missed just such a defect and the motor had burned out under too much load. Everything was fine until the second week, and then it was like someone detonated a stink bomb thousands of times more powerful than the one dropped on Mrs. Bloodworth's English class in '88. As much as I'd like to take credit for that senseless act of olfactory terrorism, that had been my buddy Simon's doing.

With Sally out of the way, I rushed upstairs and took a long hot shower.

For all that Fred's house was in disrepair, he wasn't a slob. He had soap and shampoo, clean clothes, and deodorant. Another reason to stick around. Using the safety razor and old-fashioned cup of shaving soap was a special joy, almost like a cleansing ritual.

After affixing four little pieces of toilet paper to the cuts on my face, I went downstairs and checked out the refrigerator. No heads or eyeballs or jars of human ears. Just eggs, bacon, juice, bottles of condiments, no fruits and vegetables anywhere, and a small freezer with a carton of ice cream.

Not only was my ride a predator, possibly a serial killer, but he also enjoyed Chunky Monkey. It's a small world after all.

With breakfast and grooming and cleanup squared away, I contemplated what to do next. What a great ride so far. Fred was sort of old, and slow from being way too overweight for his age, but he was strong enough to kidnap women, and he wasn't in a wheelchair. After my last ride, maybe I didn't need vigorous so much. Rest and relaxation—that'd do nicely. Something incredibly passive, requiring zero thinking on my part. No work, no guns or torture, and possibly a trip to the Dairy Queen if I found one in the wild.

"The mall," I said, finally.

Though I knew all the roads, it didn't mean I knew where all the malls were. But that's why they have gas stations.

"I'm looking for a big mall," I said to the guy behind the counter. "The biggest you got."

He laughed good-naturedly. "We don't sell any here, but if you head down to the light and hang a right..."

When he finished, I paid for my little apple pie and carton of milk, thanked him, and left. Ten minutes later I was parked outside a big mall, all boxes and elevations and tacked-on sections flung out in every direction. It was amazing.

I love malls—people from all walks of life coming together to engage in commerce, crowding from place to place, oblivious and preoccupied, yet somehow never actually colliding with one another. Malls were temperature-controlled, too, and nobody smoked indoors anymore so I didn't have to deal with that.

One of the best days of my life was when I was sixteen and snuck off to ditch a low-calorie diet my parents had put me on when I'd gotten too heavy. I'd taken the bus to the mall and bought a mixed bag of jelly doughnuts and Boston Creams. Then I sat on a bench with a carton of milk and letched over an endless parade of other people's girlfriends. Near the end of the bag, right when my body was telling me it wasn't hungry anymore, I found a lemon-filled doughnut—delicious, tart, and sweet—and that stoked the fire a little longer. For the next thirty minutes, I sat there with my arms hooked over the back of the bench. Just me and my empty bag of doughnuts and an avalanche of powdered sugar decorating my shirt.

Ah, the good ol' days.

After checking the backlit marquis, I hiked way to the other side of the mall and took the escalators up a level to the only bookstore they had.

The escalators were great, but that was a long walk for Fred. I had to sit on a bench for a while to catch my breath. A good time to resume my favorite mall pastime: staring at women.

One thing about Fred: the pigment around his eyes was darker than the rest of his face, giving him a faintly brooding appearance. I didn't want anyone complaining to mall security, so I made sure to look around innocently whenever a woman passed by. I settled for two seconds coming, five seconds going, which I deemed a good gawking-to-looking-around ratio.

When I felt I was ready, I lurched to my feet and went into the bookstore.

First, I poked through the new releases, judging each book by its cover. Then I visited the little lounge and coffee area they had, bought a large cup of coffee and six different pastries, and found a table in a more or less central location where I could eyeball everyone coming and going. A tactical decision. People were less likely to catch me staring at them because it would be impolite to watch me eat.

A little social judo, that—using people's good manners against them.

After finishing a peach danish and a bran muffin, I held off eating my next pastry—a huge creampuff, cold and heavy with cream. Needing something to read—part of my cover—I jaunted over to the newsstand to find something that wasn't too boring: *National Geographic, Scientific American,* and a science fiction magazine. Just the basics. The *Black Belt Magazine* I added on impulse would teach me some neat moves in case I was ever attacked by ninjas.

Looking for anything cool I'd missed, my gaze strayed to the newspapers. If my eyes could have bugged out, they would have, but probably they just widened a little. And with good reason: every paper had a story about Ernest Prescott's house of horrors plastered across the front page.

I put the *National Geographic* and *Scientific American* back, grabbed three newspapers, and returned to my table.

USA Today had a scary picture of Ernest on the front, captioned, "Truth or Scare?" It talked about the unidentified woman who'd been kidnapped and how she shot her way to freedom. It covered the wild parties Lana and Ernest threw at the mansion, and the cultish following that had sprung up since his first book, *Clench,* had hit the shelves.

What I found most interesting were the eleven bodies found decomposing in the mansion's oversized septic tanks. Each news source confirmed the FBI was running DNA on the remains. One of the corpses had been fresh and easily identifiable—a security guard working for Lana Sandway named Sean Galloway. It turned out Sean and Brian had been ex-military security specialists who'd done mercenary work overseas, possibly for third-world dictators.

The press spent a lot of time focusing on reports of a "sex pentangle"—the phrase of the week, repeated in all three newspapers—between Sean, Brian, Lana, Ernest, and rising MMA star Jacob Sandway. The kinky pentangle rumors and the connection to Jacob's father allowed the press to spread the sleaze so thin it covered and tainted everything. One paper went so far as to suggest it had really been a "sexagon" before the rich man's death. Other than the names, almost nothing resembled the truth I'd experienced.

Recalling the bizarre events at the mansion, which to me seemed like only yesterday and would for as long as I existed, I suddenly didn't feel like eating my last creampuff. I ate it anyway, though, because wasting food is a sin.

I paid for my magazines, and a book I snagged on the way to the checkout line, and left.

The mall had a theater, but *Sliced* wasn't playing on any of the screens. Taken down, most likely, as an outward display of respect for the victims, though I doubted the self-censorship applied to online video sales or books.

It was a weird feeling, being the center of the nation's collective astonishment. A real mover and shaker, I was. You line 'em up and I knock 'em down. A dangerous feeling, and faintly intoxicating.

I'd always thought serial killers left clues behind to see their names in the paper, to feel like big men and watch the world dance. Though that was obviously still true for many of them, I sensed an additional reason. In a weird way, knowing all those people were out there thinking about me and what I'd done at the mansion, I didn't feel so alone.

"I'm *not* a serial killer," I stated firmly, then glanced around to see if anyone heard me.

At some point in my wandering from store to store, I found myself in an open section of the mall on the ground floor occupied by an enormous jungle gym, safely contained with thick netting to keep kids from toppling out.

If I'd grown up with a jungle gym like that, who knows where I'd be today? All that self-actualization and delirious joy. Maybe I would have lived past my first broken heart and become a movie director like I'd wanted. But then Denise and her baby, and all those other people over the years, wouldn't be alive today.

Out of nowhere, the jungle gym offered up an altogether different sort of actualization, though very little joy.

In 2004, a man named Gerald Ross had been tried on multiple counts of possession of child pornography, counts of felony child molestation, charges of sexual misconduct with a minor, contributing to the delinquency of a child, aggravated sexual assault and, as if it were somehow on par with those other crimes, obstruction of justice.

Following the trial, after weeks of argument on both sides, Gerald beat most of the charges. But even his incredibly lenient judge, roundly criticized for siding so often with the defense, couldn't rescue him from one of the counts of possession of illegal porn—because Gerald had been an active participant in the one picture the prosecution managed to rescue as admissible. That one picture should have been enough to nail Gerald on a molestation charge, but the child—a little girl, about eight years old—couldn't be found.

After that, an expert witness said *this* little girl had never existed, that *this* picture had been doctored. No other pictures were examined by the expert because the defense proved (with the judge's help) that the prosecution had severely botched the chain of custody.

Before the trial, Gerald had been something of a celebrity in his hometown. He'd had a kids' television show called *Gerald's House* on a local station. *Gerald's House* featured puppets, games, singing, educational skits like on *Sesame Street,* and prizes for lucky kids who wrote in with answers to his weekly question: "What do you want to be when you grow up?" When his show got picked up for syndication, *People Magazine* called him "the next Mr. Rogers."

After the news broke about the real Gerald Ross, almost nobody covered the story. What finally brought the story to national attention wasn't the crime itself, but the sentence. The judge presiding over the case, despite objections from the prosecutor and almost anyone with a conscience, sentenced Gerald to a mere thirty days in jail for his single count of possession of child pornography, going so far as to override the jury's much harsher, maximum sentence.

The judge explained his verdict: "Almost nothing in the state's sentencing request was crafted with the goal of rehabilitation. It appears to have been born out of a need for retaliation in a case they couldn't carry, and I cannot in good conscience allow the establishment of another crime, as if the one will somehow cancel out the other."

Gerald wouldn't get off *too* easily, the judge added. As a condition of his release, he'd be forced to seek therapy for his condition.

For the next four days, the judge's bizarre verdict was all the media would talk about. Then something happened in the Middle East and Gerald's story got bumped to make room for talking heads, war correspondents, and ancient cities on fire.

Some months later, the story took an unexpected twist. The judge in the case, His Honor, Mark Simmons, had been arrested for possession of child pornography. But that wasn't the interesting part. The pictures found on his computer were of the same victims in the Gerald Ross case—the very case he had so leniently presided over.

Judge Simmons went to prison, but there was nothing anyone could do about Gerald—the laws against double jeopardy forbade another trial. After release, he quickly disappeared from the scene, and the news moved on to whichever outrage made the most sense to cover next.

Nine years later, the world may have forgotten about the case, but I hadn't.

Standing on the other side of the jungle gym was a slightly older Gerald Ross, about fifty now, and a little heavier than his showbiz days. He was carrying a teddy bear in one hand and a pink backpack in the other. He stood there with a patient smile on his face, as if waiting for his own child to finish playing so he could take him or her home. He chatted with nearby parents, laughing and getting along—even tussling the hair of the odd kid here or there. I stood out of his direct line of sight for about thirty minutes, waiting to see if a kid burst forth from one of the colored tubes and called him Daddy, but that never happened.

In time, Gerald stopped talking to parents and tussling hairdos. He drifted back from the circle of parents and nannies, turned around, and walked away.

And because I am who I am, I followed him.

SIXTEEN

Gerald didn't look around at the stores, people, and colorful sale signs. He didn't stare at other people's big pretzels or soft-serve cones, like I did. He walked with purpose, too quickly, such that Fred's large, aging body was having trouble keeping up. My heart sank briefly when I lost sight of him. He'd cut through a thickening in the crowd, then slipped around a corner jewelry store. When I finally turned the corner, I found to my annoyance he'd vanished.

He could have gone into one of the nearby shops, or he could have continued to where the corridor bent left about thirty feet down. If I continued on and didn't see him, I could always double back and check the shops one by one.

Picking up the pace as best I could, I turned the bend and pushed through the glass doors leading outside.

I caught sight of him walking down the sidewalk alongside the building toward a big parking structure. He didn't look back, and I tailed him into the garage.

Gerald took the stairs to the next level, and despite the possibility of a heart attack before my three weeks concluded, I kept after him—tiredly, doggedly, gasping for breath by the time I got even one flight up. No wonder Fred picked on scarecrows like Sally.

When I crested the third landing, Gerald had vanished

FOOL'S RIDE

again, and this time I knew I couldn't catch him. Possibly he'd gone left around the numerous columns and parked cars. Or maybe he'd kept going up to the fourth floor. Maybe the fifth. Why not the sixth?

Wherever he went, I knew I was done.

"That's that," I said to myself, and stumped back down again.

Pausing at the bottom, leaning heavily against the concrete entrance, I wondered whether I had free will. It was interesting, me coming to the mall today and seeing Gerald Ross. Like I'd been guided here. And if I was guided here, and thus not under my own control, what was the point of the whole free will charade to begin with?

Back in the Great Wherever, if I'd taken the other portal to that innocent man, would I have found my way to the same mall? Perhaps that ride would have been younger with more endurance. And if I'd caught Gerald, killed him, and gotten caught in the process, an innocent man would have gone to jail.

Just when I pushed off the wall to resume walking, Gerald Ross pulled up next to me in a blue car, neither high-end nor a clunker. He slowed before turning onto the access road that led out, glanced casually at me, then faced back to the road. Then he calmly pulled away.

I couldn't stop him, but I did note one distinguishing feature of his otherwise unremarkable car. On the back fender, positioned under the left taillight, was a bumper sticker reading: *I Love Kids*.

"Son of a bitch," I said.

Twenty seconds later, he was gone.

When I got back in the mall, I found the food court, then went to a place with no line and ordered a large soda.

"And a slice of pizza," I added.

Being in the body of an old heavy guy had become sort of a bummer. Fred was strong, but he tired too easily from walking. And his blood sugar had begun to crash when I'd taken those stairs in the parking garage. Dangerous signs in an older guy.

Now I was shaky and weak, and when I finished my pizza I went back to the counter for another slice. The soda helped replenish the sugar that had been sucked away by too much insulin. Fred didn't do well with sugar, and I knew I'd have to reduce my intake. Diet sodas going forward, and no more than two pastries next time. No need to go cold turkey, right? I wasn't trying to save Fred's life, but I didn't want to blow my ride through reckless gluttony, either.

The rest of the day was spent watching back-to-back movies at the mall theater and reading my book on a bench just outside a Victoria's Secret.

On the way back to the house, I picked up some groceries to go with all that ketchup and mustard Fred had. Then I took a nap. After I got up, I didn't feel like cooking so I ordered Chinese food. For dessert, I had a technically smaller bowl of Chunky Monkey than normal—in light of Fred's condition—then stayed up watching his surprisingly skimpy television setup. No DVD player, no cable TV, not even satellite, and no computer or Internet access.

Tired from the day and loaded with things to read, I was fine with that.

* * *

That night, just as I was thinking about heading to bed, a phone started ringing from somewhere in the house. I got up and followed the sound to the room with Harriet's death certificate. I'd been too slow, and whoever it was gave up after eight rings.

A desk stood against the wall stacked with junk mail and boxes of Harriet's Medicare papers. On it was an old yellow rotary telephone. I didn't see an answering machine, and because it was a rotary, I assumed Fred didn't have a service.

A minute later, from the kitchen, Fred's cell began ringing.

I hurried to the kitchen, picked it up and said, "Hello?"

"Fred, where were you last night?" a man said. He sounded young, with a heavy New England accent. "Lucky for you I needed the hours, but I can't cover you again. You wanna get fired or what?"

"I've been sick," I said, then coughed for effect.

"Too sick to call Cliff and let him know?"

"Exactly."

"I don't get you," he said. "You come in early every day, then every month or so you don't show up and you don't call. Something I should know?"

"Probably," I said.

"What?"

"There's probably something you should know."

He laughed. "Like what?"

"I need a favor," I said. "What's the mailing address of our ... uh, where we work?"

"Why you wanna know the address for?"

I thought for a second and said, "I need to fill out a survey for jury duty."

He laughed. "Oh yeah? Like they can't get that from their computer, right? Hold on..." The phone went quiet for several seconds before he picked back up. "You know, Fred, I don't think they care about the warehouse. They probably just want the office address."

"Can you give me both?"

Whoever he was mumbled something that rhymed with duck. "One second..."

When he picked up again, he quickly rattled off two addresses, then told me the first one was for headquarters.

"Seriously, Fred, I gotta go home tonight," he said. "How long you gonna be?"

"I'm leaving now."

"Good," he said, and hung up.

Though I was tired, I was also interested in anything Fred was up to, including his job. If I didn't like whatever it was, I could always leave. Warehouse work sounded difficult. Fred didn't strike me as the kind of guy who'd be up for moving heavy boxes, so I was curious about what he did.

It was around midnight when I pulled into an industrial park with big white buildings spanning huge blocks. I drove around slowly, wondering where the heck the front door was to wherever I was supposed to be. When I got to the end of a long road that ended in a chain link fence, I circled back.

In the middle of the street was a man standing and

waving a flashlight at me. He'd come out of a tiny trailer I'd driven past. There weren't any parking spots, just a gravely ramp up to where the trailer was. A big black pickup truck was parked next to it.

I pulled up beside it, parked, and got out.

The man was young with wiry brown hair and tough-looking facial hair trimmed to look like spikes flaring up from his jaw. He had on a security guard's uniform and carried a big long flashlight, as much weapon as light source. He didn't look happy to see me.

"You forgot your uniform, too?" he said, shaking his head at all the rules I was breaking.

I tried to say something but he waved me to silence.

"Never mind that," he said. "I need to go. This happens again, I gotta say something to Cliff, okay? Nothing personal, you know I like you. But you also know I can't leave until you get here. It's just not fair, man."

He didn't wait for a reply. He got in his truck, backed out, tossed me a grudging wave, and then drove off.

I stared around at all the big warehouses, holding however many millions of dollars in merchandise and equipment, then at the trailer.

"I'm actually in charge," I said, mildly surprised at the absurd notion. It was pretty cool.

Such power...

I climbed the two metal steps and opened the door to the trailer. It was a singlewide with lots of shelves and a few tables, so it was hard to maneuver around. Ten monitors were mounted on one wall over a desk where I assumed Fred and the other guards sat to fight crime. On the desk was a thick three-ring binder opened to a half-filled page. Some sort of status log with entries for every hour and a signature beside each one. The entries were a long string of the same thing written over and over: "Nothing to report."

A small refrigerator sat in the corner with a stack of magazines on top. After looking in the refrigerator, which was empty, I picked up a magazine: *Deer and Deer Hunters*. The other magazines were different issues of the same periodical. A subscription sticker was affixed to each one with someone's name and address on it. Brad Ratcliff, of New Haven Connecticut. I checked the others and they were all addressed to the same person.

Using my uncanny detective skills, I noted the last entries in the ledger were by someone whose first name might have been Brad if I squinted, but whose last name was definitely Ratcliff.

"Very interesting, Mr. Ratcliff," I said, savoring the triumph of my clever observation. It had been so long since I'd had one I'd forgotten how fun they were.

I looked up from the ledger and examined the monitors. The top row showed the insides of different warehouses, and each of the lower monitors covered various outside locations. Each of those was sectioned off into four small windows. There was a row of buttons that, when I pushed them randomly for fun, cycled one of the monitors through all the other views for a closer look.

It was late and I was tired. Fred was feeling his age, so I didn't go back outside. I tried reading one of the magazines, but then dozed off. Some hours later, I woke up with a full bladder and a dry mouth.

Out of nowhere, a car drove through the corner view of one of the monitors. The view wasn't great, but I caught a brief image of a smiling young woman in the passenger seat. The car passed through one monitor and then through another. Then another and another. Finally, it pulled into a dark patch way behind one of the buildings and parked.

SEVENTEEN

The woman had seemed happy, not a kidnap victim, which was my chief worry considering how fond the Great Whomever was of coincidence.

I figured out how to angle the camera where I wanted and also how to zoom in. Mainly I hoped to see another smile—to be sure whatever was going on was consensual. I'd seen so much bad in the world. Sometimes it was hard to whistle and look on the bright side of life. To imagine a world where people didn't cut up other people and paint the walls with bloody satanic symbols.

The camera was zoomed-in as far as it would go, focused on the windshield, but I couldn't see anything. Then, after a while, the car began rocking.

Which begged the question: *should I go a'knocking?*

In high school, taking a date to a hotel was a mythical idea. Hotels cost way too much. Also, they'd ask for an ID, and no guy really believed he'd be allowed to get a hotel room at seventeen. The idea of sex with another human was foreign enough to begin with, never mind where it happened. When I talked about it with my friends, it was a given that any such miracles would happen in a park or somewhere called "lover's lane," or possibly with a prostitute way out in a swamp like in the movie *Porky's*. Just our luck, none of us knew where any swamps were.

I'd been a virgin until I met Sandra, in college, so I'd missed out on whatever was going on in that car out there. Part of me mourned for those missing experiences—to be the good-looking kid with the cheerleader girlfriend, the fast car and the cool friends. Shy as I was back then, I never dated.

Having a car was the dream that kept me going, and with permission from Mom and Dad, it could have come true. Such a wonder would have snagged me a shallow girlfriend who only wanted me for my car—thus rounding out my high school experience perfectly and setting me on the path to a suicide-free life.

As it happened, I'd ridden the bus until the very last day of twelfth grade. And whether through laziness or some desire to turn back the clock, I left whoever was in the car alone and minded my own business.

By morning, I'd fallen so soundly asleep I didn't notice when my relief arrived.

"Fred, wake up, man," a voice said, laughing.

My eyes snapped open and I wondered where I was. Then I saw an old man wearing a security uniform, like Brad Ratcliff from last night.

"Hi," I said, rubbing my eyes.

"You look half dead," the man said.

The clock on the wall showed it was seven o'clock in the morning. Brad had called me sometime after eleven last night. So, an eight-hour shift.

Glancing at the monitors, I saw the lovebirds had moved on. Probably hours ago.

"Jesus, Fred," the guy said, disgusted. "You didn't fill out your report."

"It's not that hard. Everyone just writes in 'Nothing to report.' Gimme a second."

"Sleeping on the job, not doing your report? And where's your uniform? What if Cliff sees you without your uniform?"

What indeed?

I stopped writing and gazed at him fearlessly, as if *I* were the mighty Cliff. The man held my gaze a moment, mumbled something about coffee, then turned to brew a fresh pot.

A minute later, after writing *Nothing to report* eight times in a row and feeling like a schoolboy in a teensy weensy amount of trouble, I said, "All done."

Then I got up and left.

Sleeping in a chair all night hadn't been very comfortable. So when I got to the house, I went back to bed and snagged two more hours. After that, I made a Jenkins-sized breakfast with the food I'd bought the day before.

As a precaution, I also checked on Sally to make sure the motor hadn't blown out or the breaker hadn't tripped from cooling an entire human body down to freezing. When I lifted the lid and felt around with my hand, the air in the box seemed cold enough. Also, Sally was frozen solid when I poked her with a spoon.

Day two into my Fred adventures and everything appeared to be going perfectly: working credit cards, a comfortable house with a creepy kidnapping room in the basement, and a job I could actually do. Weird as it seemed, I loved the security guard job. Having to show up and be a productive member of society was a rare experience for me. What a special joy, this strange fear I might get in trouble if I showed up late. There had never been a time in my life when I'd had to fill out a report.

Nice as all that was, there was a sicko running loose named Gerald Ross. There were sickos everywhere, but few of them had been on TV before.

Years ago, Gerald had gotten away from justice, then yesterday from me. I consoled myself with the knowledge that even if I had caught him, there wasn't much I could have done. He was about twenty years younger and in better shape, and my casual search of Fred's house hadn't turned up any weapons.

But the Great Whomever doesn't care about excuses. And when it comes to kids, I guess I don't either.

I went back to the mall. More magazines, more books, more food court fun, and the rest of the day spent staking out children's stores and the big jungle gym where I'd first spotted Gerald.

All for nothing. I'd either missed him or he hadn't come

to the mall that day.

When I showed up to work that night, wearing a uniform I found in Fred's closet, there was a different guy there—young, like Brad was—and he chuckled when he saw me.

"It's your day off, man," he said. "What are you doing here?"

"Day off?"

"You don't remember? You better hope Cliff don't see you here. All that guy needs is an excuse to bitch."

He pointed at a dry-erase calendar I'd overlooked. There were names in all the little boxes for this month. Fred had the eleven to seven shift, Sunday through Thursday. I saw the problem right away: today was Friday. Brad's days paced with mine, except he worked three to eleven.

I didn't see Cliff's name anywhere. He sounded like a hard-ass. I wondered if he owned the warehouses or if he was just the security supervisor.

"So, Bill," I said, inferring the man's name from today's spot on the calendar, "how's Cliff doing these days?"

Bill laughed. "Don't go asking for trouble. That guy has *issues*. He sees you here, he'll make a big deal about it and show up more often. I don't want to be rude or anything, but..."

He looked at the door, then back at me, and shrugged apologetically.

"Oh," I said. "Should I go?"

I'd hoped to stick around and give it my all, be part of the solution, take a licking and keep on ticking, rise to the occasion, burn the midnight oil, push the envelope, hit the ground running—

Bill said, "It's just he'll wonder why you're here, you know?"

It was nice having something to do. I liked walking around the big warehouses at night and looking at the constellations. I knew them by heart, and they were fun to find. Also, if I were being honest, staying in the house at night with Sally's corpse creeped me out a little bit.

"What if I took your place tonight?" I said. "Tomorrow too?"

Bill eyed me warily. "What the hell you talking about?"

"You gotta get sick sometimes, don't you?"

Nodding slowly, Bill said, "Yeah, so?"

"Well, what do you do when you get sick?"

He shrugged. "Cliff calls around and gets it covered. But I'm not sick. And I need the money."

"Of course you need the money," I said. "What if I worked for you and you still got paid?"

Bill's eyes narrowed. "What, like for free?"

I nodded.

"Why the hell would anyone do that?"

For a second I wasn't sure who he meant.

"Me or you?" I said.

"*You*—what's this about, man?"

Sighing like I was about to admit something embarrassing, I said, "You're a young guy, Bill. You live alone?"

Bill shook his head.

"Well I do," I said. "And I'm going to be up all night, alone at home on a Friday night. If I have to be alone, I sort of like there being a reason for it, know what I mean?"

"So you don't care about being paid?"

"Nope," I said. "I'll sign your name for you like you were here, and you can do something better than waste your best years sitting in this crummy trailer."

I could see him thinking about it, trying to convince himself it made sense.

"What if Cliff comes by and sees you here?"

"Then I'll tell him you're sick and I'm covering for you."

He smirked like he'd found me out. "So then I *don't* get paid."

"If that happens," I said, "I'll pay you myself. I don't need the money."

Bill laughed nervously. "So then why do you ... oh. Yeah. Right. Sorry..."

I smiled sadly.

"All right," Bill said. "But ... you know ... with Cliff, if you see him, you gotta tell him I'm *really* sick, okay? Not just a cold. Got it?"

I nodded. "Typhoid, yeah, totally got it."

Bill's eyes grew wide. "Not typhoid, man. Jesus! Just like the flu, see?"

"Swine flu," I said. "Got it."

Bill shook his head. Then he shrugged, picked up a small blue canvas lunch cooler off the desk, and left.

I stood in the door and followed Bill's slow, hesitant progress to his car. When he looked back, I smiled encouragingly. Thumbs-up. He didn't smile back, he didn't thumbs-up back—but he did get in his car and leave.

I went out to Fred's minivan and brought in my books, magazines, and a six-pack of diet soda for the empty refrigerator. Then I leaned back in my chair and caught up on my reading.

That night, the lovebirds stayed away, and I fell asleep around 3 a.m. Later that morning, when my relief showed up—someone named Steve—I told him Bill and I were switching spots and not to tell Cliff.

Steve shook his head like I was crazy.

"I don't want to know about it," he said.

For the next two days and nights, I kept a steady schedule: the mall during the day and work at night. On the second night, a different group of people showed up with entirely different intentions. For the next half hour, I watched them spray-paint an incredible graffiti mural on one of the pristine-white warehouses, visible from the main road. All kinds of colors and shadings and big cartoon bubbles for words. I couldn't make out the letters, let alone the words, but it was pretty cool. I did recognize a question mark in there, which made me think it was something socially relevant. It was an election year, so maybe that was it. I wondered who the candidates were.

Technically, I should have done something about the vandalism, but I'd wanted to see how it came out. Now that they were done and it looked so cool, I didn't have the heart to call the cops. Also, I hated talking to cops. They were pushy, and I never did well with pushy.

When my relief arrived, he asked me about the graffiti.

"Pretty cool, isn't it?" I said.

The guy laughed and said, "Make sure you put that in *your* report. I don't want Cliff thinking it happened on my watch."

After adding my first reportable incident to the logbook, I decided I really had to meet this Cliff character.

EIGHTEEN

Later that afternoon, after my nap, I caught a break—Gerald Ross had returned to the mall.

He was at the jungle gym again, clutching that pink backpack in one hand and carrying that same teddy bear under his arm, smiling and watching the kids like he was just another parent. Most of his attention was focused on the entrance to the shiny red tube that led up into the thing. But he was also eyeing the parents, some of whom weren't watching their kids half as much as they needed to be.

Torn between wanting to protect any kids he tried to snatch and a desire for a more permanent solution, I left Gerald there and followed the same course he'd taken last time, out to the parking garage.

This time, I'd parked Fred's minivan in the same garage.

Hoping he wouldn't give up and leave too quickly, I got in and drove slowly through the structure, level by level, examining every bumper in search of Gerald's blue car. It would have been so much easier if he'd parked like a normal person, with the back bumper facing out, but after going through every level twice I concluded he hadn't. And of course I'd been too caught off guard that day to remember the model. So much easier if I could die and come back with the memory permanently etched in my mind, but the Great Whomever sucked at easier.

I found a likely candidate on the second level of the garage. A blue sedan, unremarkable. After a quick look around to see if anyone was coming, I got out and checked the back bumper, about a foot from the concrete wall.

There it was, just under the left taillight, creepy and sinister: *I Love Kids!*

Unfortunately for Gerald, I happened to love kids, too.

There were several exits out of the garage, but the one he'd used last time was the quickest way to the access road. I would have parked near it but all those spots were taken. There were plenty near where Gerald had parked, up on the third level.

The best place to hide, if I didn't want to lose him, was directly across from his car, sandwiched between a white car and a red minivan. Like Gerald, I backed into the spot. Then I put my seat back and slouched down out of sight. Gerald didn't know me, but he knew he was hated and that people meant him harm. Likely he went through the world a little more cautiously than your average scumbag.

Waiting with the radio on, I cycled back and forth between classic rock and a seventies soul channel that had a lot of great tunes. Just waiting.

Still waiting.

My original plan was to follow Gerald home. Thanks to the security job, I had a half-formed plan for dealing with him later. But now I was worried. What if he showed up with some kid he'd snatched? I cursed myself for not thinking of that before.

If he had a kid with him, I could pull out and block him from leaving. Then what? Would he get in his car and try to push me out of the way? Overpower me and take my keys? Maybe he had a gun. If so, he had the perfect hostage.

Crap.

An hour later, it all became academic when Gerald came strolling to his car from the corner stairs closest to the mall. He was alone, but he didn't seem upset about it. He still had that weird smile on his face. There was a point where I could have sped up and rammed him into the car next to his, possibly killing him, but the moment passed with me hunched down, torn with indecision.

Gerald chucked the backpack and teddy into the back seat. He didn't act like he'd seen me, and when he pulled out he did so at a safe speed. Right before he turned to go down the ramp to level two, I followed him.

Just like the other day, he exited out the same spot on the lower level, a creature of habit. He passed the exit to the interstate, heading deeper into the city. At one point, he turned and drove through a dense residential area of multi-level townhouses, making me think he was heading home. Then, for no discernable reason, he left and got back on the main road.

Two minutes later, I followed him into a busy area with lots of apartments.

He seemed to pause overly long at stop signs. Traffic was heavy, and one old lady beeped at him. From two cars back, I could see him craning his neck this way and that as he searched the streets.

No, not streets—the *playgrounds*. All of them empty, thank goodness.

In time he sped up and left, then drove two more miles and pulled into a supermarket parking lot.

Even though there were plenty of spots in the middle and close to the front, Gerald parked way off to the side. I didn't want to spook him, so I chose a somewhat closer spot between him and the front doors and parked.

Gerald got out carrying the backpack, leaving the teddy behind this time. He didn't look my way. Dropping his weird smile, he affected a worried expression, like he had a flat tire or needed help or something equally important. Then he ducked into the store.

About ten minutes later, he came back out—briskly, grumpily, shaking his head as if offended. When I glanced back at the sliding glass doors, a male worker in a red apron was standing beside a woman with a little girl. They were talking together and staring after Gerald, and they didn't look happy.

Gerald didn't waste any time. He hopped in his car and was moving before anyone could get his license or a good description. He didn't speed or cut anyone off or act like he was fleeing, but he didn't slow down for the yellow light onto the main road—which caused me to run the red light just to keep up with him.

This time he went much more quickly through the city, driven by a different motivator. Still not speeding, but when he shifted lanes it wasn't with the same smooth motion I knew he was capable of.

Ten minutes later he pulled into a rundown neighborhood of single-family homes, all quite small.

With the decrease in traffic, I eased the distance between us, but still had no problem keeping pace as he wormed his way into the neighborhood. A minute later, he pulled into a driveway in front of a small blue house. Because I wasn't supposed to be following him, I drove past and took the next right turn. After I cleared his line of sight, I sped up to the next house, pulled into the drive, and backed out. Then I crept to the corner to see if he was still there.

Gerald was out of his car now, carrying neither teddy nor backpack. He stared down at the ground with his fists balled, talking to himself. Cursing, it seemed like. Certainly upset. He stalked into the house, struggling with the keys briefly before going in and slamming the door behind him.

To think this was the same guy who'd had a happy smiley kids' show.

His was the only car in the driveway, and he didn't have a garage. I couldn't imagine him living with anyone. But after all the things I'd seen thriving in the dark cracks of the world, I knew anything was possible.

It was just after four in the afternoon. According to the calendar in the trailer, Brad would have been at work an hour now. He seemed like a nice guy. Punctual, dependable. I was counting on it.

Staring at Gerald's empty front yard, I thought through my options. Then I went back to Fred's house for my second nap that day.

* * *

Fred was a good napper. When I woke up, I wasn't achy or sore, and I was hungry—my favorite thing to be, because it meant I could eat.

I didn't need to work for four more hours, so I ordered a pizza. Much safer than eating out because I couldn't be sure how much credit Fred had on his card. I didn't know his PIN number, so I couldn't call the eight hundred number on the back of the card to get a balance. The pizza place charged me first, and thirty minutes later I was chewing my way to Heaven. I even got Cinnasticks, with the sugary spread they give you.

After dinner, I went to work.

Thinking back, if I'd lived long enough to survive my first girlfriend, maybe I would have become a security guard. Plenty of time for reading, nice and quiet, and nobody to bother me. That way, during the daylight hours, I could do other things, like hiking and woodworking. An economical solution to the problem of having to work a job and get in one's reading time, while still engaging the world. Also, at night, when I stepped away from the streetlights near the trailer and stared at the sky, I could see the occasional falling star.

Around midnight, I saw a huge one zipping along Orion's belt, and for a moment I felt a vast and terrible loneliness because there was no one there to share it with.

I realized I was wrong. If I could do it all again, the last place I'd work was a night job outside a warehouse. Maybe an amusement park—somewhere with lots of people. Then I could hang with my friends all day and after work, too, and I wouldn't read as much because I wouldn't have time.

When I turned around to head back to the trailer, there was someone coming my way from a fancy black car parked next to Fred's minivan. I pointed my flashlight at him and he covered his eyes.

"You!" he shouted, pointing at me. "Get over here!"

Since I was heading there anyway, I obliged him. And because it would seem weird if I just kept walking, I stopped when we were within easy talking distance.

He was a big guy with fake blond hair, and he wore several gold chains. He had on a silk shirt with the sleeves rolled up, shiny leather shoes, big-shot gold rings, and he was about forty years old. Unlike the other people I'd seen so far, he didn't have a guard's uniform on.

I smiled. "Howdy."

"Howdy?" he said, making a face like he was talking to a dingbat. "What are you, a dingbat? I been calling that goddamned phone all night."

"What, you mean in the trailer?"

Sneering, he said, "*What, in the trailer? Where the hell have you been?*"

Then it dawned on me.

"Ah ha," I said. "You're Cliff, aren't you?"

"Shut up, asshole. You know how much shit you're in for that fuckin' mess on Twenty-three East? It's gonna cost a fortune to get it scrubbed and repainted."

"You could always leave it that way," I said. "I can't read the words but it looks pretty cool. And I think it might be socially relevant."

Ignoring me, Cliff said, "If I had my way I'd fire the lot of you losers. You don't do shit. Only here for the insurance break."

"Sorry, Cliff. I—"

"Shut up," he said. "And another thing—you don't work overtime. Someone gets sick—yeah, that's right, I heard about that. Someone gets sick, they goddamn well call *me*, not *you*. We clear?"

For a guy with gold chains and a silk shirt, he seemed like kind of a hothead, so I paused thoughtfully before answering. "What if you're sick? Then who do I call?"

Cliff bit his lip. "What was that?"

"Just trying to cover all the bases, boss. Wouldn't want to get in trouble."

Quietly, he said, "Listen, you wrinkled piece of shit. You wanna fuck with me, I got ten people who want your job. But if you really wanna fuck with me, I—"

"—like to cuddle?" I said, smiling.

Cliff glanced around him, as if at an invisible posse, and said, "The fuck you say?"

Tired of Cliff, no longer worried about the job, I thought up something even more irritating, but then he punched me in the stomach. Coughing and struggling for breath, I fell hard to my knees. Then I came to an important realization: bullies may be fun to mess with, but *none* of them like to cuddle.

"You're done, fat ass," he said. "If I see you again, I'll bury you. Now get off the property before I kick the shit outta you."

Down through the row of warehouses, a familiar set of headlights drove past—the graffiti artists, oblivious to the violence going down not a hundred yards away. That got me laughing, though I totally tried not to because it hurt.

Laughter turned to coughing, and I felt light-headed from lack of oxygen. Old guys like Fred weren't resilient, and young guys like Cliff should have known better than to hit them. Or anyone, for that matter. Briefly, I wondered if all security jobs were this rough. Maybe the warehouse had illegal guns, or refugees off to work in black market textile jobs in New York, like in this movie I once saw...

I tried to stand but wasn't fast enough. Cliff grabbed my collar and yanked me up, somehow angrier. And before I knew what I was doing, I slammed him in the balls with the eighteen-inch flashlight.

Cliff dropped to his side, groaning. Boy it must have hurt. Now he was bicycling around on the ground with his mouth open and his eyes very wide in his head.

He was a first rate jerk, and I was pretty sure he'd call the cops on me and ruin my ride. So I did what any rational person would do in my situation—when he got to his knees, I hit him on the back of the head with the flashlight. Pretty hard, too.

"*Uhng!*" he gasped, falling down flat. When he tried to rise, I reared back for another hit, but he fell back down again.

I leaned down and checked his breathing, suddenly worried I may have killed him. Being a jerk didn't mean he deserved to die—then *I'd* be a jerk. Talk about bad karma.

Cliff was breathing, though it sounded staggered and raspy.

"Dammit," I said.

This was bad. Real bad.

For the first time in sixteen years, I was officially in big trouble.

NINETEEN

Fred was seventy years old, and he was unhealthy, but he wasn't weak. Being big like that adds muscle, even if it tired me out when I did too much at once. For the next twenty minutes, in full view of anyone who cared to drive by and look, I tested the limits of Fred's endurance.

The first thing I did was search the trailer for something to tie Cliff up with. I didn't find any rope, but I did find a thick roll of duct tape, which was actually better. Using that, I taped Cliff's arms behind his back, and then taped his legs together. It was hard because I had to hold him up one-handed while I wrapped the spool around him, feeding it out like a spider, making sure to apply enough pressure so he couldn't slip out. I considered taping his mouth shut, but for all I knew he had allergies and a stuffy nose. If I killed this guy ... scratch that. I could *not* kill this guy. Not unless he had a dead hooker somewhere I didn't know about, and that wasn't something I was ready to bet on.

Cliff wasn't a huge man, but he had muscles. Guys like him went to the gym and ate protein powder and took steroids to get big and meaty. Probably why he was such a jerk.

Through tremendous effort, I got him up and over the bumper of his fancy car—a shiny Mercedes—and into the trunk, leaving it open. Afterward, my heart was hammering in my chest and I saw little flashes of color, making me think I was about to black out—something that couldn't happen if I wanted to stay out of jail.

Panting and sweating, I climbed the two steps back into the trailer, popped open the fridge, and grabbed a soda. Gulp gulp, breathe. Gulp gulp, breathe. I checked the clock—1:07 a.m. Plenty of time before my relief arrived.

Gulp gulp, breathe.

When it was safe to start moving again, I closed the door to the trailer, fished Cliff's keys out of his pocket, and shut the trunk. After a final look around, I got in his car.

Fred was a little taller than Cliff, so I had to adjust the seat back, and then I had to adjust the mirrors. When I turned the car on, some kind of easy listening kicked in, so I had to adjust the radio or risk being miserable yet somehow more mellow. And since I was hot and sweaty from all that exertion...

With the AC and the radio and the mirrors and the seat situated, I set out for Fred's house. Hopefully I wouldn't get stuck at a light next to someone with an open window, or a motorcycle cop, because that's when Cliff would come to and start screaming.

As it happened, I did pull up next to a cop. He even turned toward me, not smiling of course. I smiled at him and nodded, because that's what you do. It was late at night and I wasn't drunk and weaving around the road. And Cliff had a nice new car—not a sports car or a monster truck or a clunker with a busted taillight. The cop pulled ahead of me when the light changed, and I continued at the posted speed limit.

By the time I got to the house I felt stronger, and my breathing was back under control.

I remembered seeing a rusty wheelbarrow in the garage. If the garage hadn't been so packed with stuff I would have backed the car into it. Instead, I dug out the wheelbarrow and set it close to the back fender.

Cliff was beginning to wake up when I opened the trunk. He was still too groggy to fight, and wonder of all, he actually popped his feet out for me and leaned forward when I tugged his arms.

"...the fuck," he muttered, then gasped when he landed butt-first in the wheelbarrow.

For a moment, I struggled to keep it upright on the top-heavy tripod, but got it leveled out. Behind him now, I tugged Cliff into a sitting position, then grabbed the handles and wheeled him to the side door leading to the mudroom. A lip up into the house caused me a moment of worry, but I was able to get him over it by pulling from behind. The sides of the barrow barely cleared the doorframe without scraping.

"...dead. Kill you," Cliff said, struggling now and jerking around.

Before he got too much of his strength back, I pulled him through the foyer and into the hall leading to the kitchen. Then my foot caught something and down we went together in a noisy mess.

Cliff kicked the wall with his taped legs, shouting how I was going to die.

No way could I get him back in the wheelbarrow, and he couldn't stay in the middle of the floor like that.

Mustering the remainder of my strength, I seized him around the middle and pulled him backwards toward the basement stairs. Then, careful not to trip and fall backward, I dragged him down into the basement and over to the ratty mattress.

When Cliff was close enough to the chain and the steel collar with the key in it, I set him down and unlocked it. He was grunting and twisting and making it harder than it needed to be, but I resisted the urge to hit him again. Eventually I got the collar around his neck and latched it shut, then pulled out the key.

Briefly, I wondered where they sold stuff like that. It had to be the Internet. Everything was on the Internet.

"Be right back," I said, pocketing the key.

I went upstairs, got a drink, and found a paring knife. Fred's heart was hammering in his chest, making me worry he'd have a heart attack. I splashed water on my face to cool down, then blotted it dry with my sleeve.

I went back down.

Cliff said, "You're so dead it's not funny!"

There was a puddle of puke on the corner of the mattress near his head.

"So you're going to kill me?" I said.

"Soon as I get outta here."

"Have you ever killed anyone before?"

"Just you, asshole. Wait and see."

I stepped over to him and showed him the knife. He yelled more bad words and thrashed around and I said, "Dammit, Cliff, if you move I'll cut you, now just hold still."

He wasn't a big one for holding still, but I was careful and managed to cut the tape off his wrists without nicking him. Then I hurried out of reach. The chain was about four feet long.

"You can do your feet if you want," I said.

Cliff glowered at me, not saying anything, working the tape with his fingernails to find the seam. Then he set to unraveling it.

"You sure you never killed anyone?" I said, trying not to sound desperate.

"No, dick, I never killed no one. The fuck you keep asking for?"

I sighed.

"What about selling drugs," I said. "You ever do that?"

"What? Me?" He laughed derisively. "Clifftonite makes good money, what the hell I wanna screw that up for?"

"Clifftonite? What's that mean?"

"That's what they call me," he said. "Like kryptonite. Only thing stronger than Superman. They call me that."

Just my luck—a punchy jerk who said no to drugs and referred to himself in third person.

Cliff finished with his legs and stood up. Then he took the chain and tugged hard against the support beam like that'd actually work.

"Who calls you that?" I said.

He was pulling at the collar now, working his finger in the keyhole.

"What?" he said.

"Who calls you Clifftonite?"

"Never-fuckin'-mind who calls me that! Now let me go!"

"These people who call you Clifftonite," I said. "Are they

women?"

"What if they are?"

"You ever knock them around a little?" I said, and winked to show it was just us guys here. "You know, when they get out of line?"

"Clifftonite don't hit women," he said. "What do you think I am, huh?"

He hadn't met my eyes that time, not until the end—almost like he realized he needed to look me in the eyes or it'd seem like he was lying.

"What's this really about?" he said. "Did Sherry ... you been talking to Sherry?"

"I'm guessing you like to hit people and talk later. You definitely seem like a hothead. None of the other guards like you very much. You ever hit any of them?"

"Fuck no!" he said, more believably than when I'd asked if he hit women.

Maybe none of the others mouthed off to him the way I had tonight, so he'd never had to get physical with them.

"Why don't you sit down?" I said.

"I don't wanna sit down!" he yelled. "Let me go!" Cupping his mouth, he tilted his head to the ceiling. "Help! Someone! *Help!*"

I turned my back on him and went upstairs. He was still yelling for help when I shut the over-built door on him, cutting off his cries until I had to strain to hear them. Whatever Fred's problems, he did good soundproofing. As an afterthought, I latched the throw bolts shut in case Clifftonite burned through the chain with his heat vision.

Quickly, I gathered paper towels, some linen from an upstairs closet, a few sodas, some packs of cookies from my trip to the store, and stuffed them all in a bucket from the garage.

Cliff was still screaming for help when I carried it all down to him.

Keeping out of reach of his Popeye arms, I tugged the mattress away from him. I cleaned up as much of the puke as I could, turned the mattress over, and covered it with the fresh linen.

"What are you doing?" Cliff said. "I'm *not* sleeping down

here—you need to let me go right now, goddammit, or ... I swear to God when I get out..."

The tenor of his threats sounded more desperate than furious, as if he were losing hope.

"Couldn't keep your hands to yourself," I said. "This is sort of your fault, you know."

"*I'm sorry!*" he yelled, hands together, imploring me. "I'm sorry a hundred times, okay? If I knew you was a crazy sonofabitch I would have been nicer. Let me go, I won't tell no one. My fuckin' word. My word's good, just ask anyone."

I said, "But you do hit women..."

"*I don't hit no fuckin' women!*"

"And all that profanity..."

After the linen was arranged, I took out the sodas and cookies and set them on top, then nudged the mattress closer to him so he could reach it.

"Use the bucket if you have to," I said. "I know it's gross, but ... Dammit, Cliff. You ruined everything, you know that? The Dan of Steel had a perfectly good trip this time and now you've gone and messed it up."

Cliff stared at me, mystified, like I was spouting fourth-grade math problems at him and told him no calculators.

"Messed what up?" he said.

"Now listen," I said. "I need to get back to work. After I deal with Gerald tomorrow, you'll be free."

"Gerald who?" he said. "What do you mean *back to work?*"

"When I die, don't worry, they'll send someone to investigate. I'll carry a note in my pocket with something creepy on it so they check the basement and freezer." I sighed, feeling bad again. "For what it's worth, I'm sorry. You're kind of a dirtbag, but I don't think you're a murderer."

"I'm *not a murderer*, I keep *telling you!*" he shouted, sobbing a little now. "You let me go now, goddammit!"

I started up the stairs.

"Turn the light back on!" he screamed.

"Whoops, sorry," I said, and flipped it back on. "Force of habit."

Turning my back again, I left him chained there, crying

and pitiful in his big muscles and steel collar.

TWENTY

Until I finished my business, I needed to keep Cliff's car at the house. Fred's minivan was stuck in the warehouse district, and I still needed it. I also needed to finish my shift, to stave off suspicion if Cliff was reported missing. So I called a cab to take me back to the security trailer.

Forty minutes later, I paid my fare and waved goodbye to my laconic cabbie. He didn't wave back. Sam would have waved and followed up with an offer to take me home when I was ready. I wondered how ol' Sam was doing and if he realized who was in his cab that day. Was he following the media sensation and telling his friends and family how he'd driven evil Ernest Prescott to his own movie?

I sighed. Of all the dumb things I'd done, losing my temper with Cliff stood out as one of the big ones. He liked to hit people, so what? Maybe that's as far as it went. Maybe it went farther, but how would I know? He didn't hurt kids, he wasn't a killer, he just seemed like a hothead. Working with the best knowledge I had, purely on facts, nothing he'd done warranted me killing or crippling him with irreversible brain damage. But chaining him up like that ... I'd go so far as a possible *maybe* on that one, because who doesn't need a good scare to straighten them out once in a while?

If this had happened even two rides back, I wouldn't

have been so concerned. But that terrible smokestack of death—with the dying over and over *a thousand and one times*—that was solid confirmation the Great Whomever was real and not some figment of my imagination. He could punish and he could reward, and I needed to be careful.

After the night's exertions, I didn't feel like reading anything. A check of the monitors showed the graffiti artists were gone, and I felt a little bit sad about that. I was also wiped out.

I closed my eyes and leaned back in my chair. Then, in a while, I wasn't so sad anymore.

* * *

"Fred, man, wake up," a voice said after no time at all.

It was bright out, which didn't make sense at first. There was a guy standing over me—my relief.

"Hold on," I said, and scrawled *Nothing to report* on the first line, then double quotes down the next seven lines.

"Can you get any lazier?" he said, shaking his head.

"If I felt like it," I said, and left.

Like every other night, I was still tired by the time I got to the house. The Mercedes remained parked in the driveway. I'd left Cliff's keys on the counter in the kitchen and they were still there. I almost went down to check on him, but I had a big day ahead and needed my rest.

Around noon, I woke up with a headache and a stiff neck. After a shower and clean clothes I felt a little better, but could have really used some aspirin. Sadly, none of the cabinets had any medicine. Maybe Fred liked pain? Come to think of it, I didn't know much about the guy except he liked to kidnap people. Sort of scary, thinking of it that way, considering my own behavior last night with Cliff.

I put off eating long enough to go down and check on my prisoner.

He was sitting with his back against the post, staring at me.

"How's your head?" I said.

"It hurts, that's how."

"My head hurts too," I said. "I need to go out and get some stuff. You want anything?"

"You could come a little closer."

"Other than that?"

Cliff turned away and shook his head. Then he seemed to deflate. "Some toothpaste? Water?"

I nodded, and turned to go.

"And some TP," he added. "You sick son of a bitch."

"Will do," I said.

The more time I spent with him, the more I realized he wasn't evil, he just wasn't that smart. He thought with his emotions. Me too I supposed, and if that made him dumb what did it make me?

Thirty minutes later, I came back with a bunch of stuff from a nearby drugstore: pain killers, toilet paper, toothpaste, a soft-bristled toothbrush, and a case of bottled water.

"Now, Cliff," I said. "This is your big day. If everything goes as planned, you'll be out within twenty-four hours."

"I want out *now!*"

"You brought this on yourself," I said. "Don't forget it. Now just hang tight and a little later the cops will be here to let you go. I'll even leave you the key, for when they arrive."

Way on the other side of the room, which was empty except for the things I'd brought down, I placed the key on the floor against the wall.

"How am I supposed to reach it?"

"You're not," I said.

Then, pursued by cries and threats, I left him there, shut the door, and went upstairs to write the note:

Dear Mortal Authorities,

In my basement, you will find one of your race called "Clifftonite." He is a terrible person, much given to profanity and hitting women and old men. It was my intent to destroy him, but I changed my mind for mysterious reasons known only to me. Perhaps I am simply lazy.

In the garage, resting in the freezer, is a woman named "Sally." She overdosed when I spiked her drink during a kidnapping attempt. You should assume there were more women before her.

All hail Ernest Prescott!

I signed the note *Fred*, added his address as an extra precaution, folded it up, and stuffed it in my pocket.

I was about to leave when the phone rang.

I answered it. "Hello?"

"Fred? It's me, Larry from work. You seen Cliff around?"

"Nope," I said, and became seized with the certainty that the fight and kidnapping had been recorded on video.

"His girlfriend dropped by looking for him—says he was coming out here to see you."

"Is that right?" I said. "Well, you know Cliff..."

Whatever that means.

Larry laughed and said, "I know what you mean. I'll tell her something. Sorry to bug you."

"No problem," I said and hung up.

Cliff had a girlfriend who cared enough to go looking for him. Maybe he was a jerk with guys and a pussycat at home.

By the time I left the house, it was just after one o'clock in the afternoon. I was tempted to take the Mercedes, but no way could I do that now.

I still had two hours to kill before I could make my next move, so I went to a fast food place. I couldn't be sure when Fred's credit card would give out on me, and I didn't have any more cash, so I needed a place that could accept or deny me at point of sale.

Though nothing fancy, the food was great. Especially the milkshake.

At two thirty, I closed the book I'd brought with me, got in the minivan, and drove two miles to Brad Ratcliff's neighborhood. Using the address I'd gleaned from his magazine subscriptions, I found the house easily—a corner townhouse in a low-income section of New Haven. I recognized his big truck right away.

I parked a few cars back and waited.

Maybe a minute later, the door opened and Brad came out wearing his guard's uniform. He didn't lean back in and yell something to anyone, and he didn't stoop down and give an attack dog a big snuggly head rub. Both very good signs.

After he left, I got out, walked up the sidewalk to his house, and pressed the doorbell. I didn't hear it ring, so I knocked loudly while glancing around to see if anyone was watching. I gave it another twenty seconds, then leaned down low and slammed the door with my shoulder. When it didn't budge, I leaned back even more, putting all Fred's ponderous girth into it, and this time it not only flew open, the middle of the door caved in, too, almost folding. I hadn't busted through the frame so much as the deadbolt had slipped out of the latch.

The laws of motion, however, are nothing to be trifled with—I crashed inside and sprawled forward, painfully. The floor I was lying on was a section of purple tiling, veined like marble, separating the entryway from wall-to-wall purple carpeting. Tacky, sure, but it was someone's home, and way more than I had.

I got my knees under me and staggered to my feet, breathing heavily for my efforts. Then, after a quick look outside, I shut the door as best I could, pushing it in the middle so it flattened out like it wasn't made of hollow cardboard.

Leaning back against the door, I surveyed the room: yellow walls in a small living room, and a low wall separating it from the kitchen. There was a set of stairs on the right, going up. Farther along the wall, under the stairs, was a door that probably led to the basement. Leather couches in the living room, modern art prints on the walls, and bicycles near the front casement windows.

Bicycles...

One for a man, the other for a woman.

"Hello?" I called out, hoping nobody answered. Then louder: "*Hello?*"

Nobody answered.

I took the stairs and headed up to where I figured the bedrooms were. At the top were three doors: one on the left, one on the right, and one straight ahead opened wide to an empty bathroom.

I almost shouted *hello* again, but something stopped me. Cautiously, I reached for the door on the right and turned the knob, pulling back a little so it'd make less noise. I cracked it open and saw a woman, about twenty-five years old. She was sitting at a computer with a big monitor playing a video game.

"Someone cover me," she said in a serious tone, startling me clear out of my skin. But she wasn't talking to me. She had on a hands-free headset.

I'd played the same game on another ride several years ago. Very fun, very addictive. I hoped to play it again one day.

Judging from all the movement on the screen and the rigid way she was sitting, she appeared to be in an epic battle for all Mankind. Hoping she'd be occupied for the next few minutes, I quietly shut the door.

The other room, a bedroom with nightstands bracketing a king-sized bed, was unoccupied. I went to the closest end table and opened the top drawer. Just as I'd hoped, Brad owned a handgun. My only reason for being there.

It had been a leap of faith Brad would have one at all. But what manly hunter-guy with a big tough truck didn't also like handguns? My biggest worry was he'd only have rifles and long shotguns. They'd do in a pinch, but I couldn't hide them under my shirt no matter how big Fred was.

Resting beside the gun was an extra magazine, nine millimeter. Quickly, I grabbed it and the gun and left the room, being careful not to bump anything. With luck, the woman wouldn't know they'd been robbed until she went out later and saw the messed-up front door. By then I'd be long gone.

After closing the bedroom door behind me, I hurried down the stairs, slipped the gun in my waistband, and left.

TWENTY-ONE

I now had a gun. This should have made me feel better, but now I had something else to worry about: I was having chest pains.

They'd started after I fell through the door. At the time, I'd shrugged them off, lumping them in with the general pain of crashing to the ground in Fred's large body. I'd been pushing the old guy pretty hard, and I was feeling jittery again, like at the mall after those pastries.

"Then why'd you drink that milkshake?" I said.

I didn't care for my tone, so I chose not to answer that. Also, traffic was tight due to roadwork ahead and I needed to pay attention.

My plan for dealing with Gerald was simple: knock on his door and gun him down. The direct approach. Then I'd wait for the cops to show up before shooting myself. I needed them to be there when it happened to ensure they got the note. I couldn't risk some opportunist rifling through Fred's pockets and robbing his corpse. An unlikely possibility, sure, but I was responsible for Cliff until he was free again.

When I got to Gerald's house, it was just after four in the afternoon.

"Dammit," I said.

I'd arrived too late—he was backing down his drive.

Probably off to hunt for more kids at malls and supermarkets.

I followed him closely at first, then pulled back. My desperation was going to get me noticed. If I lost him today, something told me I'd never get another chance.

The new plan was almost as simple as the old plan: wait until he parked at the supermarket or mall or playground, or wherever he was heading, then pull up and shoot him in the head. Preferably not at a playground. Bad for anyone to see something like that, let alone kids, but I'd do it rather than let him go free.

Ten minutes later, Gerald got on I-91 heading north. I doubted he had run out of places to lurk with that awful backpack and unloved teddy. Briefly, I considered ramming him off the road, or pulling up to him and shooting him through the passenger window—plan C, if you will. But with my luck, I'd bump into him, spin out, then veer off an overpass into a bus loaded with nuns and supermodels.

In the middle of my car chase, we hit several miles of bumper-to-bumper traffic that lasted an hour due to a bad accident. When it cleared, we kept going. Twenty minutes later I became curious. Intrigued, even. Why was a guy like Gerald Ross taking road trips? Some new job? Family that still talked to him? A kid of his own, of all things?

After a while, I noticed my fuel gauge dipping down near a quarter full. Also, I needed to use the bathroom. If I thought I might lose him, I'd take a chance and try shooting him anyway.

Eventually, the decision was made for me when Gerald exited east to a place called North Bradford. This was a particularly country area with big houses, open land, rich vegetation, and good old-fashioned distance separating people from their neighbors.

The farther we drove, the more secluded it became.

At this point in the tail, I'd pulled back even more. If he turned, I'd speed up to keep pace with him, but he kept going straight. About ten minutes later, he put on his blinkers and pulled down a long driveway bisecting a wide field of bright green grass. Way out in the middle of it, a large white house blazed in the day's last light, a shock of white sail on a painted sea.

I pulled off the road and watched Gerald drive up to the house. There were eight other cars parked there. He got out. The lights on his car flashed once when he locked it, then he approached the house. Up the stairs onto a porch, now, where he pulled open the storm door and knocked.

I slipped out of the minivan for a clearer look.

The inner door opened and Gerald shook someone's hand. The contrast of white on shadow hid whoever was there. A snatch of conversation carried across the field, but the words escaped me. Shouting between the two of them, then Gerald threw up his hands and headed back to his car. Just as he reached for the door a man with white hair came out, waving for him to stop. Gerald turned around. The white-haired man approached him and the two began talking again.

Something in the house caught my eye. In the doorway, standing in silhouette yet somehow discernible, was a small girl with dark hair. Though she was too far away for Fred's seventy-year-old eyes to tell, I somehow knew she was watching me.

My gaze was pulled away by Gerald and the man walking together back to the house. Whatever they'd disagreed about must have been resolved. When I looked back to the door, the girl was gone.

The two men went inside and the door shut behind them.

I stood there leaning against the minivan, watching the house and worrying about the girl. I waited five minutes, twisting in indecision, growing more worried. No one else came out of the house, and there were no new arrivals.

I sat behind the wheel, inserted the key, and then took it back out. If I drove up and they heard me, they'd be ready and I'd be just one person.

I got out, walked to the entrance, and turned up the long driveway. I made sure to keep close to the fence, trusting the lengthening shadows to hide me. With every step, whatever semblance the house had to a sailing ship evaporated. Now it seemed more like a toadstool—looming and sickly and poisoning the world.

Fred's heart thudded heavily in his chest, and I took deeper breaths.

"Just a little more," I said.

As I struggled ahead, the air grew heavier, weighing me down even more than all the excess flab I was carrying. My steps felt too short for the distance I had to travel, and the house seemed impossibly far away now.

Halfway to the house, I felt a brief moment of panic when I thought I'd left the gun in the minivan. I took five steps to go back before realizing it was clutched in my hand all along. I lifted it up and stared at it, just to be sure ... of something ... before lowering it and turning around again.

I tried to continue ... and then realized I was sitting in the middle of the gravel drive, less than thirty feet from the house. But I'd dropped the gun ... I needed the gun. Where was it? Breathing was difficult, like being squished under an enormous invisible bubble pressing me from all sides.

My chest tightened painfully and I saw little sparks of light, like fireflies. More colorful, less cheerful. The door of the toadstool opened again, and the little girl from before was standing there looking at me. I could see her clearly now, so beautiful, her face a mask of concern mixed with resolve—too much of either for a girl so young.

While I lay like a cow pie in the middle of the road, the pressure on my chest began to lighten. I dragged in several ragged lungfuls of air, and with each draw my oxygen-starved brain recovered. Soon my vision cleared and the burning in my chest cooled to a distant smoldering.

My hand hurt. Looking at it, I found I was squeezing the gun in a white-knuckled grip.

When I searched for the girl, she was gone. But the door was open.

The way was clear.

TWENTY-TWO

On entering the house, I was hit by the syrupy smell of cheap perfume mingled with marijuana. The second thing I noticed was a young boy, naked, sprawled on the floor watching TV. Maybe nine years old, he didn't look up when I came in. He was too focused on the frenetic motion of cartoon characters. I didn't see the girl anywhere, or Gerald, or the man with the white hair.

Thumping music carried down from upstairs, not terribly loud or I would have heard it from outside.

A powder room was to my left and a flight of stairs just beyond that, also on the left. The room with the television stretched right, out of my field of vision. I stepped around the boy, turned the corner, and found myself in the dining room. The table was loaded with sandwiches, deviled eggs, cookies, chips, meat and vegetable platters, sodas, and bottles of hard liquor.

There was another child, sitting at the dining table in her pajamas holding a Barbie. Not the girl I'd seen twice now. This girl was about five or six and looked Hispanic. She didn't react to my presence in any way. She stared ahead with drugged, lidded eyes.

In the middle of the table, next to the deviled eggs, was a candy bowl filled with little white pills. I leaned over and picked it up. Each pill was smooth and free of branding. I moved to put the bowl back, then thought better of it and set it out of the girl's reach. She didn't appear to notice.

I saw a cordless phone up on the wall where the dining room turned into a kitchen. I walked over, picked it up, and dialed 911.

A lady came on asking me what my emergency was.

"Hurry," I said, and set the phone down facing out to the room.

From somewhere upstairs came the voice of a man asking a question I didn't catch.

"...still downstairs," another man said.

A slender steak knife was on the table near the folded cold cuts. Though I had a gun, I grabbed it anyway.

Leaving the little girl, I stepped around the boy on the floor and over to the powder room near the entrance and hid inside—barely avoiding a face-to-face with a burly black guy who clumped down the stairs and walked into the living room wearing...

What the hell?

The guy was wearing a spandex cow outfit. It hugged his body tightly, with black and white shapes everywhere. Though it seemed almost like camouflage, the effect accentuated his muscles. He shifted my way to stand over the boy, and the tight spandex revealed way more than anyone needed to see. If that wasn't bizarre enough, he stretched his arms out wide and flexed like a bodybuilder, his gaze sweeping over his arms and body in a lurid display of self-infatuation.

"Come on," he said to the boy, his voice husky and deep. "I got plans for you, little friend."

Time seemed to slow down for me, not unlike the attack outside, but with an important difference. Where before I'd been nearly undone by Fred's flagging health, now I shook with white-hot rage.

The man bent down, reaching for the boy. When I came up behind him, he turned toward me, his eyes widening in surprise. The knife flashed hard and fast, like a sword, slicing deep through his neck in a geyser of oxygen-rich spray. I kicked him before he could fall on the child, who kept watching the television as if it were the only thing in the world that mattered.

From behind me, near the stairs, came a startled sound and a scrabbling of feet.

I turned around and shot the white-haired man in the face, splattering the yellow wallpaper behind him with blood and brains and chunks of his white-haired skull.

Upstairs, over the sound of thumping music, someone shouted in fear.

When I looked up the stairs, she was there—the brown-haired girl. I'd seen her face before. Her eyes were blue like the sky from another age, back when the world was new.

"Wait!" I shouted.

She turned and walked away.

Gun in one hand, knife in the other, I climbed the stairs. With every step I felt a growing and overwhelming hatred—a need to destroy. When I got to the top, the world turned funhouse strange, and for a while I became lost to myself...

* * *

Dan Jenkins stands in the middle of a short hallway that veers off to the right. Along its length are four doors, two per side. The music is loud and there are three adults visible, all men. Two are peeking out of the various rooms, and one stands in the middle wearing a green bathrobe and nothing else. Dan recognizes him—His Honor, judge Mark Simmons, the same judge who'd let Gerald Ross go and later went to jail himself—falling now after Dan's bullets catch him high in the chest. Judged.

Down the hall, the two faces duck back into the rooms.

Dan looks in the room to his right and sees a man lying on the bed with two children clutched in his arms like pillows. Dan takes careful aim, shoots him through his screaming mouth, and turns back to the hall.

A man rushes to get past him, fleeing to the safety of the stairs, but Dan catches him in the stomach with the steak knife. Mustering Fred's thick meaty strength, backed by adrenaline, he lifts the man onto his toes, splitting him navel to sternum. Dan pulls the knife out and kicks him down the stairs, where he stumbles, falls, and doesn't get back up.

Heedlessly, Dan enters the room the man came from. He blinks away tears for the children who stare back listlessly, too drugged to care. He backs out, takes a breath, and moves to the next room. Again two men on a bed, again clutching children as human shields. Dan strides up to one of them. The man foolishly lets go of the girl he holds to cover his head, and Dan shoots him in the chest. The other man gets up to run and Dan guns him down from behind.

The final room is empty of adults. The children don't cry or seem to notice him. Like the child in the dining room, and the ones in the room near the stairs, they appear drugged.

The bend ahead leads to a closed door. Dan kicks it open. A bathroom. The shower curtain is closed. When Dan pulls it wide, he finds Gerald Ross lying naked in the empty tub staring at him in terror.

Dan points his gun, pulls the trigger, and nothing happens. He looks at the gun, confused, and Gerald leaps at him. The ferocity of the attack drives Dan back, knocking him over. Gerald falls on top of him, punching and scratching savagely, eyes wild, his teeth pulled back in a triumphant snarl. For a while. In time, the frenzy slows and he rolls off, shuddering and gasping.

Dan uses his knees to nudge himself away. The knife is sticking out of Gerald's stomach.

Gerald lies on the ground shaking and coughing.

Dan jacks the spare magazine into the pistol and chambers the next round. He could have shot him in the head and killed him quickly, but he misses and hits him in the stomach. A cruel way to die. Dan shoots again, missing the head again, and hits him three more times with shots to both knees and then the crotch. The screaming is almost satisfying, but it ends too soon.

With Gerald dead and no more adults left to shoot in the stomach, Dan steps into the hallway...

* * *

It was the stinging chest pains and the wheezing and rattling of my breath that brought me out of my rage.

Ignoring the pain, I struggled from room to room

checking on the kids. None of them were crying, just staring, and all seemed physically unharmed. One of the things about the Great Whomever: he's always had good timing.

I shook my head, disgusted and used up.

The music was thumping like a heartbeat I hadn't killed yet, and the smell of marijuana and perfume warred with the gun smoke, cooling guts, and human waste, such that every breath was a desecration. Pain flared hotly in my chest, and the ground came rushing up.

When I came to, it was to the sound of sirens from outside. Gunshots over a 911 call, works every time.

I tried to raise the gun to my head but my arm wouldn't move—it was numb all the way down, and my chest felt like someone was stabbing it repeatedly with broken glass.

Someone was there now, looking down at me. The girl from before.

Outside, when I'd seen her in the doorway, she'd been too far away to get a good look at. Later, at the top of the stairs, I'd had other concerns. Now that I was dying, I recognized her. I'd seen her before. I'd been dying one of many heart attacks in that Scheherazade smokestack of death and she'd been there for one of them, looking down at me like she was now. *Exactly* as she was now.

Like before, the girl touched my face. Then she leaned down and whispered, "It's okay."

Moments later, it was.

TWENTY-THREE

I had to assume Cliff was safely rescued. Of all the things that had happened, none of them were more troubling to me than the idea I'd contributed to the death of a more or less innocent dirtbag. Not even a dirtbag really, just a jerk.

The girl at the house was a mystery. Of all the children I'd seen, she was the only one who hadn't seemed drugged. Also, she'd been dressed. And when I walked the hall looking from room to room, she hadn't been in any of them.

Which was fine.

It's like I always say: sometimes when you come back from the dead through mysterious portals for no good reason and you do it going on sixteen years, and when a strange child guides you into a house so you can kill a bunch of awful people, and then that child disappears as if by magic ... you roll with it.

Stuff like that had happened before, most recently with a disappearing camera during my brief ride as Peter—not there one minute and suddenly there after I'd killed Erika, the amoral fiancée of a lottery winner named Nate. Before that, she'd pointed a gun right at my head and fired. And though her aim had seemed perfect, she'd missed.

Magic bullets and spooky cameras. Smokestacks of deaths and disappearing girls. It was enough to drive me

FOOL'S RIDE

crazy. But in the Great Wherever, even that comfort was denied to me. So what did I do?

I rolled with that too. Having seen too much, I no longer cared and just wanted it over with.

I'm ready now, I willed into the nether. *I'm ready to move on. I'm sorry for my sins, is that what you want to hear? It's even true—you know it is. No more, I'm done.*

But as had happened every time before when I'd tried to communicate, no voice spoke back to me. I did not move on.

Ages, it seemed, passed for me in the Great Wherever. Far longer than I remembered it lasting before. And though it was boring in a general sense, it was never tiring. I wasn't standing in an empty room somewhere, aching and weary and wishing for sleep. I was living consciousness and nothing more. I existed, I remembered, I imagined.

* * *

Virtual years after Fred and Gerald and blued-eyed mysteries, I was thinking about that time I used to steal from supermarkets.

When I was twelve years old, when kids were expected to play outside and video games weren't remotely as fun as the commercials on TV made them out to be, I'd walk the quarter mile to the local shopping center and steal candy.

To this day, it remains one of the few things in life I was ever an expert at. I had the system down perfectly. I'd stroll into McCrory's, a chain of five and dime stores that isn't around anymore, then go to the section with the books and magazines and browse—all while keeping tabs on the checkout area where the sales clerks were. When things got busy, I'd pop over to the candy aisle and steal something big and unusual—like the giant candy bars with the fruits and nuts in them, or the Chunkys, or the enormous Snickers bars Mom always refused to buy me with her hard-earned money. Then I'd grab a cheap piece of chewing gum and stand in line. If nobody paid attention to me in line ... well, maybe I *wouldn't* buy that gum. Maybe I'd rethink my choice and put it back. Then I'd waltz out of there, chin up, spurning the meager choices offered at McCrory's. I'd spend my money elsewhere, thank you very much.

I had a rule of never stealing two things from the same place on the same day. But I couldn't steal candy from the shoe store or the ice cream shop or the picture framing shop. Emboldened by my success, I'd head four shops down to my next score: the supermarket.

Safeway was a little more difficult to steal from. They had food stockers in the aisles and adults everywhere doing serious grocery shopping, and not browsing for cheap junk to make them happy. If that wasn't bad enough, the candy aisle shared floor space with the chips and cookies and other snacks—in the middle of the store, with the highest visibility. Only the very best candy thieves dared steal from Safeway.

My method was to pick up the candy like I was buying it, browse around until I knew nobody was watching me, and then pocket it. Then I'd visit the public restroom behind the produce section. Adjacent to the restroom was a storage room with employee lockers. It had an access door in the wall to get at the pipes. Provided the locker area was empty, I'd place the candy on the inside lip right above the access hole. Then, with the goods safely stashed, I'd waltz out of the store, chin up, spurning the meager choices offered at Safeway. I'd spend my money elsewhere, thank you very much.

The next day, after the heat had died down, I'd return and claim my prize with no one the wiser.

Things went fine until, one day, the manager of Safeway came to my elementary school and lectured everyone about criminals and how bad stealing was, and how if we stole then that made us criminals in the eyes of the law.

"Everyone who steals gets caught," he told us, and went on to say how nobody escapes justice forever, and that our crimes would come back on us if we strayed from the honest path. He added that jails were full of hardened criminals who'd launched their lives of crime by stealing candy. And because he was an adult and not a teacher, I actually believed him.

From that day on, I never stole candy again. Not because I was afraid of getting in trouble. Getting in trouble was annoying and loud, but ultimately survivable. The reason I quit stealing candy was pride: I wanted to be the only candy thief who'd never gotten caught.

And as far as anyone knows, I am.

Sometime after my memories of McCrory's and Safeway and candy thieving, while leafing through the past for something fresh to think about, a portal opened in the nether. Enough time had passed since that bummer of a ride in Connecticut, and I was curious as to what was on the other side.

What the heck, I thought.

It couldn't be worse than last time. Maybe I was the world's biggest sucker, but I still held out hope for a good ride.

Ever the optimist, I projected: *Beam me down, Scottie...*

* * *

I was sitting in a plush leather chair, staring down at a stack of pictures. One of them looked like a beautiful woman holding a machine gun in each hand. Another looked like two women, back to back, holding cakes or pies. Still another looked like a beautiful woman surrounded by angry spiders. To anyone normal, these pictures probably looked like inkblots in a Rorschach psychological test.

Which, in fact, they were.

Across from me, facing away at an angle, was a man in his late twenties. Brown-haired and slight of build, he sat in a similarly plush chair. Behind him, against the wall, was a couch. There was a landscape painting above it and a couple of bookcases around the room, and everything appeared clean and safe and pastel. The air smelled great, with a hint of real, actual flowers. Not cloying like cheap perfume or spray in a purple or pink or powder-blue can.

"...then I watched more TV until I got tired, and that was my weekend," the man said.

He had a thin, unsure voice—like he expected someone to interrupt him at any moment. He stole a glance at me and shrugged.

On my right was a glass table. I reached over the high arms of the cushy chair and put the inkblot cards down next to a pad of paper and a glittery gold pen.

The man said, "Dr. Schaefer? Were you going to show me those cards again?"

I was still looking around, trying to get my bearings. "Just a second."

"Okay," he said, nodding.

Behind me stood a desk with a curtained window behind it. The room was some kind of office. Not a small office, and not a big one. It was a just right office.

"What was that, Dr. Schaefer?"

"Sorry?" I said.

"You said 'baby bear.' "

"Yes." Then I peered at him and added, "How does that make you feel?"

Faint relief replaced his previous look of confusion, and he slumped back in his chair.

The man closed his eyes and told me how he'd gone to the zoo once when he was little and saw some bears. He had a lot to say about how the bears just slept and his mom kept tapping the railing to wake them up, and how he was afraid she'd abandon him at the zoo with the bears and snakes and monkeys.

While the man droned on about abandonment, I snuck away to the desk and sat behind it.

A neat stack of folders sat next to a closed laptop. I opened the first one and found what looked like medical files, with the name "Psychiatric Associates of Toledo" at the top of every page. The top file belonged to Will Dingle, age twenty-nine, with an address in Bowling Green. Lots of notes and commentary by my ride—Scott Schaefer—focusing on Will Dingle's anxiety issues, his inability to make friends, and his depression. Will was also on two kinds of medication.

I wondered whether my ride was a psychologist or a psychiatrist.

"Will?" I said, coming around the desk.

His eyes were still closed.

"Yes, Dr. Schaefer?"

"Can I see your medication?"

Will picked up a backpack I hadn't seen and took out a blue case for organizing pills.

"Never mind," I said, waving him off.

If he'd had a bottle with a prescription I could have checked if Schaefer's name was on it, which would have meant he was a psychiatrist.

"Let me ask you something," I said, and sat back down. "What do you think about psychiatrists?"

Will laughed nervously and said, "You serious? I haven't seen one in years." He laughed again and rubbed his hands. "Not since I set my house on fire."

"That long, huh?"

Will nodded proudly.

If I'd come back in the body of a psychiatrist, no way could I prescribe medication all day for patients without killing someone. But as a *psychologist*, I could do nothing at all and let them refill their prescriptions until my last kick.

"Good," I said. "Psychologists are cooler anyway."

Will smiled. "You're a pretty good therapist, Dr. Schaefer."

I'd had a therapist once. I'd gotten bullied in junior high and refused to go back. But that wasn't why I was in therapy. To get me to return, Dad gave me the talk about bullies being more afraid of me than I was of them, how the bigger they were the harder they fell, and then he'd topped it off with, "That which doesn't kill you makes you stronger."

To this day, I'm not sure why I believed him when other kids knew not to listen to their Machiavellian fathers.

I'd returned to school. Then I'd approached Randy Cobb from behind and said, "Hey Randy." When he turned around, I hit him with my book bag—the same book bag I'd loaded with a couple of large rocks plucked from someone's garden on the way to the bus stop. He went down hard, knocked-out but otherwise okay, and the school forced me into therapy.

In all my sessions, the therapist made me call him by his first name. He was a nice guy who enjoyed asking me how I felt about anything I said. After two months of that, I told my parents I wasn't going back.

That time, Dad kept his sagely advice to himself and I

got my way.

Will Dingle droned on for ten more minutes about all the things he worried about. He started to say how he couldn't go in pet stores because talking birds scared him, and then a soft tone sounded in the room.

"Thanks Dr. Schaefer," Will said, and stood up to go.

His eyes widened in surprise when I reached out to shake his hand.

"Next time I see you," I said, "I want you to come with a list of places in the world you'd like to visit one day."

I knew all my old psychologist's questions and responses by heart. He'd been a big one for setting goals to reach before every session.

Will nodded vigorously and said, "Ok."

After he left, I poked my head out the door and learned I was in a sort of communal facility. There was a staff desk surrounded by a sprawling great room with a number of sofas, tables, and chairs. Around the perimeter were doors to offices just like mine. At the desk sat a middle-aged white woman and a young, pretty, Asian woman, talking together. They were the only ones there besides me.

I went over.

"Hey, you two," I said, throwing them my hundred-watt smile.

"Hey yourself," the older woman said in a frosty tone. Her name tag had the name "Pam" on it. The younger woman—Melody—wouldn't look at me.

I wondered if my ride had bad teeth.

"Sure," I said. "Do, uh, either of you know what time it is?"

"Four o'clock," Pam said, glaring at me.

"Do you ... is uh," I said, kind of nodding toward the door. "Do I have any more patients today?"

Pam snorted disdainfully. "How the hell would we know?"

That got a small, appreciative, smile from Melody.

I didn't trust myself to answer so I smiled too, then turned around and went back to Scott's office.

I searched the desk for an appointment book but didn't find one. I tried the computer but it was locked, so I searched for anything with a password on it. Just as I was about to go through Scott's weirdly advanced cell phone to see what day it was, the door flew open and Pam marched in.

She slammed the door behind her and pointed at me from across the room.

"You stay the hell away from her, you miserable son of a bitch. And me too, if you know what's good for you!"

Then she turned around, stormed back out, and slammed the door again for good measure.

"And stay out," I said.

TWENTY-FOUR

If Pam and Melody were good indicators, Scott had problems with women. Maybe he liked to boss people around, something simple like that, and had hurt Melody's feelings.

I waited until well after five o'clock on the off chance I'd have another patient, but nobody showed up. To be honest, I was waiting for Pam and Melody to leave. I wasn't sure what was going on with all the finger wagging and profanity, and I hoped I wouldn't need to find out. Nobody was dead or dying by my hand, and that was good enough for me. The rest was Scott Schaefer's business.

When I finally peeked out, I saw a man carrying a laptop case waiting near the main entrance, looking back past the front desk. A second later, a thirty-something woman came rushing out of another office carrying a laptop case of her own. The man said something funny and she laughed. Then they left together.

I wasn't sure what to do with the whole therapist thing. It wasn't like with Fred and the security guard job where all I had to do was write *Nothing to report* over and over again. I'd inherited some serious responsibilities for which I had no training. If one of Scott's patients thought I'd abandoned him or her and then committed suicide, that'd be on me.

Scott's keys were in a rain slicker hanging in a shallow closet. After pocketing the keys, I grabbed the coat and had another look at Scott's phone. It was like looking at something from the future. At first I didn't know what to do, then found I could touch the icons on the screen and little windows would pop up. Also, if I moved my finger while touching the screen, all the buttons moved at the same time, and then a new screen with new buttons popped up. I was like a caveman playing with a flashlight.

It had an icon that said *Calendar*, so I clicked it. The date showed May 28, 2013. An astonishing five years had passed since my last ride.

My exile had seemed unbearably long this time, and I'd suspected ... well, not *years*. Maybe a year at most. But five? Unbelievable. I wondered if the Cubs had managed to win the World Series, or if someone had cured cancer, or if aliens had shared their technology with us, because this phone was *cool*.

Then something else happened: I got a phone call.

Now look—I wasn't completely prehistoric here. But the moving screen-thing was throwing me off my game. And when the call came in, all the icons disappeared, replaced by a picture of a pretty brunette named *Tara* with a green *Answer* bubble underneath it. I stood there staring at it, frozen with indecision. Where were the damn buttons?

After it stopped ringing, just as I was about to figure out how the voicemail worked, Tara called back, and again I didn't answer it. When she called back yet again, I almost touched the *Answer* bubble, but the ringing cut off abruptly.

Whenever a ride comes along with significant others in his life, it complicates things. Particularly when those significant others were as pretty as Tara. Even worse when the ride has kids, and I'm stuck with the knowledge their father will soon be dead or in jail because of me. Whatever my ride had done to them or their mother before I got there, for the rest of my stay I'd be quite harmless. Friendly, even. Almost like ol' Dad changed his mind and decided not to be abusive or scary or a drunk anymore. Then I'd do what I always did and nothing would be the same for them again.

I looked at my brand new left hand and saw I wasn't wearing a wedding band. Maybe Tara was Scott's sister? Or another patient?

Through a series of clicks and swipes I found the button for voicemail, called it back, and gave up when it asked for a passcode. If needed, I could always find a store for the carrier and have it reset, but it wasn't a priority. For now, I'd wait until she called back. Lots of options.

I put on my jacket, locked the office door behind me, and left the building. It was warm outside, the ground was wet, and the sky overcast. Water pooled in the gutters halfway into the parking lot, as if from a recent storm. Careful not to get my feet wet, I found Scott's car using my normal method—walking around clicking the *Lock* button.

Scott's driver's license showed him living in Perrysburg. I pulled out of the parking lot and saw I was on West Central Avenue. When I got to the corner I knew exactly where I was. More than eleven years after looking at a map of Toledo and the surrounding area, I still felt comfortable the streets were the same. Especially in so rundown a city, where the economy was historically so bad it wasn't uncommon for people to burn down houses for insurance money.

The ride to Perrysburg was quick and relatively free of traffic. Traffic would have meant the employment rate had improved since my last visit, but I got over the Maumee River in ten minutes. The change couldn't have been more marked. Where before the landscape was spotted with vacant lots and buildings for rent on every corner, now there were tidy subdivisions and decorative split rail fences between the houses, and not a crumbly sidewalk in sight.

I found Scott's house at the end of a comfortable cul-de-sac with a wide disk of green in the middle that was probably home to snowmen and snow forts in the winter. The house was blue and white and new looking, had a two-car garage, and there wasn't a stray toy anywhere. Hurray for no kids.

The remote for the garage was clipped to the visor, and when I clicked it, my heart sank a little when I saw another car parked inside. Tara's, I supposed.

Frowning, I looked at my hand again and saw a thin circle of white in Scott's already light skin—on his ring finger. I checked both pockets, and wonder of all, I pulled out a shiny gold wedding ring.

"My precious," I said, and put it on.

Resignedly, I pulled in beside the other car and got out. I came around and peeked in the car's window and saw a bottle of hand lotion, an open can of diet soda, and a pink hairband on a little shelf in the dashboard.

I considered my options. Maybe Scott had a toothache and couldn't talk much and I'd just nod a lot. Or maybe Scott had a bad day at the office and just wanted to watch TV. Partially true—I did want to watch TV. Or maybe I'd ask about her day, thereby learning more and getting her used to me being home—go on the offensive right away. And *then* watch TV.

Before I could come up with another strategy, the inside door to the garage opened and there was Tara, looking prettier than her phone picture. She was about thirty-five. Tall, with shoulder-length brown hair, and a small, attractive mouth.

"What are you doing?" she said, eyeing me suspiciously.

I turned my head and examined the side mirror, like she'd caught me in the process of doing just that—and got a close-up look at my new ride. White guy, but I knew that by looking at my hands. But this guy was pasty white, with red hair and red eyebrows. No bristly red mustache, thank goodness, or I'd clip that sucker off at the first opportunity. Some things I cannot abide. When I smiled, Scott's teeth were even and healthy looking.

"Toothache," I said, standing up straight.

She looked upset.

"I got tired of waiting at the restaurant," Tara said. "I thought you were serious when you said ... Never mind. Guess I was wrong. Again."

Everyone's wrong sometimes.

I followed her inside and shut the door behind me, sniffing the air as I went. No cooking smells. I wondered if that meant microwave dinner or pizza. My vote was for pizza.

The Schaefers had a modern-looking kitchen with a shiny double stove and lots of great appliances. Thankfully, one of them was a microwave.

"Something wrong with your phone?" she said.

I rubbed my jaw. "It hurts when I talk on the phone."

"Oh that's right," she said drily. "You have a toothache. Listen, next time, don't even bother, okay?"

"It's no bother," I said. "We could still go out. Or maybe get pizza."

Tara gazed coldly at me for several seconds. "Why don't you call your little slut to come over and cook for you?"

"Baby..."

"Don't you fucking call me baby!" she yelled. "Stop the lies! Do you even have a toothache?"

She waited for an answer, then rolled her eyes and pushed past me.

"I never lie about pizza," I said.

Tara stopped midstride and threw me an odd look. That was a Dan thing to say, and I was supposed to be out of my Dan mind.

"You lie about everything," she said, and walked out of the kitchen.

A minute later she returned carrying a patent leather clutch purse and wearing a shiny white jacket.

"Don't wait up," she said, and opened the door to the garage.

Nodding, trying to appease, I said, "I promise not to."

Tara threw me another of those odd looks. "What's with you, anyway?"

"Toothache," I said. Then, because I was supposed to be a psychologist, I added, "How does that make you feel?"

She threw me a final look of disgust and left, which was actually okay.

More pizza for me.

TWENTY-FIVE

Before I even touched the television, I researched all the must-watch stuff on the blessedly password-free computer upstairs in the little office they had. I briefly checked the news and saw the world was just as messed up as ever, a few different names mixed-in for variety. I also found an article about Nate Cantrell, the lotto winner—how he'd founded a charity for needy kids and donated half his wealth to it, all while keeping his job at the elementary school. That guy was totally going to Heaven.

A very quick search turned up what I wanted to know from my adventures in Connecticut—Fred Evans had died in that house after killing eight men. The article had more to say, but I didn't feel like reading it and moved on.

I almost tried logging into my free email account to see if the minister had written me back all those years ago. It was nice knowing there was someone out there who knew the real me, even if he tended toward grumpy and judgmental and a little bit scary. But if whatever Scott Schaefer was up to was illegal, I didn't want my online activity traced back to the minister. Besides, after five years of inactivity, my account had probably expired.

When last I'd been in the world, on-demand television was still in its infancy, relegated mostly to sporting events or movies you could watch in your hotel room. So imagine my joy when, after hitting *Menu* on the remote and clicking around, I found whole video stores of movies and a staggering number of TV shows available. Most of them you had to pay for, but I'd be gone before it showed on the Schaefers' cable bill.

There were so many shows I hadn't seen, so many movies. I'd missed years of Oscars and Oscar nominees and award-winning TV dramas like *Breaking Bad* and *The Walking Dead*.

For the rest of the evening and into the morning, I drank Scott's gourmet coffee and ate pizza while watching back-to-back perfection. All the very best stuff and none of the junk, all at my finger tips while I sat there giggling my butt off and having a blast. This was the most fun I'd had in forever—with extra cheese.

Tara came home around 2 a.m. I heard her keys jangle on the countertop in the kitchen. She came into the living room smelling faintly of cigarettes and beer. She'd obviously been out having fun.

"What are *you* doing up?" she said, slurring a little at the end of it. She wasn't wobbling around yet, but she was getting there. She'd obviously driven home that way, but now was not the time to lecture Scott's wife about the dangers of drinking and driving.

"Watching TV," I said. "You wanna join me? I saved you a slice."

I pointed out the pizza box in case she'd missed it on the way in.

For the first time, a smile flashed across her pretty face, and then it was gone. She opened the pizza box lid.

"I thought you had a toothache," she said.

"I do," I said. "I had to chew on the other side."

I could feel her thinking about it.

"You seriously ate all that?" she said.

"Seriously, I did. And we're going to need more cookies, too. Also, we're out of milk."

Tara held up an unsteady finger—*hold on*—and walked back to the kitchen. I heard the refrigerator open and close, followed by the little metal trashcan with the foot lever clank open and shut. Then she came back.

"You really drank all the milk?" she said.

I nodded. "I ate all the cookies, too ... I'm sorry, did you want—"

Tara threw back her head and laughed. She had great laugh, full of scorn and personality. And even though she'd been nothing but mean to me since I arrived, I was able to distance myself from it. I mean she was mad at Scott, right? And I suspected Scott was the kind of guy people frequently got mad at.

"See you in the morning, asshole," she said, and gave me a toodles sort of wave, then headed toward the stairs. I thought I heard more laughing from upstairs, and then it was just me and my big TV again and, oh yeah, that extra slice I was saving for Tara. Her loss, my gain, and Heisenberg just blew up a bunch of bad guys with some sort of chemical stuff.

What an easy ride. Scott had money, great television, and a good-looking wife who didn't get along with him. It was almost like the Great Whomever was easing me back into the cycle again. I didn't care why, because mine was not to reason why...

"Mine is but to *chew*," I said, and took a bite of Tara's pizza.

By 4 a.m. I couldn't keep my eyes open any longer. I went upstairs, entered the master bedroom, stripped down to my underwear, and approached the bed.

Tara was sprawled naked in the middle—wow, she looked great. In some ways, this was the hardest part of being me. I stared at her for about ten more seconds—being me—then scooted in and did my best to nudge her over to make room. She was tall, which meant she wasn't light like most girls.

After what seemed like no time later, I woke up to someone yelling, "Get out of my bed, you son of a bitch!"

Hard slaps rained down from above, and I covered my head to protect myself. I glanced back and saw Tara on her knees, still naked, with her hands raised like claws and her lips pulled back in a snarl that was ferocious and sexy at the same time. When she reared back to slap me again, I slipped off the bed and landed on my butt and elbows and scrabbled clumsily to my feet.

"Would you calm down?" I said.

Tara told me my room was down the hall, "for being a cheating son of a bitch."

Shuddering suddenly in pain, I said, "Oh boy," and rushed through the open door to the master bath.

"Don't you *dare!*" she shouted, chasing after me.

Boy I dared. I sat down in the preferred location and dared loudly, majestically, with gusto. Tara came in with claws raised, still yelling at me. She held off long enough to see the look of horror on my face and ... and ... *screamed with laughter.*

"Seriously?" I said.

Something felt terribly wrong, and I worried she'd somehow poisoned me. Was that why I'd been sent back? Was it the Nate and Erika situation again, with the crazy fiancée replaced by a jilted, vindictive wife?

Tara stood there shaking with laughter and pointing at me. Somewhere inside, it felt like a monster was trying to claw its way free, like something from a scary movie. Soon, even Tara couldn't stand being in there with me. She left and shut the door. A few seconds later, the door cracked open again and a can of air freshener sailed into the room and rolled to a stop about five feet away, then the door shut again.

Minutes later, after the initial pains had subsided, I realized what Tara's strange pizza perplexity had been about last night. She'd known something about Scott I hadn't: he was lactose intolerant. *Violently* so.

Years ago, I'd caught a ride in a street corner drug dealer who survived by killing other drug dealers and taking over their turf. It had been a weird feeling, always looking over my shoulder for a car to come barreling through an intersection, guns-a-blazin'. Somehow I'd kept from being shot for the entirety of the ride. Then, one day, I bought some shrimp cocktail at a supermarket. I'd eaten a few pieces, then a few more—and then suffocated to death in the parking lot. Ever since, I've always tried to be careful around shellfish and peanut butter.

I'd been in one other lactose intolerant ride before, but

it had been nothing like this. I wasn't going to die from it, but if it kept up like this I'd want to.

About ten minutes later, I finally got up and limped over to the sink to wash my hands. I glanced at myself in the mirror—and nearly went blind. I mean, this guy was *white*. I had red gashes along my neck from where Tara's Wolverine claws had raked me, but I wasn't bleeding.

When I got to the bedroom, the bed was made up but nobody was there, and my clothes from the night before were gone. I found them in another room down the hall, tossed on *my* bed.

I took a shower in another bathroom on the same floor, then got dressed with the clothes I found in the closet and a chest of drawers. When I went downstairs, Tara was in the kitchen making bacon and eggs—for herself. Which was fine. I wasn't that hungry anyway, though it did smell good.

I cupped my rumbling stomach and bent over in another spasm of pain. Seconds later, it went away.

"Tara, sorry about..."

"Just stay out of my room," she said, snapping her words off at the end like she was mad at them. "You lost those privileges when you fucked that slut at your job. If she calls here again I'm calling the police."

Melody, I figured. This guy was a piece of work.

"It's your room, I know," I said. "I was just tired. Wasn't thinking straight and went in there automatically."

She shook her head and scrambled her eggs more vigorously.

I rooted through the cabinets looking for a cup, but opened the one with the tupperware in it.

"What are you looking for?" she said.

"Not sure," I said, and opened another cabinet. This one had the dinner plates and bowls. The next one over had the glassware. I got a glass down and filled it with water.

"You're acting really weird," she said, pouring her eggs into the pan.

"I'm just not feeling well."

"What were you thinking of, eating like that? Drinking milk?"

I shrugged: *you know me.*

"Well, it was stupid," she said.

For once, she didn't sound as angry as she normally did, which was refreshing. Even though it wasn't my fault she was mad at me, my psyche didn't like it, and it was wearisome.

Tara took her eggs and bacon and left the room. In the living room, the television came on. I considered joining her, but she could barely stand me, and I desperately needed to find a bathroom nobody cared about.

TWENTY-SIX

As soon as Tara got up to put her dishes away, I shot into the living room and took over the TV. When she came back, she gave me another of those funny looks. She couldn't understand why I was so fascinated with television. She said it was like I just discovered we had one, and how come I never watched it before?

The Walking Dead was on now. Technically a horror show, but I didn't find it scary. To me it was simply a neat concept: civilization coming to an end, strangers banding together for survival.

"I thought you hated the whole zombie thing," she said.

"Have you seen *The Walking Dead*?" I said.

If we'd had shows like that in the eighties, there's no way we'd have put up with the *A-Team* shooting thousands of rounds a week and never hitting anybody. TV had crept slowly away from tame make-believe in the nineties to gritty realism in the early 2000s. But the things they were getting away with now...

"Can you imagine if something like that actually happened?" I said, pointing at the screen. "Zombies running loose everywhere?"

Tara looked at me strangely and left me alone on the couch.

About an hour later, something like a conscience reared

its sheepish head, and I went looking for her. First the kitchen, then upstairs, but she was gone.

Maybe I was taking the whole "Tara hates me, yippee" thing too far. Scott and Tara were still married, whatever their problems were, and she was obviously still talking to him. Now that I thought about it, had all that laughing at my expense been malicious?

A person doesn't go from marriage to breaking up and then suddenly start waltzing around the house acting like nothing is wrong. Bad relationships have minefields of treacherous politics in every tiny thing. Lower or raise the TV volume when someone enters the room and it means something: consideration for her, or lack thereof. Wash the dishes after breakfast? One less thing she has to do, and thank you very much Honey.

Scott could have been trying to fix things between them, and here I was not fixing things anymore. Or maybe he'd been walking around hating her, being a real ass about it, and now I was acting polite and nice and cruelly messing with her head.

And here I thought I'd caught an easy ride.

Sometime in the early afternoon, just when I felt it was safe to leave the house, I heard Scott's phone ringing in the kitchen. I went in, picked it up, and checked for a picture on the front, but all I saw was a phone number. I answered it.

"Hello?" I said.

"Fuck you!" someone yelled. A woman, but not Tara. And not Pam from the mental clinic. Whoever she was, she hung up before I could put her in her place.

After a brief hesitation, I clicked and swiped until I figured out how to call her back and then did so. Nobody answered the first time, and nobody answered the second time, either. I went to put the phone in my pocket and it rang again. This time from a different number.

"You're gonna fucking die, asshole," a man's voice said, and then he hung up. I was so shocked by the rudeness I forgot to put this guy in his place, too.

Both the man and the woman were angry, and anger makes people do reckless things. Reckless people worried me. That's why, when I left the house for a drive, I noticed a silver sports car following me a little too closely. Whoever it was made sure to stay a few lengths behind.

I took a sudden turn after the bridge, hoping to lose him or her, but the silver car revved and squealed after me. I took another turn and it followed along easily, keeping pace. I would have turned again, but the sports car shot in front of me and slowed. Beer bottles flew from the driver's side window landing on and around my car. One came crashing into the windshield, fracturing it with a lovely spider web of cracks that made it hard to see through.

The silver car angled across the narrow lane, blocking me in. The area looked beaten down and derelict and forgotten. With a chain link fence on one side and a hydrant poking out of the sidewalk on the other side, there was no way I could move forward. I put Scott's car in reverse, already turning the wheel—and promptly bumped into something. When I looked back, I saw a big black Jeep blocking my way.

A young, muscular, Asian guy got out of the silver car waving his hands around and telling me to get out. I stole a glance behind me and saw a tubby white guy get out of the Jeep.

Curious, but unafraid, I got out too.

Casually, Jeep Guy reached in and pulled out a long hunting rifle with a glossy stock and a decorative fur strap.

"Where you think *you're* going, dickwad?" he said.

Meanwhile, the Asian guy had gotten out his own weapon—an aluminum baseball bat.

"I told you to leave my sister alone, asshole," he said with a flawless Midwest American accent.

He rushed me with the bat held low. I hid behind the still open door and crouched down for the first swing. It broke the side window and sent a shower of glass everywhere. I shoved the door hard with my back against the car and he gave a surprised yelp and fell over. As he was getting up, I came around and kicked him a glancing blow to the head, knocking him back down again.

Despite all that, I'm not Bruce Lee. I can't fight ten people at a time, or even two people. Jeep Guy must have hit me with the butt of his rifle, because I saw stars and dropped to my knees, then my hands and knees, and then my face hit the asphalt.

Someone said, "You okay, Johnny?"

Someone else said, "Smashed my knee."

My vision was blurry and the world seemed spinnier than I was used to. Someone dragged me up by my shirt and then slammed me against the car.

"He warned you once, and now I'm gonna shoot you," Jeep Guy said.

"Let me do it," Johnny said.

Johnny was maybe twenty-five, buzz cut, with a sculpted physique from too many hours in the gym. He would have been scary to someone who hadn't died as many times as I had.

"I told you I'd kill you if you touched my sister again," he said, getting in my face, angling his gaze back and forth like he was cornering me.

Then it dawned on me. "Melody's brother?"

"Shut up!" Johnny said, and punched me in the stomach, causing me to double over in pain.

Somewhat comically, my lactose intolerance blared forth in what may have been a B flat tone, and the air filled with the noxious stench of indigestible milk sugar.

Johnny chuckled.

"Oh, Jesus," Jeep Guy said, crinkling his nose. "Looks like you hit him too hard. So hey, you want me to shoot him now?"

"I don't know, George," Johnny said, pretending to think about it. "I wanna see him cry before we kill him."

Now it was my turn to chuckle, though I had to force it out over the pain in my sour stomach and my stinging face.

"Hey look," Jeep Guy George said. "He thinks we're kidding. Hold him higher."

Johnny grabbed my shirt and held me up. Then George unslung his expensive-looking hunting rifle and pointed it at my head.

"You want me to do it now?" he said.

Johnny opened his mouth to say something but I laughed again. Not because I wasn't afraid of death, but because I didn't think I was in any danger beyond the cooling trickle of blood from my nose.

"Think we won't do it?" Johnny said. He grabbed my hair and jerked me ouchingly close to his face. "I told you ... but you couldn't leave her alone, could you? Why you wanna die?"

"He's not going to kill me," I said. "And you won't either. Not here, not anywhere. He's just some guy who likes hunting and country music. Probably has a big mouth, and that's why you asked him to go on this little adventure. I get it, you love your sister and I'm bad news, and—oh *no*, who's *that*?"

"What?" Johnny said, turning to see where I was looking, loosening his grip on my hair at the same time.

I twisted painfully from his grasp, losing some of Scott's frizzy red hair in the process, and grabbed the barrel of the gun. Bracing my back against the car, I held on tightly and kicked George away. The rifle came out of his hands like a sword from a scabbard. I used it like a sword, bashing Johnny hard in his arm, and that brought a not-so-tough yelp out of him. Then I reversed the rifle and pointed it back and forth between Johnny and George, who was scrabbling backwards like a crab.

"Yeah right," Johnny said, smiling evilly, waving the bat around like he was winding up. "You won't shoot anyone. You're gonna stand there while I beat the shit out of you."

I aimed at the bat, following it carefully, affecting a look of supreme concentration.

"What are you doing?" Johnny said, still swinging the bat, though less fluidly, looking from me to his bat and back again.

"Nobody'll get hurt," I said, "if you hold perfectly still. I think I can shoot it out of your hands..."

Johnny's eyes widened and he dropped the bat. "Don't do it man!"

"I thought you said he was a pussy!" George screamed, and dove into his Jeep. Then, out the window, he yelled, "You better not mess up my gun!"

Ensconced in his shiny expensive-looking vehicle, George backed up to make room, then accelerated halfheartedly toward me, like he wanted to take me and the still-open car door for a ride. I didn't bother moving. No way was he going to mess up his Jeep, and he didn't.

Moments later, they were both gone.

This section of Toledo didn't look like it got much traffic, so if they'd wanted to really hurt me I suppose they could have. I examined the rifle—a bolt-action, with the safety off. George couldn't have been dumb enough to point a loaded weapon at me.

On a lark, I opened the breach.

"Seriously?" I said, and picked up the ejected round.

TWENTY-SEVEN

I pulled in behind Tony Packo's and parked. After all the hoopla with Johnny and George, I felt like having the Greatest Hungarian Hotdog ever.

Tony Packo's had been mentioned several times by Klinger in the TV series *M*A*S*H,* one of my all-time favorite shows. I'd only been there once before but the food had been good. Lots of memorabilia, and all those hotdog buns signed by celebrities. I'd always wanted to meet a real celebrity (Ernest Prescott didn't count), and maybe today I would.

I'd gotten most of the blood off my face with half a bottle of water found on the floor under the passenger seat. I thought I looked fine, but the hostess gave me a suspicious once over.

"Table for one," I said.

"You have blood on your shirt," she said.

I glanced down. It looked like someone had dipped their hands in blood and then shaken them at me.

"Oh that's just paint," I said, laughing at the absurd misunderstanding. *These aren't the droids you're looking for.*

A look of relief washed over her face. "Right this way."

The place had a lot of people in it. A tourist attraction of sorts, Tony Packo's had been busy last time, too. Which was fine. It gave me time to ponder the craziness with the rifle and Johnny and his dumb bat.

Until I knew more about my ride, I couldn't let anything happen to him. Not until I knew he'd done something warranting it. Rules were rules, even if I was the only one following them.

Thinking back, Scott's portal in the Great Wherever hadn't had that weird sense of ... I don't know what you'd call it. Like it was okay to take over, with limits. Like with Nate Cantrell, and later with Peter. Both those guys had ended up being relatively innocent. So what did that make Scott? Did it mean he was a butchering killer, like Ernest and Lana, or whatever Fred had been?

Eventually my waiter arrived. His name tag said his name was Troy. Troy-the-waiter was in his mid-twenties. He had enormous circle things in his stretchy earlobes, wide enough to poke a finger through, and his arms were sleeved in an indecipherable confusion of colorful tattoos. His eyes were wise beyond his physical age, and he was very, very cool.

He gave my bloody shirt a quick glance.

"Hello, welcome to Tony Packo's," he said in a reserved tone that was technically still polite.

"I know this is going to sound funny," I said, "but have the Cubs won the World Series in the last, oh say, five years?"

I wasn't that big of a baseball fan, but I was a little, and on those occasions when I missed the Series I always hoped to find the curse had been lifted. Also, I was trying to cheer myself up.

"You mean baseball?" he said.

"Yeah."

"Can't say I follow baseball."

"What's your sport?" I said, happy to talk to anyone who didn't hate me yet. "Football?"

He shook his head. "Not really."

"Why not?"

Troy shrugged, turning his indifference into something cool and interesting and wise and no big deal all at the same time.

"Just the whole machismo thing, I guess. Objectification of women, male hegemony, strong is good, weak is bad, commercialism, big corporations and banks ... you know, that kind of thing. Basically a microcosm of all that's wrong with America."

"Microcosms," I said, shaking my head at the shame of it. "Those are the worst kind of cosms."

Troy blinked, then threw me a sharp look.

"Whataya have?" he said, a few degrees cooler.

"You're kidding, right? Hungarian dog. Fries too. But please, hold the American-*cheese*-mo—makes me fart. Thank you."

"Right," he said, pulling a thin smile before leaving.

On his way to the kitchen, he passed a waitress and said something. The girl snuck a glance at me and smirked, and the patron she was supposed to be helping sighed impatiently. I felt a little like that infamous butterfly flapping his wings and causing hurricanes around the world.

A different server brought me a drink, and somewhere in the restaurant a cell phone started playing Yakety Sax, the Benny Hill theme, which brought me back to the old days when Dad stayed up late to watch it when he thought Mom was asleep. Mom hated the show, called it *smut*, and one time over dinner she accused Dad of liking it because the women ran around in their underwear.

Dad's deadpan response had been: "Sometimes they walk." Then he smiled the classic Benny Hill mugging-for-the-camera face, and my sister and I took his side while Mom pretended to be offended.

Hotdogs and fries was normally a quick order, but my food hadn't arrived yet.

Ok, why not...

I got out Scott's phone, pecked-out a familiar number and wondered, as I always did, if someone would answer it this time. I always expected the number to have changed or been disconnected, but someone picked up after a few rings and said, "Hello?"

Her voice was a little rougher than when I'd called five years ago from Sandra's house. Tired-sounding. More so than she deserved.

"Hello?" she said again.

My throat tightened and I swallowed.

"I'm sorry," I blurted.

"Who is this?" she said.

"I mean I think I have the wrong number. Sorry."

"Oh yeah?" she said. "Who were you trying to reach?" There was a note of insistence in her voice, like she really wanted to know.

I faked a laugh and rattled off her phone number, with the last digit a seven instead of an eight.

"Funny how that happens," she said. "We've had this number for thirty years, and though every telemarketer and charity group in the world seems to know it, we've never changed it."

"Funny," I said, stalling, hoping to hear more of her voice before it got too weird and I had to hang up. "Uh ... why?"

"Twenty-one years ago we started getting calls every few months, then maybe once or twice a year. Different people, different places. Something about those calls always seemed odd. Whenever I asked who they were looking for, they said they hit seven and not eight, just like you did now."

"Is that so?"

"Yes," she said. "Then, about five years ago, the calls suddenly stopped."

My mouth was dry, so I took a sip of water.

"And I don't know why," she said, "but I miss them. Those strange calls."

Tears came to my eyes, unbidden, causing them to sting. I needed to hang up the phone and never call that number again.

Instead I said, "Does ... um ... your husband, or children ... do they also miss those calls?"

Hang up now!

"Paul died four years ago," she said softly. "Jane, my daughter, lives in Toledo. Same area code you're calling from now, matter of fact."

Cursing myself for being weak, I said, "Sorry, ma'am.

For the wrong number. Small world, huh?"
   I ended the call before I could say anything else.

TWENTY-EIGHT

The next day, Tara made us both eggs and bacon and served them with orange juice. She was less hostile than normal, didn't use any swear words even once. She made the bacon the way I liked it—a little rubbery, just this side of trichinosis. But I couldn't enjoy it because my sister was somewhere in town and Mom liked chatting with stalkers on the phone. Also, I'd just found out my father was dead.

"How are your eggs?" Tara said.

"Great," I said, and took a bite to prove it.

Through an astonishing degree of stupidity on my part, Mom had noticed a pattern in the calls I'd made over the years. How could I have been so careless, saying the same lame thing every time?

Tara and I were sitting across from each other at the glass-topped breakfast table in the kitchen.

"What are you doing?" she said, staring at me over her coffee mug.

"Looking at the ceiling."

"For answers?"

I didn't know what I was looking for.

"You've been weird since you came home yesterday," Tara said. "Weirder than usual. I know we're ... you know. But that doesn't mean ... Look, we go back a ways. So if there's something wrong. Other than, you know..."

I needed to get back in the game.

"Everything's fine," I said. "My tooth's hurting me, that's all."

The old failsafe.

Tara shrugged and began fiddling with her phone. She had a fancy swipey phone like Scott's, and she was tapping away at an astonishing speed. She had clear smooth skin and pretty white teeth, and her tongue stuck out daintily when she was concentrating, and boy was she concentrating. Glossy brown hair like Sandra Bullock. No perfume.

"What?" she said when she caught me staring.

"Nothing," I said.

Tara shook her head and went back to tapping on her cell phone, and I went back to my bacon. When I was done, I got up to put my plate in the sink.

Tara glanced up and said, "Are you going to church with me?" Her tone was rigidly casual, and I wasn't sure whether to say yes or no.

Growing up, I never liked church and I hated nice clothes. Something about all those people dressed up and being friendly to one another made me nervous. As if any moment someone would go bananas and start yelling profanity and throwing punches. Churches were mostly empty and echoed like caves, and for some reason people thought it made perfect sense to burst into song every three to four minutes, even if they couldn't hit all the notes. Those times I'd gone, I mouthed the words and spent a lot of time wondering if anyone would notice if I didn't keep standing up to sing.

A few rides back, my dubious relationship with all things churchy took a slide when I'd run into Anthony Hendricks, the man I mostly thought of as the minister. He'd touched me once, on the shoulder, and nearly kicked me out of my ride. And when he looked at me I felt like running away or passing out or confessing my sins right there and begging for forgiveness. So when Tara asked if I'd go to church with her...

"Yeah, I'll go," I said, surprising myself.

After breakfast, Tara went upstairs to get dressed.

I had on shorts and a T-shirt, which God hates. Looking through Scott's guest-room closet, I found a white long-sleeved shirt and dark pants and put those on. Then I switched out my sneakers for loafers and dress socks, which God likes.

Tara came down in a short-sleeved blue dress with a dark hemline just above the knees, appropriately snug, and a black leather belt around the middle. On her left wrist was a matching black bracelet, and she wore a tiny cross on a delicate gold chain around her neck. Her hair was twisted in a rope over her shoulder. She stood at the base of the stairs watching me, her bright eyes shining like the first light of creation itself.

"Jesus," I breathed.

"What?"

I cleared my throat and pointed at her cross. "That's him right there."

Tara smiled briefly, then stepped past me on the way to the garage, trailing an elusive floral scent. And me.

Upon entering the garage, she said, "Scott ... what happened to our car?"

Yesterday, in my preoccupation with Mom and the news about my father and sister, I'd forgotten those idiots had broken the window and messed up the door. To me it was just a car. I didn't have to get it inspected or repaired or have the tires rotated or any of that. Unlike Tara. To her, anything bad that happened to one of the family cars was a big deal.

"I forgot to tell you," I said.

"Well, what happened to it?"

She circled it carefully, looking at the smashed-in side window and the glinting cracks in the windshield. The side panel was bent inward from where I'd kicked the door into Johnny.

"Vandals," I said, shaking my head. Crime's a terrible thing.

Tara gaped at me like I had a spider on my face.

"Did you call the police?" she said. "Did you call the insurance company? What the hell, Scott? When did this happen?"

Found out and sick of the lies, I told her how I'd come out Tony Packo's after a healthy lunch of salad and water and found the car all beaten up. A couple of other cars nearby were worse, and when their owners came out and saw the damage we called the police and filed a report.

Tara said, "You didn't make separate police reports?"

"There was a lawyer in the group," I said. "He said this way's more efficient. Trust me, that guy knew his stuff."

The moment stretched with neither of us saying anything.

"I'll never trust you again," she said at last.

Just like that, all the barriers from that first night returned and flew up around her, shutting me off again. Scott was a cheat, and I needed to watch it when I threw around words like *trust*.

Tara handed me her keys. I said my toothache was bothering me and handed them back, that way she wouldn't get suspicious when we drove all over the city for no good reason. She didn't suggest I go to the dentist. She didn't ask if I'd taken any medicine. She took the keys, got in, and didn't talk to me the whole way to church.

After parking, Tara gave me a pointed look and said, "You know what? You need to make this count. Not just for me, but for you."

We got out.

St. Stephen's was close to the river in an area more densely populated than Perrysburg. Across the street stretched a row of small single-family homes. On this side, the church towered without pity over the world and its sinners. It was brick and big and quite beautiful in an early romantic neo-Byzantium rococo impressionist sort of way. Upon entering through the central door, one of three, I didn't blow away in a puff of smoke or get attacked by beatific beings with flaming sabers. So I was able to enjoy the distillation of a thousand years of early Pleistocene, upper gothic, lower renaissance, eastern realist, and western iconoclastic architecture. Sculpture and columns, ceiling murals and all that horrible echoing from my childhood multiplied by a thousand, all of it collected in one place to add to my feeling of insignificance.

Ah, church.

There were glossy wooden pews, and people were grabbing the good seats left, right, and center. Before Tara could pick one of those, I snagged a spot in the back, way off on the side. She tossed me a funny look and then sat down next to me.

Cautiously, I poked one of the pleather-bound prayer books in the holder in front of me. Nothing happened.

"Why did you do that?" she said.

I quirked her a tiny Mr. Spock and said, "I'm being ... mysterious."

Tara half smiled, shook her head, then turned toward the front of the church.

Yesterday, I'd found out where the games were on Scott's phone. I was playing one of them when an echoing voice asked us all to bow our heads in prayer. Organ music groaned loudly from regions groany, and Tara poked me in the side until I put the phone away. Then everyone got up and sang a song while the altar boys walked solemnly around carrying things and doing stuff with the candles.

I made like I was singing while the others sang actual words. Tara had a beautiful voice, and I wondered if she ever did karaoke. I stole a glance at her: pure singing, lovely profile, so alive, so nice.

It was the best moment I'd ever had in a church.

When the singing ended everyone sat down, and a familiar voice said, "The Lord be with you."

"And also with you," droned the congregation.

When I looked to the pulpit, Anthony Hendricks, aka "the minister," was standing there in white and gold robes surrounded by altar boys on either side.

* * *

I was so shocked by the absurd development I sat with my mouth open through the next song and into the next prayer:

"God our Father, your gift of water brings life and freshness to the earth. It washes away our sins and brings us eternal life. We ask you now to bless this water, and to give us your protection on this day which you have made your own. Renew the living spring of your life within us and protect us in spirit and body, that we may be free from sin and come into your presence to receive your gift of salvation. We ask this through Christ our Lord."

Then, like the world's most reverent hecklers, the congregation said, "Amen."

Time seemed to fly in that suddenly too-small church as I absorbed the shock of the minister's presence over and over again. It was him. It was *him.*

At one point Tara said, "Are you ready for communion?"

She stared at me intently while I sat there not getting up for crackers and grape juice. I didn't dare for fear of being shunted into the line with the minister. And no, I wasn't ready to think of him as *the priest* yet.

"I'm not hungry," I said absently, and immediately wished I could take it back.

"That's not funny," she whispered, her expression hurt.

Why couldn't I keep my big mouth shut?

As if proving something, Tara got into the middle line. The one with the minister.

Near the end of the service I said I needed air and went outside. My plan was to slip home and tell Tara I'd left because I wasn't feeling good, which would get me off the hook for my lack of zeal. Then I remembered we'd come in the same car.

It was almost like Someone was interfering with things. First, Mom says my sister's in town, and now the minister shows up in Toledo at Scott and Tara's church. A lot of coincidence in the span of two days.

About ten minutes later the people let out—the women chatting and taking their time, the men shuffling, waiting to grill burgers and drink and watch sports. It wasn't football season, so at least they were safe from all that hegemony and objectification of women.

I craned my neck, hoping for a glimpse of Tara making her way out, but didn't see her. I climbed the steps, poked my head inside, and found her and the minister just inside the doors talking like best friends.

"Scott!" he said, and reached over to shake my hand.

Before the unthinkable happened, I faked a noisy sneeze into both my hands.

Almost as quickly, the minister's hand retracted.

"Coming down with a cold?" he said, an amused smile on his kindly face.

His supernatural voodoo didn't appear to be working, because I didn't feel like throwing up or running away or any of that. If he touched me, that'd change. Might even kick me out. Even if it didn't, he'd know who I was, and I wasn't ready for another long theological discussion with him. Also, I had no idea what he was doing here. As a priest, no less. The old minister had seemed to scoff at such religious rigidity, preferring Universalism to Catholicism. Could it be that our running into each other, years ago, had somehow kicked him back the other way?

"Must be dusty in here," I said, and made a show of wiping my hands on my pants. "Sorry about that."

Tara was staring at me in disgust. When the minister turned to her, her face morphed into sweetness and light and cheery amusement, and for a second I wondered if maybe ... ah, nope, as soon as he looked back at me, Tara made with the mean look again.

The minister leaned closer.

"I've been meaning to talk to you, Scott," he said in a low voice. "The church offers marriage counseling for free, as I'm sure you're aware. And as a psychologist, I'm sure you also know the power of a shoulder to lean on, even if it's attached to an old celibate like myself." This last with a soft chuckle.

A line of people stood nearby waiting to talk to him.

The minister stepped back, gave me a significant look, and added, "I hold confession here every Wednesday at 8 a.m." Then he was off to greet other people.

As soon as his back was turned, Tara stormed out.

TWENTY-NINE

When I was a one year old baby, I couldn't understand what my parents were saying to each other, though it all sounded very funny at the time. After dying, I'd pieced it together—a harder task than you'd think. Being a baby was a world of sound, color, and sensation, all perfectly mingled with this pervasive sense of either *happy* or *sad*. Mom and Dad were *happy*. My toy was *happy*. And sometimes the world was *sad*, like when I woke up and it was dark for no reason and I was alone. When I remember my babyhood, there's this annoying happy-sad stuff saturating all those funny sounds my parents were making, such that I have to consciously say to myself, "Aha! After Dad picked me up, he said, 'We're going to Grandma's.'"

When Tara and I arrived home, I poured myself a quick glass of orange juice and headed toward the living room, hoping to snag the television before certain other people got there first.

"I've decided to move back with my mom," Tara said suddenly, stopping me in my tracks. "She said she'd fix a room up for me."

Even though Tara was Scott's wife, I felt that same primal feeling of *sad*, just like when I was a baby.

"Just for a few months," she said. "We need time. You need to decide if we make this work or if we ... you know.

Like we talked about that night when ... when *she* called here. Divorce."

They were Catholic, which made it a bigger deal than for others.

"When are you leaving?" I said.

"She's bringing the truck down next weekend."

I nodded.

"Why did you have to mess it up?" Tara said. She was crying a little. "What's wrong with *me*? Why couldn't I be enough? Was fucking that stupid woman so important that you had to ruin everything else, too? We were gonna have children and do everything right."

Openly weeping now, Tara fled the kitchen.

The Great Whomever must really have hated suicide, to put me through this. That poor woman, all that pain, and it was my job to take the brunt of it and keep from somehow making it worse. I assumed. It wasn't always obvious why he sent me back, but back I went, obvious or not. Usually there was a lot more blood and screaming and guns.

Standing in the kitchen listening to Tara crying upstairs, I almost wished for one of those rides.

Tara avoided me for the rest of the day, and I contented myself with doing housework. Laundry, vacuuming, and other mundane tasks kept me occupied and gave me time to think about my own problems for once. My dad, after all, had died. How, I didn't know, nor when exactly. I missed him terribly. Him and Mom, both.

Back when it all began, on my first ride ever, I came close to returning and convincing them I was still alive ... around ... whatever I was. I'd regale them with incredibly specific anecdotes, verbatim quotes, and other impossible-to-know information—like how many stitches my sister got when she fell down the stairs. Or how, at five years old, I'd gotten out of bed and walked almost a mile to the supermarket to steal a rubber ball. Then, parroting my babysitter and her mean friends, I'd cussed-out the cops when they questioned me.

There were plenty of stories to go with that one. They'd have been convinced by the time I finished, as well as horrified—their world turned upside down, their memories of me transformed into something twisted and nightmarish and wrong. So I'd done the right thing and stayed away.

Before going to bed that night, I thought about locating my sister, Jane. She was sure to be in the City Directory, available at any library. It'd be no big deal—bump into her at a supermarket or something. Strike up a conversation. I was good at worming information out of people. I'd tell her she looked Dutch. I'd be pleasant, not weird, because I'd have flowers in one hand and wine in the other. Like I already had a girl. So it must be a real compliment and not some creepy pickup line. Dad always called Jane his little Dutch girl, and given enough time with her I'd know how he died.

Maybe I'd do that tomorrow.

My last thought before falling asleep was, *But I have work tomorrow...*

* * *

Sometime in the middle of the night, I awoke to someone shaking my shoulder. It was Tara, crouched by my side with a robe thrown hastily around her.

"What?" I said. "Huh?"

"Shh! There's someone in the house."

When my eyes gained focus, I saw by the meager light through the curtains she was frightened.

"Here's the gun," Tara said, and thrust a pistol into my hands.

"Did you call the cops?" I said.

"Not yet."

"Why not?"

"Because," she said, "what if it's just an animal or something? I'll look silly."

That's a funny thing about humans. They'd rather die than look too silly to take basic defensive measures to save their precious lives. Rather than go to the other side of the street to avoid a group of young men in gang colors, they'll keep walking along. Maybe even say hello as they pass, just to prove a point. Wouldn't want to seem sexist or racist or classist or whichever *ist* was eating at them. They'd spin that wheel and see what happened, but they wouldn't look silly.

I shook my head. "Tara..."

"Don't Tara me," she said, pulling her robe tighter and glaring at me.

I listened carefully, and she listened too.

"I don't hear anything," I said.

"Can you just go look? And *please* be careful with that gun."

I smiled at the concern in her voice.

"If you hear gunshots, call the cops. Deal?"

"Yes, now *go*."

Scott's gun was a silvery .38 snub-nosed revolver. I checked the cylinder and it would fire on the next pull, provided it wasn't a dud. If it was, I'd pull again. Better than a semi-auto for dealing with duds.

I crept down the stairs, straining to hear something. At first it was quiet, and then I heard a door open in the kitchen. I came around the corner, gun pointed down. Nobody was in the kitchen, but the door to the garage was wide open. I stepped past the dishwasher and the little table we'd eaten breakfast at and peeked into the garage.

Someone was in Scott's car with a flashlight. I flipped the light switch and squinted at too much light in my night-adjusted eyes. Whoever was in the car yelped and scrambled out. I held my gun steady and pointed it at him, squinting to see if *he* had a gun pointed at *me*.

It was a tense moment, and then George the Jeep guy said, "I just want my rifle, Schaefer."

"What?"

"You took my rifle," he said "It was a Christmas gift and I want it back."

He didn't have a gun on him, I could see that now. Maybe he had one hidden under his shirt.

"Why didn't you come ask me during normal hours?" I said.

"Would you have given it to me?"

"Probably. So long as you promised not to shoot me with it."

"I was just supposed to scare you," George said. "Johnny..."

"Yeah," I said, "what's up with that? Why's he so pissed

at me?"

George pulled a big, goofy grin, like I must have been kidding him.

"You serious?" he said. "You, uh ... that is ... Melody said you were stalking her. That's what *she* said, man, not me, and would you *please* stop pointing that pistol at me?"

Finally I knew why I was here. Scott the big fat stalker. Easy enough to fix. If he'd gone further than that I'd find out eventually, and Tara had even handed me the right tool to deal with it. She was a good person, Tara. I hated to see her made a widow, or married to a prisoner and all that entailed. At least if I killed myself, she wouldn't need to do the whole divorce thing. I could admit my crimes in a note, like I'd done so many times before. There wouldn't be any doubt about whether to love me or hate me ... I mean Scott. Or maybe she'd blame herself anyway, the way everyone did.

Dammit.

"I'm sorry, man," George said, sounding blubbery and afraid. "Please lower that gun, would you? I'll just leave, okay?"

"Hold on," I said, and walked over to a cabinet against the wall. I opened it and pulled out his dumb hunting rifle, then handed it to him.

"Jeez, thanks," he said.

Just then, Tara walked in and shouted, "He's got a gun!"

George appeared more afraid of her than she was of him. He held the gun tightly, not pointing it at anyone.

"Tara, it's okay," I said.

"I'm calling the police!"

She marched back to the kitchen.

To George I said, "You stay put," and followed after her.

I grabbed her shoulder just as she picked up the landline and said, "He's a patient. I'm working with him on something important and if you call the police it'll ruin everything."

Tara slapped my hand away and said, "What? He's got a gun! What kind of breakthrough is that?"

"He was trying to *give* me his gun, not shoot me. I'm trying to get him to give up hunting to help his ...

reattachment to nature."

She had her thumb poised over the numbers, no doubt ready to dial 911.

"Tara, seriously," I said. "Hold on a minute and listen, okay? Please?"

Still holding the phone, almost like a weapon, she said, "Make it good."

"I'm trying to tell you he's a hunter, and getting him to stop shooting animals is part of his therapy. It's the Jungian Pentangle technique—a breakthrough development in psychotherapy. Cutting edge stuff."

Tara's eyes widened a little, and then she laughed.

"Jungian *Pentangle* therapy? That's what that is in our garage? At..." She looked at the clock. "Two in the morning?"

I nodded gravely. "Cutting edge."

Tara shook her head and put the phone down. "Get him out of my house."

Then she stomped out of the room.

"*Our* house," I corrected, though low enough she wouldn't hear me.

Moments later, I heard the sound of a bedroom door being slammed. In addition to good cable, the Schaefers also had impressively sturdy architecture.

Back in the garage, I said to George, "Okay, you got your gun. You know where Melody lives?"

He nodded.

"I'll drive behind you," I said. "You're going to take me past her house. Got it?"

Again, George nodded. He was looking at the gun in my hand.

Reluctantly, I stopped pointing it at him.

THIRTY

George had jimmied the front door open with a screwdriver and left dents in the jamb. The lock still worked when I tested it, but the wood was all chewed up. Tara wasn't going to be happy ... which wasn't unusual for her, granted.

"I got a friend who can fix that," George said, when I pointed it out to him.

"Send him," I said. "Tomorrow. Now let's go."

George nodded and got in his Jeep and I got in Scott's car to follow him. He didn't drive fast, and ten minutes later we were in a poorer part of town on the other side of the river. Older single-family homes—in name only. They appeared to have been subdivided from bigger houses.

When we got to one such house on a corner lot, George slowed down and pointed at it through his window, then drove off.

I'd left the gun in the guest room at the house. It was no use to me here, and could only get me in more trouble. Tonight was purely an intelligence-gathering mission.

After parking, I strolled up to Melody's door like I had every right to be there at that hour. If I was right, when she opened the door she'd act afraid. Maybe she'd yell at me. Maybe she'd call the police. I didn't like the idea of scaring her, but I needed to know if what George had said about

Scott stalking her was true. Bad stuff, but it would make things much simpler going forward. Then I'd just need to find out how far the stalking had gone.

I pushed the doorbell and waited. A minute later, light streamed down through a window on the second floor, and not long after that I heard someone fiddling with the latch.

The door opened and Melody was standing there naked. B-cups, shining abs, slender, and beautiful. Her shiny black hair draped around her shoulders while she eyed me coldly. But only for a second—she threw herself into my arms and proceeded to make out with me.

That's right, *with* me, but let me explain...

For years, I'd remained celibate and did my best to ignore the advances of the various women I met on my rides. Then, one day, I'd met a stunningly beautiful killer named Erika. She was bad, but not psycho Lana Sandway bad. Also, she seemed to like me. One thing led to another ... and another ... and another, then a few more after that for one of the most shameful (yet amazing) nights I'd ever experienced.

Despite my fall from grace, I still feel taking advantage of someone who thinks I'm her boyfriend or husband is about as low as it gets.

But see ... it was the strangest thing. Yes, I was relieved what George said about Scott stalking Melody was not true. I processed that rather quickly. But I knew I shouldn't have been kissing her back. She didn't know me, Dan Jenkins. She thought I was Scott, the cheating psychologist. But Melody was evil, wasn't she? What she'd said about Scott—lying to her brother about him being a stalker—that had to be evil, right? Also, she was an *adulteress*, which was against every one of the Ten Commandments. And hadn't I gotten away with it with Erika? Totally had. Also, and perhaps most importantly, Melody was *Asian*. Did it make me a racist that I'd always wanted to kiss an Asian woman and now I was actually kissing one?

Her breath was minty, like she'd swished with mouthwash and hadn't rinsed enough. For my part, I totally appreciated the thoughtfulness.

Melody pulled me inside and said, "What took you so

long, you big goof?"

Morality, I thought, and shut the door to the night and my morality, both.

* * *

The next hour passed amazingly, and then it was morning and Melody was shaking me awake.

"Come on, sleepy pants," she said. "Time for work."

She skipped around the room, bouncing and jiggling and looking really athletic and cute and Asian all over the place. But all I could think was, *Oh my God, what have I done?*

Melody's room in the morning light was a disaster area of clothes, makeup, hangers, curlers, and magazines strewn everywhere. She didn't even have a proper bed, just a mattress on the floor.

She poked through her closet and found a short skirt, then chose a frilly yellow blouse from a mostly pink pile of clothing over by the window.

I got up to use the bathroom.

Despite the weird night and my relative lack of sleep, I still wanted to work today. I was looking forward to the psychologist thing. Much like my stint as a security guard in Fred's body, this was something I could do. It'd be nice to be needed, and who knew, maybe I could help someone?

"Everything okay in there?" Melody said from outside the door.

"Just peachy," I said.

When I came out, I found yesterday's clothes and put them on.

"We going in together?" she said.

I shook my head. "Separate."

Melody frowned, then poked me in the chest.

"What's wrong, don't wanna be seen with me?"

"My car's here," I said. "I need to go right home after work."

She pushed me away and said, "I knew it! You're going back to her!"

"That's where I'm living now," I said.

"I don't know what you see in her," she said. "Ugly and tall, like a big white man with fake boobs. What about me?"

Tara's breasts hadn't looked fake to me.

I shook my head, gave her my two hundred-watt smile and said, "What did I tell you about my marriage before you got mad at me?"

"You said we wouldn't have to worry about her after last week. But then nothing happened."

That was odd. Here we were in *this* week and Tara was still a factor. I'd only arrived on Friday, at the end of the day, with a patient going on about the zoo and his fear of abandonment. So whatever it was Scott wanted to do—file for divorce, kick her out, kick himself out—it hadn't happened.

Momentumis interruptis, as they say in psychology.

"That's why I was mad at you," Melody said, mock pouting, then giggled and squeezed my arm. "You sure scared the hell out of Johnny. Who knew you were such a tough guy?"

"That's me," I said.

What a horrible, horrible, mistake coming here. I actually felt bad, like I'd cheated on Tara. Which I had, in a way, because my ride was her husband. If this got back to Tara, after all the apologizing Scott must have done when he'd gotten caught...

How'd he get caught to begin with?

And then I remembered: Tara said if Melody called the house again she'd call the police. Maybe Melody had spilled the beans, hoping to nudge the relationship to where she thought it should be.

"What did you say to Tara?" I said.

"Huh?"

"When you called the house."

"Which time?" she said.

"*Each* time."

Melody's face grew pinched, like she was about to cry.

"What's wrong?" I said.

"You're still mad at me..."

"Nope," I said. "Totally not mad. So what did you tell her?"

"Fuck you!" she shouted, and moved to push past me.

"Hey," I said, grabbing her hand. "I'm sorry, okay? I just

wanted to—"

"What about me?" she said, wiping her eyes.

"You're right, I'm sorry. We'll talk about it later."

Sniffling and hiccupping, Melody buried her head in my shoulder and hugged me around the middle. I stroked her hair and closed my eyes and pretended she was someone else.

"We're good now, right?" I said to her after she pulled away.

Melody nodded halfheartedly, which was all the heartedly I needed to get dressed, give her a chaste kiss on the cheek, and then get the heck out of there.

It was raining when I left. On the way to the clinic, Tara called me. I pulled over to talk to her.

"Hello?" I said.

"Where have you been?"

"With George," I said. "Jungian Pentangle therapy, remember?"

"Cut the shit," she said. "I looked it up as soon as I got upstairs. There's no such thing."

Tall, pretty, and tech-savvy.

"It's still very new. Cutting edge."

"Don't bother coming home," she said. "Just stay with ... *Go to hell!*"

I pulled back onto the road, seeming to hit every rain-filled pothole and feeling dirtier than the Toledo gutters.

It wasn't my place to speak for the Great Whomever, but whatever Scott had been trying to do, he didn't need my help. If I hadn't shown up, they would have gone to dinner that night. What had Tara said, something about him *wanting to talk*? Maybe Scott had wanted to fix things up, and I needed to call her back now and apologize. Or maybe he'd wanted a divorce and had planned to spring it on her over lobster. If that was the case, no amount of fence mending would help once I was gone. Scott would show up and the train would resume its normal course—except he'd be missing three weeks and freaked out of his mind.

This just wasn't fair.

I tried calling Tara back, but she didn't answer.

"Shit," I said.

When I entered the clinic, I saw Melody had arrived first. She blew me little kisses all the way from the front doors to my office, while Pam frowned at her in disbelief.

I tossed Melody a small wave, then entered my office and shut the door.

Scott's office was warm and muggy. I checked the thermostat, but it was set to seventy-three degrees. When I put my hand over the vent, it was blowing cold dry air. The landlord obviously skimped on the AC over the weekends.

Sexually satisfied and guilty about Tara, I relaxed on the big puffy couch and waited. I wondered what to do about Melody. I'd basically used her, and I was guilty about that, too.

I couldn't go back to her house or make kissy faces at her or whatever she expected. But if I didn't, she had that crazy brother she could sic on me again. Maybe next time he'd have a better wingman than George.

Eventually it got cooler and drier, and around nine thirty there was a knock on the door. When I opened it, I was so happy to see someone other than Pam or Melody or anyone sexy that I almost hugged the balding middle-aged man standing on the other side.

Noting my weird grin, he smiled uncertainly and stepped inside.

I moved toward the comfy chairs and stopped when I saw him heading to Scott's desk.

"Where's the sheet?" he said, looking around.

"Sorry?" I said.

"Come on, Doc, quit clowning."

He started ruffling through papers and opening desk drawers.

Though I was tempted to shout, "How dare you, my good man!" or other appropriate words of outrage, I held back. He seemed like he knew what he was doing.

In retrospect, I should have searched harder for Scott's appointment book. Then at least I'd know who to expect.

"So how you been?" I said.

Whoever-he-was laughed. "You gonna pscho-*anal*-ize me?"

I smiled and spread my hands wide. "That's why they

pay me the big bucks."

"Good on you," he said, still rummaging.

A moment later, he found a clipboard in one of the drawers. He flipped a few pages and wrote something using one of Scott's pens. Then he gazed pointedly at me.

"You gonna sign this or what?" he said.

I went over to see what it was and he handed it to me. It was an attendance sheet with a bunch of signatures on it—a different person's and Scott's, each time, with time-in/time-out boxes next to them. The man had conveniently filled in his boxes: 9:30 a.m. and 10:30 a.m., respectively.

"Well?" he said.

"Sure," I said, and signed Scott's name next to his. I moved to hand it back and he just laughed at me.

"See you in two weeks, Doc," he said, and then left.

THIRTY-ONE

The sheet we'd signed was an official-looking form titled, "PROOF OF ATTENDANCE." At the bottom, in small writing, was the address to a Social Security office on Monroe Street.

I thumbed through the last few filled-out pages on the clipboard and saw entries going back to the beginning of the month. There were about thirty different names, each showing up on the half-hour, Monday through Friday, starting at 9:30 a.m. and lasting an hour each. Signing in could have been a state requirement, for all I knew. I'd only had that movie theater job back in college and the world was a complicated place, especially anything to do with medicine.

It would have been nice to look in Scott's computer at his calendar to see everyone's appointments, but the attendance sheet solved that problem. Mostly. Looking at all the names and times, I noticed there were gaps here and there on various days, and I didn't see my first patient's name anywhere. In fact, his session last Friday had fallen on one of those gaps.

My next patient was either someone named Stephanie Ellis, based on last week's attendance, or Andrew Cope, who'd come at ten thirty two weeks ago. I quickly scanned Andrew's file and learned he suffered from extreme depression with a number of debilitating symptoms: loss of interest in activities, loss of appetite, sleep problems, lack of energy, and thoughts of suicide. Stephanie's was almost exactly the same. Maybe Scott specialized in certain types of patients?

At ten thirty there was a knock on the door.

I opened it to find a tall skinny white guy wearing a Led Zeppelin T-shirt and jeans.

"Andrew?" I said.

"Hi, Dr. Schaefer," he said cheerily, and glided past me on his way to the desk while I stared at him, mystified.

He picked up the clipboard, which I'd left sitting out, signed it, then strolled past me and out the door.

"See ya," he said.

He made his chipper way through the lobby—whistling, even throwing a jolly wave at Pam and Melody on his way out. Awfully upbeat for someone diagnosed with extreme depression.

An hour later, when the next person showed up, I was ready for her.

Monique was a heavyset black woman wearing a skintight halter and neon yellow pants. When she tried to skate by, I blocked the way.

"How you doing, Monique?" I said, staring at her and smiling.

"Uh, hi," she said, looking at me like I was the odd one here and not her.

According to her file, Monique also had sleep problems, loss of interest in activities, loss of appetite, lack of energy, and thoughts of suicide. Maybe it was a Toledo thing.

She moved to scoot past me but I followed along, herding her toward the sofa chairs.

"What are you doing?" she said.

"Just guiding you to your seat."

"I ain't got no seat," she said, stepping back, making to go around me.

As I moved to block her again, Monique did a double fake and slipped past before I could stop her. She ran over to the desk and began searching frantically. She looked hither. She looked thither. She opened all the drawers like my first patient had, but she didn't find what she wanted.

"Looking for something?" I said.

"Where the hell's the sign-in sheet?"

"Sign-in sheet?" I said as if pondering some deep philosophical question that had plagued humanity for ages.

Monique glared at me. "What the hell's going on?"

"Please have a seat, Monique."

To my surprise, she walked over to one of the sofa chairs and sat down. She didn't lean back. She sat on the edge of the chair, staring at me anxiously.

"Why you doing this?" she said.

"Doing what?"

"You know, *this*. Thought we had it all settled."

"All what settled?"

"You know…"

Monique sat glaring at me and fidgeting. She glanced from me to the desk to the door and back again. She seemed perfectly normal, just agitated. Not listless or depressed.

I remembered that other patient, last Friday, when I'd first arrived. Will Dingle. He'd seemed genuinely in need of help. But these others? It was almost as if…

"You're gonna piss me off, you don't hurry up," she growled. "I got things to do today."

"Things to do?" I said, pursing my lips and scratching my chin in my best Sigmund Freud. "How does that make you feel?"

Monique stared at me like I'd insulted her. Then she got up and walked to the desk, yelling, "Where the hell is it?" and "I don't know what game you're playing!" and "Talking to me like I'm crazy!"

I'd hidden the clipboard behind the curtains, propped against the window.

"Aren't you here for therapy?" I said helpfully, a study in sincerity.

Monique laughed. "Therapy? Me?"

She laughed again. Oh, the absurdity.

"Then why are you here?" I said.

Monique stared at me for half a minute, not saying anything. Then her eyes widened and a look of fear swept over her.

"I'm not feeling good right now!" she shouted. Not so much to me but to the entire room. "That's why I'm going home!"

Then, peering around at every little thing like something was hiding from her, Monique walked briskly to the door, opened it, and left.

I spun around, giggling and hugging myself. I wasn't here to fix anyone's love life. Scott's crime was now obvious. The Great Whomever had put the right guy on the job, and that guy was me, and *this* was the job. Monique and Andrew, and probably every name on those sheets, were scamming the system. Either a disability program or something for people with debilitating mental disorders. They had to show up or lose their assistance, and that's where Scott came in—he got a full roster of patients every day and all that government money, and he didn't even have to work.

I went over to the desk and examined his computer— sleek and modern. I wished I could log in to see what was on it. Probably state of the art video games, or maybe he was working on a zillion-dollar novel. Definitely something other than work, otherwise he'd get bored sitting here for hours every day with nothing to do.

As if on cue, there came a soft knock on the door.

"Come in," I said.

Melody slipped into the room, closed the door, and locked the doorknob. Then she bounced over and threw me backward into Scott's desk chair. Straddling my hips, she started making out with me.

That's right, *with* me.

* * *

Several shameful minutes passed and then Melody climbed off of me, panting from exertion and adjusting her skirt back around her legs.

I wasn't panting, having barely exerted. I also wasn't very happy with myself. Maybe I was having an identity crisis, or my ego had beat up my existential id.

"Pam's gonna give me so much shit," she said, giggling, and bounced over to the door to leave.

"Uh, hey, wait a minute. Before you go."

Melody spun around on the balls of her feet like a ballerina, smiled prettily, and bounced back.

"My computer," I said, pointing at it. "I can't get in. Is there something I'm supposed to do?"

Melody made a cute little pouty face and poked me in the belly.

"You forgot your password," she said.

"I guess I did."

"I'll call ArcaTech and tell them to reset it. They should call you pretty quickly." She leaned in and walked her fingers up my chest. "Bet your ugly wife doesn't fuck you like I do."

She gave me a final kiss, then left.

Yeah. She was sort of awful.

Fifteen minutes later someone knocked. When I opened it, Alex Mitchel walked in, smiling and happy to see me. I handed him the form. He signed it and then left, cured of his afflictions, and I hadn't even graduated college.

Over on my desk, the phone rang.

I went over, picked it up and said, "Hello?"

A man said, "Password reset?"

"I think so."

"What happens when you try to log in?"

"It says password incorrect."

There was a brief moment of silence on the other end.

"Okay," he said. "That means you ... Never mind. Your new password is *password123*. Try that, then change your password."

I entered it and got a new screen that let me change it.

"Thanks," I said.

"Sure," he said, and hung up.

With that settled, I sat down to have a look around Scott's computer.

THIRTY-TWO

At first I was happy to learn about Scott's little scam, but now I was confused. Put simply, it wasn't a big deal. He was stealing from the government. Depending on who you asked, that might even have been a good thing. It was still stealing, sure, but the Great Whomever was usually pickier in the *whoms* he sent me after. Who next, someone driving thirty-five in a school zone? Serial jaywalkers? Kids sneaking into R-rated movies?

Or was this about Melody?

She was something, all right. Pretty, young, athletic, and morally stunted. An adulterer, just like Scott. Bad, I supposed, but way down on the priority list of the things I gave a damn about.

I logged into Scott's computer. There weren't any obvious game icons, and I felt a momentary pang of disappointment. I thought about that ride when I'd played World of Warcraft for three weeks. Sheer bliss.

Instead of bliss, there were eight folders on the desktop, all named for various women: Beth, Teresa, Michelle, Alicia, Tammy, Melody, Carol, and Aimee.

I opened Melody's folder and found about fifty or sixty pictures in it—of her, posing naked in her messy room, and some of the shots were explicitly X-rated. There were video files, too, but I didn't bother looking at them.

I backed out of that folder and clicked into Teresa's. No pictures this time, just movie files, each of them named by date.

I clicked one of the files from February of that year and it opened to four angles in Scott's office, all focused on the couch. One of them was a close-up on one specific location of the couch. About thirty seconds later, a woman sat down on it and Scott joined her.

"How's my naughty girl?" he said.

Teresa forced a joyless laugh. "I guess I'm fine."

"And naughty," he said.

Strange as it was hearing Scott's voice on the tape, it got weirder. They began kissing. Then they took off their clothes. One thing led to another, and then I got to see what Scott's vision of love was from four different angles. At one point, Teresa went off script and scooted over to the left side of the couch, but Scott guided her gently back to the spot in front of the close-up camera. Things got noisy and anatomical at that point, and that's where I stopped the video.

The other folders were filled with movie files, just like Teresa's, but I didn't watch any of them. Not my thing. Scott had graduated from being a cheat to definitely twisted rather quickly. Which meant Melody could go on home wrecking in safety for the rest of her life.

I opened a browser and scrolled through Scott's bookmarks. Porn sites, and lots of them. So that's what he did every day instead of writing zillion-dollar novels. I checked his browsing history and saw he had a free email account. When I went there the site got pushy and asked for a password, so I gave up and closed the browser.

I walked over to the couch and looked around. Three of the cameras had to be in those tall bookshelves he had around the room. But that close-up shot of the couch...

Taped underneath the small table between the couch and the sofa chairs, I found a tiny black camera. I left it there and checked out the bookcases and found better cameras aiming down from the top shelves, each one lodged between a couple of heavy books.

A quick check of Scott's phone showed it was almost one

thirty. I'd been here four hours and the walls were closing in on me a little. I was also starving.

When I stepped out of the office, the only person at the front desk was Pam. She ignored me—pointedly.

I walked past the desk over to the other side of the big room. I'd spied some vending machines there on my way in. After inserting a five into the slot, I chose a package of Pop-Tarts. Then I loaded the change back in and got some cookies. Then again and got a package of little orange peanut butter crackers.

Off to the side, next to the sink, was a big and beautiful coffee pot filled all the way up. There was a stack of paper cups next to it, but they were too tiny for my coffee needs. I checked the little cabinet above the sink and found an actual coffee mug, which I cleaned out and then filled to the brim. I reached for the non-dairy creamer and—

"Hi, Dr. Schaefer!" a loud voice said behind me.

I was so startled I seized up and spilled coffee everywhere.

"Oh, jeez, I'm sorry," the woman said.

She grabbed a bunch of paper towels and started cleaning up the counter and the floor.

"No problem," I said. "You scared me, is all."

She was very young—about nineteen or twenty—with long blond hair and fair skin. She had a wonderful smile, and when she stared into my eyes it was as if we were sharing a very special and important connection. And let me tell you something—we weren't.

"Thanks again," I said, and raised my cup to her.

I headed back to Scott's office. When I got there, something made me glance back—causing the girl to collide with me and making me spill more coffee.

"Sorry again, Dr. Schaefer," she said, smiling and shrugging and bobbing her head and biting her lip and giggling all in the span of about two seconds. Any two of which would have rendered her merely a cute kid, respectful of her elders. Sometimes less is more.

"No problem," I said.

She followed me into the office and I closed the door. She didn't ask where the attendance sheet was or go looking for it on my desk or get irate like Monique. She went over and sat down in one of the soft chairs without being asked to. Not the couch, thank goodness. After seeing Scott's other girlfriends or prostitutes or whatever they were, what it needed was a good cleaning.

The girl sat with her hands folded, smiling at me like I was the most important person in the world.

"Right," I said and sat down across from her.

She wore a knee-length skirt, white blouse, black flats, and red-and-white striped knee socks. Her long hair was pulled back in a ponytail. No braces, no lollipop.

"So how have you been?" I said.

"Just great, Dr. Schaefer. I worked on asserting myself on Saturday. My brother wanted me to come over for dinner at six, and I suggested six thirty. He agreed!"

I nodded. Impressive stuff.

"What did you have for dinner?" I said, and then popped a peanut butter cracker into my mouth.

As an afterthought, I offered her one. She accepted.

"Let's see," she said, looking at the ceiling and biting her lip. "Peas. Mashed potatoes. Chicken. And I drank water. My brother had the same thing, except he had his dinner with soda. I think it was Pepsi, but I'm not sure. My sister-in-law had water."

"Did you have dessert?"

"Yes!"

"My favorite meal," I said. She was sunny and upbeat, if a little weird. "What kind of dessert?"

"Ice cream."

"I love ice cream," I said, smiling. "What did you do after dessert? Movies, games?"

"I cleaned the house, of course."

"Huh?"

The girl put the whole cracker in her mouth and started chewing—then began violently coughing up cracker dust.

I ran over to the drawer with the water bottles and brought one back. She tried apologizing while opening the bottle but all she did was cough more. Finally, she took a sip. Her face was red from choking and she kept wiping her eyes.

"Thanks..." she said and coughed again. "...the water."

"No problem," I said. "Just take your time. Don't want people thinking all my patients are crackers, do you?"

She just nodded, coughing a little more and wiping her eyes.

I opened my mouth to ask why she'd been cleaning her brother's house on a Saturday night when she suddenly checked her watch, stood up straight, and said, "Oh no!"

Then she rushed over to the couch, pulled her skirt up over her waist, and lay back.

THIRTY-THREE

For a brief, disheartening moment, the needs of my inner college kid struggled against the demands of my outer grownup, and then I turned my head.

"Hey, listen," I said.

"Yes, Dr. Schaefer?"

"Can you do me a favor and say your name for me?"

"Beth," she said. Helpful, compliant, blonde, pretty, ready...

Shut up, inner college kid!

"Beth, we're gonna do something different today. If you can, uh ... pull those, that is, your skirt. Pull it back up ... uh, I mean, down? Please?"

"Is something wrong?" she said.

A quick glance revealed the first frown I'd seen from her that day.

"Just do what I said, okay?"

"What did I *do?*" Beth said loudly.

She shook her head and bawled at the top of her lungs, her skirt still hiked up around her waist. Then, pounding the fluffy couch, she got *louder*, frightening in her intensity.

"Beth!" I shouted, to get her attention. "Come on. Get up and fix your skirt. It's okay, I promise you're not in trouble."

Beth stood up and let her skirt drop back. She was still crying, though more quietly. She wouldn't look at me. She stood there ashamed, staring down and a little to the right, with her hands stiffly by her sides. She seemed like she needed a hug. Just not by me.

The door to Scott's office flew open and Pam poked her head in.

"What's going on in here?" she said, her gaze sweeping from me to Beth, who stood sniffling and hiccupping and refusing to make eye-contact with anyone.

"What do you want?" I said.

"I thought I heard..."

"I'm with a patient—get the hell out!"

Beth flinched at my tone.

Pam threw me a poisonous look and shut the door.

An angry red haze swept over me—at Scott, at Melody, and at Pam. I was even angry at this poor, screwed-up girl for making me feel like the real Scott, if only for a moment. And then I was mad at myself, Dan, for thinking she'd had anything to do with my failings.

"How did you get here today?" I said.

"M-my mother b-brought me."

"How old are you?"

"N-nineteen," she said, glancing at me and back down again.

"I want you to relax, okay?"

Beth nodded and sat back down.

I went over to Scott's desk and got his cell phone, then asked Beth, "What's your mom's phone number?"

Dutifully, Beth rattled it off. She seemed to perk up at the opportunity to help out.

I entered the number and waited.

Moments later, a woman answered. "Hello?"

"This is Dr. Schaefer. Beth's therapist."

"Oh hello, Scott. How lovely of you to call."

"There's been a development with your daughter," I said. "I was hoping you could come by and discuss it with me."

"Oh dear, what is it?"

"I'd rather discuss it in person, if that's okay."

"Oh, well I ... certainly," she said. "I'll come over right now."

"Thank you," I said, and hung up.

Over on the couch, Beth sat watching me, a small, hopeful smile teasing around the edges of her mouth.

"Maybe come sit over here," I said, and pointed to one of the chairs.

Nodding, her smile back in full bloom, Beth got up and switched seats.

Man I hated Scott. I hated being in his horrible body. I never liked any of my rides, except maybe Nate. The truth was, I didn't want any more of those rides, either. Why mess up a good person's life? Give me a normal bad guy any day of the week, preferably someone who liked to rob banks or beat people up. Easy slam dunk stuff.

On the next half-hour mark, while we were waiting for Beth's mom to show, there came a knock on the door. When I opened it, the woman in the first video I'd seen was there. She wasn't like my ever helpful and smiling Beth. She didn't seem unhappy either. Kind of in the middle.

"Teresa," I said. "How are you?"

She shrugged. "You know."

"Hey," I said, "we have to cancel our session today. Developments. Ok?"

She peered over my shoulder at Beth sitting in the chair watching us. Beth offered a small wave.

"Developments?" Teresa said, then barked a cynical laugh. "Good for her. Just sign the form for me, will you? Don't forget, either, or no more nookie for you."

Before I could reply, Teresa turned and walked out with her head tilted a little to the side, almost like nothing was wrong. Maybe for her nothing was.

About fifteen minutes later there came another knock. When I answered it, a woman was there, late forties, with a low cut top, thigh-high skirt, stiletto pumps, and a shiny gold handbag. She wore a silver crucifix sinfully close to her yawning cleavage. Her hair was teased, primped, colored, highlighted, curled, straightened, swished, whooshed, wrapped, and strategically all over the place. Lots of makeup, too, and her lip-gloss made her mouth look like strawberry jelly.

"Beth's mom?" I said.

"It's been too long," she said, breathing out heavily and smelling faintly of alcohol. "What seems to be the trouble?"

"Please come in," I said.

When she walked past, I saw she had an angel tattoo on one shoulder and a devil on the other. I escorted her to Scott's desk and offered her a seat, which she accepted with a demure smile.

Beth came over and sat next to her mother. I took my seat across from them.

Beth's mom said, "Dr. Schaefer, what's all this about?"

"Ma'am, I'm not sure how to begin."

"You used to call me Joan."

I took a deep breath and folded my hands in my lap. The poor woman. What a mess. She'd sent her child to a place of healing and gotten the exact opposite.

"Joan," I said. "I'll just say it. I've been having sex with your daughter. Here in my office, whenever she comes in for treatment."

Just barely, I held off saying I'm sorry. The real Scott wouldn't be sorry, and I wasn't trying to get him off the hook.

Joan looked at me without expression, then at Beth. "What did you do?"

"I'm sorry," Beth said quietly, leaning away.

Joan raised her hand to strike her and Beth flinched.

"Hey, stop!" I said. "What are you doing? She didn't do anything. I'm trying to tell you, it was me."

"I told her to do everything you wanted," Joan said, sighing theatrically, her face a mask of disappointment. "I'll straighten her out, Dr. Schaefer, don't you worry. She'll be back here in no time and ready to please, I promise."

Next to her, Beth was crying again. This time more quietly—staring ahead, looking at nothing while big fat tears ran down her sad confused face.

"Hold on," I said. "You knew about this? What we were doing?"

Joan laughed like we were old friends sharing an inside joke.

"Dr. Schaefer, please. She's a little small, granted, but she's got that nice hair. But maybe you want a fuller-figured woman. I don't normally go for red-headed men, but you've grown on me since we first met."

The moment stretched between us—her looking at me and me looking back.

Beth was a troubling case. I'd seen a lot of messed-up people on my rides, but never anyone like her before. She spoke eloquently enough, used multi-syllabic words. And her inflection was that of an adult. What's more, she was a physically mature woman. But there was something about her ... the way she looked at me, hanging on my every word and doing her best to keep from getting in trouble. Like a ten-year-old inside a nineteen-year-old's body.

"Beth?" I said.

"Yes, Dr. Schaefer?"

"Your mom and I are going to play a game," I said. "You like games?"

Beth laughed a high, happy laugh. "Boy do I."

"Okay," I said. "Do me a favor and go over to that couch and lay down. Don't look up, no matter what. Cover your ears with your fingers and hum until I tap you on the shoulder. It might be a while, so you need to have patience. Can you do that?"

"All the way over there?" she said, her smile wavering.

"Yep, just lie down, close your eyes and put your fingers in your ears. And don't forget to hum."

Beth nodded, got up, and went over to the couch. Then she lay down, put her fingers in her ears, and hummed tunelessly. Across from me, Joan licked her jelly lips in an expression of overripe seduction. I got up and walked around the desk. I noted her legs had parted slightly, and she was breathing more heavily.

"I might actually like this," she said, looking me up and down through lidded eyes.

"Me too," I said, and punched her dead in the jaw as hard as I could.

Beth's mom yelped and fell out of her chair. I took the opportunity to kick her in the stomach, then her back, and then one more time in the back for good measure. She gasped on the carpet, trying to breathe. I reached down, grabbed that snake's nest haircut of hers and pulled her back into the chair. Then I went to the nearest bookcase, took down a video camera, and returned to my seat.

After figuring out how to make it record, I'd positioned it toward the desk so I could confess my crimes and get Scott arrested. Now it was a completely different kind of confession.

Joan sat there staring at me in shock with her hand on her jaw. Her makeup was smudged from where she'd landed on the carpet, and her upper lip was swelling by the second.

"That's your confession," I said, and tossed the camera on the desk. "Mine too."

"What do you want?" she hissed. "Money? I don't have any. That's why the little twit's here. We need the money."

Ignoring her, I said, "If you ever do this again, sell her out like this to someone, I'll do more than just hit you. I'll cut out your ugly black heart and make you eat it. I'm sure it tastes like shit. Nod if you understand. *I said nod!*"

Joan jerked her head up and down.

Over on the couch, Beth was humming away.

I needed to do something about Joan, but I worried what would happen to Beth. When the state found out what was going on, who would take care of her? She'd be easy prey for other opportunists.

And then there was Tara. I wondered if I could soften Tara's heartbreak from when the truth finally came out. Maybe if I confessed to her first, before I went to the cops?

Confess ... confession. Yeah, okay.

A sliver of hope, but I'd take it.

"Take your daughter and go," I said.

Casting me a quick, scared look, Joan went over and pulled on her humming daughter's arm to get her up.

"Bye, Dr. Schaefer!" Beth said happily, stumbling after her mom.

"Shut up," Joan said, and hurried her out the door.

* * *

It was only three thirty, and doubtless I had more patients. My guess was Scott kept a few legitimate cases for appearances—like Will Dingle, with his fear of talking birds, or anyone like Beth who came his way. The rest, I figured, were just scammers.

I left the office and shut the door, then walked to the front desk. Pam and Melody were both there. Melody was smiling at me and Pam was pretending to read a novel.

"Pam," I said. "Anyone who comes in, tell them I'm sick."

Pam looked up from her novel, which I noticed was upside down, and stared at me like I had to be joking.

"I'm not your secretary, asshole!"

Ignoring her, Melody said, "Oh honey, what's wrong?"

"You and I are through," I said. "Tara's a thousand times the woman you'll ever be. Tell your brother if he has something to say about it, I'll be here tomorrow waiting for him, regular hours."

Then I strolled out of there feeling good about myself for the first time since stepping into Scott's life.

THIRTY-FOUR

When I got to the house, the garage door opened for me and the house key still worked. The doorjamb was still chewed-up, but I'd worry about it later.

I felt famished. Pop-Tarts and little orange crackers weren't doing it for me, so I made myself a sandwich.

Tara came down from upstairs, folded her arms and said, "I want a divorce."

If I acted like I wanted one too, that might hurt her. If I acted like I didn't, maybe she'd worry I'd cause problems and wouldn't sign the papers or whatever. Or worse, she'd feel relief that Scott wanted to fix the relationship. It wasn't fixable, but there was no way I could tell her that. If she ever learned of those recordings, she'd be crushed.

"Yeah," I said.

"What's that's supposed to mean?"

"We should get a divorce," I said.

Tara wiped her cheek.

"What about the house?" she said. "I ... we can't live here together. And you're not staying here while I'm stuck at my mom's. I deserve better."

"I'll move out," I said. "You stay here until we sell it."

Tara was quiet for a time. "You'll be with her."

If I said yes, that'd seal the decision, give it permanence. I shook my head and said, "I'll get a room somewhere inexpensive."

Tara nodded.

"Good," she said, then turned and went back upstairs.

* * *

With all the sadness I'd seen in the last few hours, I decided it was time to get back to my roots. Dan Jenkins liked fun. Dan Jenkins hated evil moms who exploited their kids for money, and that's why I went online looking for a Borders Bookstore somewhere in Toledo, because I'd never seen anyone evil in a bookstore even once.

Imagine my surprise: Borders had gone out of business.

It was like when I'd found out about 9/11 a month after it happened, except way less important.

I searched for another large bookstore and found one on Secor Road. It'd do in a pinch, and things were pinchy as hell at the moment.

After entering the store and experiencing that first rush of excitement—like anything was possible—I went hunting for something good to read. And by that I mean I went through the Fantasy and Science Fiction section and picked up books with cool covers and eyeball-scanned the pages, one by one. The memories wouldn't crystalize until after I was back in the Great Wherever, but that was fine. In fact, that was the point—I'd have stuff to read.

Just like a camera, I made sure to capture every word without getting my thumbs or fingers in the way. I could do about a page a second, a book per five to six minutes on average. Starting with my favorite authors first, I scanned anything new they had, then moved to the folks I'd never heard of before.

A lot had changed since my last ride. Young adult books were overflowing in their own section, and werewolves were suddenly cool again. Vampires too. I made sure to scan a bunch of *Twilight* books to see what all the fuss was about.

"Sir, what are you doing?" a woman's voice said from my right.

"Checking for mistakes."

"Pardon?" she said.

A quick glance showed she was an employee, mid-twenties, with pink hair and a face like an angel. There's something about bookstores that attracts girls with pink hair and faces like angels.

Still flipping pages, I said, "If I find a book with no spelling errors, I usually buy it. You don't expect me to buy a defective book, do you?"

She made a brushing aside motion and said, "We've had complaints. You can't just, you know, go through all the books like that. You could rip a page or something."

I finished the last page of the third book in the *Twilight* series before putting it back on the shelf. Then I turned and gave her my full attention.

"What if I find a spelling error when I get home? Can I get a refund?"

In a suffering tone, she said, "You're worried about *spelling* errors?"

I nodded. "Your website said you give refunds for defective books."

I'd never been to their website, and I doubted she had either.

Rolling her pretty eyes she said, "Refunds are for torn pages and stuff, not spelling ... this is ridiculous, just browse normally, okay?"

I picked an old favorite off the shelf and handed it to her.

"Page 256, there's a typo. Third paragraph down, the author wrote *the the* when he clearly meant to have just one *the*." I frowned and shook my head sadly. "To think I almost bought that thing."

I put my faith in the cheapness of publishers that it hadn't been fixed in five years.

The employee—Ashley, her name tag read—opened the book and thumbed through it. When she found the line, she sighed.

"Is that your big trick? Get a bunch of attention and then fool someone into thinking you're Rain Man? What's the scam?"

"No scam," I said. "Pick a random page and read a line."

For the first time, the skeptical smirk faded from her bookstore-girl face. She pursed her lips, then opened the book and read a line out loud.

"Now what, Rain Man?"

Also out loud, I read from memory from where she'd left off.

Ashley studied me with a puzzled expression, blinked in surprise, then quietly read along with me. I kept it up for two pages before picking another book off the shelf—a really thick one, *Battlefield Earth,* by L. Ron Hubbard—and handed it to her.

"Do your worst," I said.

Ashley laughed like a little girl and read another line chosen from near the back. I followed with the rest of the page and three more after that. The whole time, I watched her lips mouthing the words as she read along with me. It was like we were in tune or something. I'd think something, say it, and she'd say it at the same time. It was the closest to simpatico I'd ever been with a pink-haired woman before.

At some point I noticed we'd attracted a small crowd of mostly young people. One of them started clapping. I got another book and handed it to him, then picked up two more books I'd read before and handed them out, making it all seem random.

"Go on and read something," I said to the teenage boy.

"Anywhere?" he said.

I nodded.

He read a line and I took it from there. With every new book, I'd keep reading while putting the previous one away. That was the hard part, doing two things at once. Even harder, finding and picking new books without breaking stride.

Five minutes later, the crowd had grown to about fifteen people, each of them looking at me with expressions of admiration or shock. Then, about two minutes later, an older woman stepped through the spectators, breaching the respectful barrier they'd formed around me. Another bookstore employee, though without colored hair.

"Hel*lo*?" she said in a singsong voice. "What's going *on* here?"

Though ostensibly friendly, she glanced from Ashley to

me with an expression of thinly veiled disapproval, the set of her jaw threatening to suck the fun and joy from the atmosphere. Where Ashley had on jeans and a cool t-shirt, this woman had on less trendy, more professional, attire. Her name tag read: "Linda." And underneath that, in thick bold lettering: "Manager."

Ashley quickly told Linda what was going on. There were still four books out, so I took them back and put them away. I didn't want to get Ashley in trouble.

"Sorry, Linda," I said. "Just having a little literary fun."

Linda glanced down at her name tag and then back at me.

"Fun's *fine*," she said, smiling tightly, her thin lips threatening to crack a tooth. "But Ashley has work to do, *and* we're not supposed to have more than three people in any of the aisles at a *time*. Fire code regulations, I'm *sure* you understand."

Oh how I wish I'd read a fire code even once in my life. I would have shown her. Total nonsense, of course. Fire codes only cared about occupancy or obstructed fire exits, not people packing the aisles and enjoying themselves. She was just mad someone was having fun without her permission.

"You're right," I said. "Fun's over folks! Brun-Linda wants you to spread out, one per aisle. Make sure you don't mess up and start any fires—especially you Ashley. You're a scorcher."

Ashley covered her mouth with her hand, but I saw she was smiling behind it. Probably wasn't used to hearing stuff like that from older men with red hair and super memories. Or maybe she heard stuff like that all the time and that's how she always reacted. I almost asked her about it, but—

"You will *not* talk to my employees that way," Linda said with a look of triumph in her eyes. Now she had a reason to get rid of me that didn't involve fabricated fire codes. "Sir, I think you need to go now."

"Well, if you're only thinking about it..."

"I'm *asking* you to leave," she said.

"Well, if you're only asking me..."

"Sir," she said, "I'm *ordering* you off the premises!"

Laughing, I said, "But I'm not *selling* me off the premises."

"Get out of my store!" she shouted.

"I can throw myself out fine, thank you," I said, heading toward the front.

Linda paced me the entire way, her face fused in a granite-like grimace.

"Look, quick, moral turpitude!" I said and pointed at a young couple standing near the New Releases holding hands in a fire lane.

"Just keep going," Linda said, marching along behind me.

Still going, I said, "So, how much do you bench? Two fifty? Were you ever in Nam? Do you sometimes wear an eye patch and raid other bookstores?"

"What?" she said.

When I got outside, the manager glared at me from behind the glass doors. A few seconds later, Ashley joined her and waved sadly.

Smiling, I dipped low into a mocking bow and then left.

THIRTY-FIVE

The problem, I decided, was that the Great Wherever was incredibly boring—like living in one of those sensory deprivation things for weeks, months, and now years at a time. Assuming the Great Whomever was God, it seemed maybe he could spruce the place up a little, give me a physical body and add a few pinball machines or something. The fact he hadn't done so, after all my begging, was sort of a slap in the face. I mean I'd take anything. If I couldn't have a real body, how about a thought-powered morphine drip so I could zone-out and not be aware anymore?

Popping into a ride like Scott—with food and TV and naked women everywhere—had turned me into the Jenkins equivalent of a drunken sailor.

But that was all over now.

My little showing-off excursion had done wonders for me. I'd gotten in too deep with this crowd of cheating, exploiting, Jeep-driving specimens of humanity, and I needed to step back. I was Dan Jenkins: immortal assassin, fast food aficionado, celibate provocateur of other people's wives and girlfriends. I was aloof. I was the world's greatest loof. Nothing much fazed me, or not for very long, because the world was doomed.

"We're all doomed," Joe said again. He was one of

Scott's legitimate patients, and he had come in Tuesday morning promptly at nine thirty.

"Doomed," I said. "Absolutely."

"Come again?"

"I agree—we're all doomed."

"You're not supposed to say that," he said, blinking at me in confusion.

"Do you want me to lie to you? Ok, we're *not* doomed."

According to Joe's file, he was chronically depressed and had been ever since his wife left him, shortly after their wedding. He had a job as a mechanic, tended to overeat when he was feeling bad, and was frequently lonely. It was like talking with a more talented version of me.

"Doc, come on," Joe said, smiling. "You're supposed to cheer me up, remember?"

"Is that what I do around here?" I said, looking around and blinking.

"Someone's gotta, right?"

"How about you?" I said. "Tell me something cheerful. Perk me up. Drive my doomy feelings away."

Joe made a *huh* sort of laugh, and shook his head. "I'm not a doctor."

"Is Bill Murray a doctor? He always drives my doomy feelings away."

"I'm not Bill Murray, either," he said. "And anyway, how can anyone be happy? My great grandmother died in the Holocaust. Now there's all these wars and mass shootings and everything."

"You're Jewish?" I said.

"Yeah. That okay with you?"

"It's just a little suspicious. A Jewish mechanic?"

Joe laughed. "I know, right? But I like what I do. I'm good at it. Ma won't forgive me for it, either. Says Granny didn't die in the Holocaust so I could wear greasy clothes. Says that's why Clara left me." He shook his head. "You feeling happy yet?"

"A little happy," I said. "Genghis Khan was way worse than Hitler."

Joe made a derisive sound. "You're crazy. Hitler killed six million Jews, tore up Europe and destroyed all kinds of priceless art. Also, no offense, Doc, but you need to watch what you say. People get offended when you go around apologizing for Hitler."

"Who's apologizing?" I said. "Genghis Khan killed anywhere from twenty-five to fifty million people, and the Mongols tortured millions of men, women, and children before killing them."

Joe cocked his head and studied me. "Really? They did all that? What else did they do?"

"There was a city in China called Zhongdu," I said. "Over a million people lived there. The Chinese leaders didn't send help when the Khan was fighting the Khwarezmian Shah in Iran. The Khan wanted revenge, so the Mongols killed everyone in the city. They also killed all the populace outside the city. He left giant mounds of bones all over the landscape. Travelers approaching Zhongdu after the massacre couldn't even use the roads." I smiled. "Go ahead and ask me why."

Joe's expression grew bleak. "Do I really wanna know?"

"No," I said, "you don't."

After a moment's hesitation he said, "Tell me."

"The roads were too slippery," I said.

"With blood, right?"

I shook my head.

"Then what was it?"

"A thick layer of liquefied human fat, covering the ground for miles."

Joe jumped at that, his hands leaping up in front of him as if for protection.

"Eew!" he said.

"That was just one city," I said. "The Mongols sacked ninety-two such cities in China. They did stuff like that everywhere, and not just China."

Joe was shaking his head. "Wow. Makes Hitler look like an amateur. So they tortured all those people?"

I nodded.

"Man," he said. "Where did you learn this stuff? I thought you were just a shrink."

"Nobody's just one thing," I said. "Mostly I read science fiction and fantasy. But a few years back I went through a history phase and started reading anything that looked good. Pretty soon I discovered it all looked good, and I went a little crazy. Let's just say I've read a lot of books. One of them was about Genghis Khan."

What I didn't tell him was how I'd gone to the Library of Congress and wore out their book runners by requesting hundreds of books a day, then eyeball-scanned them like I'd done at the bookstore. Eventually, just like at the bookstore, I was asked to leave. It was worth it. Between that ride and the next I read every one of those books I'd scanned.

"Wow," Joe said. "Kind of makes me feel ignorant. All this time there was a worse guy out there than Hitler."

"Hitler was still pretty bad," I said.

"Human fat," he said shaking his head. "I can't even imagine it. Yuck."

A soft pulsing tone came from the desk. I'd re-enabled the alarm clock Scott used to let patients know their time was up.

"Looks like we're done," Joe said. "If it's okay, can you write down that Mongol book?"

"Sure," I said, and went to write it down.

"Thanks, Doc," he said when I handed it to him. "This was like the best time I ever had here."

"How so?"

Joe shrugged. "I don't know. Just different. I feel pretty good. Can't wait to read that book. Then I can tell Ma how Granny got off lucky. Maybe I'll pick a few more books. If I find something good, I'll let you know."

I nodded noncommittally and said, "Thank you. Take care, Joe."

"You too, Doc."

When my next patient showed up, she tried to take her clothes off. I stopped her and handed her the attendance sheet, then politely told her I didn't do that anymore. She shrugged, neither happy nor unhappy about it, then signed the sheet and left.

* * *

Melody hadn't been at the front desk when I showed up that day, and she wasn't there when I left, around four thirty. Once again, I cancelled any remaining appointments with a jaunty "I'm feeling sick again" thrown over my shoulder at Pam.

Pam shouted back, "I said I'm not your damn secretary!"

As much as I didn't like being hated by her, she was actually on my side without even realizing it. Go Pam.

When I got to the car, a call came from Tara.

"Are you coming straight home?" she said.

"Yes," I said. "I'm leaving soon, as a matter of fact."

"Good. There's a real estate person showing up in ten minutes, and I was hoping you could be here for that."

"I'll be there in thirty minutes," I said. "Can you get all the finance stuff out of the way?"

"Just get here," she said, and hung up.

I went to a doughnut shop I'd found online that morning. That way, Tara could talk about Scott's salary and how much was owed on the house. Also, I wanted some doughnuts, though I'd have to enjoy them without milk. Another reason to hate Scott.

When I got to the shop, I gave the old woman behind the register my order and added I'd pay anything for a lemon-filled doughnut.

"Oh, I'm sorry," she said. "We ran out of those this morning."

I finished my doughnuts before I arrived and hid the bag behind the passenger seat. Otherwise Tara or the real estate agent would wonder why I hadn't brought enough for them.

The first thing I noticed on getting out of the car was a brand new minivan parked on the road outside the house. The other first thing I noticed was the photograph plastered across the side of it.

Of my sister, Jane.

Jane looked like Jane, except more adult now. Great hair, though I couldn't tell what color it was. She was younger than me by two years, which put her at forty. And now she was a real estate agent who happened to work out of Toledo ... and happened to be in the house of a man who happened to be my ride.

I would have paused to consider my options but I didn't have any. Also, when coincidence shows up plastered on the side of a minivan with indeterminate hair color, you do what you're kind-of told—you go inside and deal with it. So that's what I tried to do, except my feet wouldn't move. Also, my hands were sweating. There had to be a reason why she was here. That's how the Great Whomever worked. He put me where I was needed. Did she need me? Was someone trying to kill her, something like that?

"Why?" I said, looking at the sky.

Suddenly, as if answering my question, several cumulus clouds formed together into the face of a wizened old man with a booming voice, and ... all right, no, that didn't happen. Would have been cool, though, and definitely more helpful.

I went inside and found Tara and my sister in the dining room. Together, they turned toward me—the one frowning, the other smiling professionally. I wanted to laugh. This was the same girl who'd spent a whole summer walking around barefoot because *that's what the Indians did.* She used to play in the mud. Now she was all dressed up and acting completely different.

"Hello," she said. "I'm Jane Jenkins."

"Scott," I said.

We shook hands. It took everything in me not to hold on a fraction too long. My sister's hand, after all these years.

Why is she a Jenkins again?

Jane had gotten married when she was nineteen, a few months before my death. We all figured it was a rebellion thing. It was a little weird, too. The groom's family had ponied up the money for a great wedding with a live band, a team of photographers, and a catered reception on a river cruiser. A thirty-one-year-old man marrying a nineteen-year-old girl, but she said she loved him, and Jane always got her way. Nobody thought it would last, and clearly it hadn't. I wondered if they'd had kids.

I checked out her rings, of which there were several. She could have re-married and hadn't changed her last name this time. Plenty of people kept their names for professional reasons, or when their husbands' last names were things like Dickmeister or Fugenheimer.

Jane Fugenheimer...

"Something funny, Mr. Schaefer?" Jane said, smiling curiously. Not at all like the girl who'd purposely burst into tears when Dad walked into the room, and then lie and say I'd hit her. Now she was talking like a grownup.

"Just something I heard on the way in," I said. "On the radio. Those shock jocks, I tell you."

"They are amusing," she said.

Tara glanced from me to Jane and back again.

"We were just going over our situation," Tara said.

"Great," I said. "How do we look?"

Jane whipped out an iPad, something that hadn't existed on my last ride, and began pecking away at it.

"I'm afraid I don't have any good news," she said. "You're upside down on the house. The government has a program for folks in your situation, but with your income, Mr. Schaefer, you don't qualify. So you'll have to come up with the additional fifty thousand at closing." She shook her head sadly. "I'm really sorry."

Tara said, "I was thinking with our savings, and some help from my mom and Scott's dad, we might be able to do it. Or maybe we can just ... you know ... walk away?"

Jane shook her head and said, "That's a really bad idea, Mrs. Schaefer. They'll auction the house off for less than I can get for it and you'll owe that much more. Plus it'll destroy your credit. Talk to your mom, and you, talk to your dad. Also, it's worth a shot to check with the bank. They might be willing to forgive a portion of the money if they thought you were entertaining ideas of walking away." She shrugged. "Worst that happens is they say no."

To think this was the same girl who'd brought a brick to school for show and tell.

Tara studied me and said, "Why are you still smiling?"

"Just keeping a positive outlook on life, that's all."

"Hey, that's right," Jane said. "Mrs. Schaefer tells me you're a psychologist."

Chuckling politely, I said, "I dabble..."

A bit loudly, Tara said, "I *insist* you call me Tara."

For the first time since arriving, Jane's professional face

slipped. She looked in my eyes and appeared momentarily confused—no longer the self-assured real estate agent. And maybe I was imagining it, but for a second it seemed some hidden knowledge passed between us, special and deep and thicker than water.

Jane blinked her eyes and smiled embarrassedly.

"Forgive me," she said. "But ... um, can I come by your office some time? Make an appointment? It's about my mother."

Then, realizing how that sounded, she added, "Not that way. It's just ... well, it's sort of personal, and that's not why I'm here today, I know. I've just been worried about her."

"Not at all," I said, grinning to put her at ease. "If it weren't for families, I'd be broke."

Jane smiled weakly.

Tara was watching me, her head cocked at an arch angle. She glanced at Jane and then back at me again.

This was my chance to throw a monkey wrench into the Great Whomever's plans. He'd set this whole scenario up just to get me alone with my sister for who knew what reason. Whatever it was, I probably wouldn't like it. Also, I was worried. People around Dan Jenkins had a statistically higher chance of getting shot or stabbed than, say, Eliot Jenkins or Marty Jenkins or even Leopold Jenkins. But if Jane was in some kind of trouble, I couldn't just walk away.

"Tell you what," I said. "Why don't you come by tomorrow? Say, nine thirty?"

In a fractionally higher octave than normal, Tara said, "Don't you have a patient then?"

Tomorrow's nine thirty was another in-and-out scammer.

"He cancelled," I said. "Schedule's wide open."

"Well, great," Jane said. "I'll see you then."

I shook her hand again—my flesh and blood—and let her go.

"I guess that's it then," Jane said. "Mrs., um ... sorry. *Tara*. I'll send you both a packet from the agency. It'll have all the information about that government program I mentioned, and tips on how to get your house ready to show when we get to that phase. And thank you so much for having me over."

"Our pleasure," Tara said, visibly relieved we were back to talking about the house again.

Tara walked Jane out.

Jane Jenkins, after all these years.

THIRTY-SIX

It was Wednesday morning, approaching eight thirty, and I was standing in front of St. Stephen's church wearing a backpack. There was nobody around outside, and the place was just as deserted when I walked in.

The confessional, when I found it, was an ornately constructed wooden affair with doors on the front. Looking around the quiet church, I wondered if I'd gotten the time wrong. What a shame that would be. I'd never gone to confession before and thought it might be fun—especially if I told the truth.

As I stood there twisting with uncertainty, one of the doors opened and an old woman with a cane came slowly out. She stumped past without saying hello, her head bowed as if from a lifetime of sins. They must have been doozies, because she didn't look up even once.

Wouldn't want to be her when she dies...

"Just in time," the minister called from the other booth, its door now open.

He stepped back in and closed it.

I entered the booth the old woman had come out of, shut the door, and sat down on the narrow bench. The window between my booth and the minister's was a wooden latticework of tiny roman crosses inside bigger roman crosses.

"Whatever you do," I said, "don't bless me."

"I don't understand," the minister said. "You're supposed to say—"

"Consider that the latest of my many sins, Anthony."

The minister chewed on that briefly, then said, "I'm sorry, Scott, what's this about?"

As fun as it was acting all mysterious and clever, I was too nervous to keep it up.

"It's me," I said. "Dan Jenkins."

And just like that, my seat in the confessional felt like sitting at the bottom of a deep dark well looking up, the walls spinning round and round and making me dizzy. Normally it was something the minister could control, but I'd surprised him.

"You're back," he said.

"We're both back," I said. "What are you doing in those wizard robes way up here in Toledo?"

The minister got up and left the booth.

Just as I worried he'd fled on foot, the door to my booth opened and he said, "Follow me."

I got up and closed the door, then followed him to another part of the church. He reached out and opened a door I hadn't even realized was there, so well did it blend with the textured wall. Kind of like a secret door—my second secret door in five years. Inside was an office with bookshelves and a desk and even a computer.

From a little radio on a shelf came the sound of a morning news program, which he lowered.

The minister sat down and invited me to do the same.

"What about the other sinners?" I said. "Don't they get to confess?"

He checked his watch. "Eight twenty-five. Close enough. So where have you been?"

No chitchat. Didn't ask me how I was doing or who I'd seen on the other side.

"Stuck in the Great Wherever," I said. "For five years."

The minister nodded. "What are you doing with Scott?"

I thought about how to proceed. He was a man, after all. And there were things I needed him to do, but only if he was the right kind of man.

"One second," I said, and got out Scott's laptop, which I'd snagged from work earlier that morning. I set it up on the minister's desk and clicked Beth's folder. There were eighty-three files. I opened the latest one and turned the laptop his way. "Go ahead and click play."

"I hope this isn't what I think it is," he said.

"All hope abandon, ye who enter here."

The minister frowned, then reached over and clicked.

I didn't need to watch to tell what was going on. Beth sitting down in front of that close-up camera and Scott sitting beside her. He told her how naughty she was and she disagreed vehemently, playing into his hands and not even realizing it. My hands were hurting, and then I remembered to unclench them. When Scott started groaning the minister slammed the laptop shut, crossed himself, and said a quick prayer.

He glared at me, his face livid—and the world turned upside down and sideways on me. Unbalanced, I fell out of my chair, overcome with that smell you get from a punch in the nose.

"Are you all right?" came the minister's voice, as if from far away.

"I'm not Scott," I said, and got up carefully. "You gotta ... wow ... remember. That was a big one."

I'd had a lot of kicks in my time, but what the minister had done was simply stunning. Like getting two kicks at once from two directions. I'd thought he had to touch me to cause the full-on kick, but righteous fury seemed to work, too.

I sat back down.

"I read that in your story," he said, shaking his head. "Hard to believe, if I hadn't felt it myself. Right here." He pointed at his face. "A jolt, like a punch."

Fascinating. The *minister* had been kicked. An intriguing development, and scary. Maybe he could get kicked out? And maybe something else could slip in?

"What's your name?" I said, warily.

"Why?" he said.

A dangerous ten seconds passed and then he said, "Anthony. Why?" Then his eyes widened in understanding.

"Oh ... *well*. Very interesting. I think we should tread carefully."

"You're the one with the super powers," I said.

"Never mind that—tell me about the video."

I gave him the bare bones of the story: Joan, Beth, the scam with his perfectly healthy patients coming in and out and signing their names. He listened carefully without interrupting.

When I finished he said, "How can I help?"

From my backpack, I took out the video camera and laid it down next to the laptop. I'd checked it before coming in. Both the visual and audio quality of the recording were excellent.

"This," I said, "has Beth's mom admitting to giving her daughter to Scott, and me admitting my part. I also hit her and expressed remorse. That's the part that worries me."

"You *hit* her?"

"I've been hitting a lot of people lately."

The minister shook his head. "What's this about remorse?"

"If I'm on camera expressing remorse..."

"Ah, yes, I see," he said. "You've helped Scott's case."

"Right. I'm remorseful, and Scott can maybe twist that into something to reduce his sentence, then let Joan take most of the blame." I frowned. "Only he's *not* getting off the hook, is he?"

The world felt stretched and narrow again, like I was at the bottom of a deep pit.

The minister said, "I cannot let you harm Scott Schaefer. He's under my protection. You still have enough to convict, so we do it the legal way. This way, nobody gets killed again."

He was still sore about Nate's evil fiancée.

"One second," I said, and opened the laptop.

"I've seen enough already."

"No you haven't," I said, and turned the computer back around so he could see. "Look at the filenames."

After a brief hesitation, he said, "So?"

"*Read* the filenames."

The minister sighed patiently and did as I asked—and

then his superpowers kicked-in again, making me dizzy. Unlike last time, he squelched the effect before it got too bad.

"Twice a month for three years," I said.

"She can't be more than twenty," he said, shaking his head slowly.

"She's nineteen. Which puts her at sixteen when he started on her. And you want the law to handle this?"

The minister grew quiet.

It was getting close to nine, and I needed to get to the office.

"That summer you sent me your story," he said, "I decided to quit the wedding business and get a job somewhere. Maybe an office building, managing a different sort of folk. Years before, I'd abandoned the church for a more personal relationship with the Almighty and an open mind. Then, after spending my whole life searching for the truth, along comes Dan Jenkins, a somewhat tiresome fool enjoying the most personal relationship with God I'd heard of in two millennia. And what did he do with it?"

"You tell me."

The minister smiled patiently. "Anything he wanted to."

Despite my being here to help Beth, in his typical negative way the minister had turned this around so I was somehow to blame for his problems. I'd trade him my so-called personal relationship any day for his lavish office with the neat secret door and all those people looking up to him. He even got to hear the confessions of sinful old ladies. And all those church bake sales...

"Keep the laptop and the recorder," I said. "Do whatever you can to help Beth. Also, take this." I handed him one of Jane's business cards. "That's my sister. For some reason, she lives up here, just like you live up here. I'd appreciate if you contacted Nate and had him buy Tara's house—for way more than the asking price. He can afford it, and he owes me big time. Tara's a good woman, married to a snake, and she could use some good fortune."

The minister nodded and said, "I'll see what I can do. Anything else?"

"Just a question—why are you in Toledo?"

The minister smiled. Then he laughed. He wasn't a big one for laughing and I found it jarring.

"I contacted a friend of mine and mentioned I wanted to come back. There was an opening here for a Parochial Vicar, so I took it."

"What's a Parochial Vicar?" I said.

"Associate priest. Mostly the same duties as the pastor, except it's harder for me to get to Heaven."

What the ... but that doesn't...

I pointed at him and said, "Almost had me there. Who knew you were funny?"

The minister shrugged.

"But why are you *here*?" I said. "In the same place as me? It can't be a coincidence."

He nodded. "I'm inclined to agree with you. For some reason, your Great Whomever—who may be God, though I have an altogether different theory—has thrown us together again. For now, the best we can do is pray for guidance and see where that takes us."

He was an awfully cool cat when it came to divine intervention.

"So what's this theory of yours?" I said. "Because I've been thinking he's not God, either."

The minister shook his head. "Not yet. Call me when you're ready. Did you get that email I sent? The one with my phone number?"

"Yeah," I said, turning to go.

"Good," he said. "One more thing: if you harm Scott, other than sending his sorry ass to jail, whatever understanding we've had is over."

I glanced back and said, "So that's how it is, now."

The minister smiled in a way that seemed both kindly and dangerous at the same time.

"You bet."

THIRTY-SEVEN

It was after nine and I needed to move if I didn't want to miss seeing Jane. As I approached my car, I flinched at the screeching of tires. When I turned around, Melody's brother jumped out of his silver sports car, baseball bat in hand.

"Don't got no gun *now*, asshole!" Johnny yelled, and moved toward me. Probably to teach me a lesson, or show me who was boss, or fix my little red wagon.

I pulled out the gun Tara had given me and pointed it at him.

He yelped and hit the deck, eyes wide with terror, bat raised to block any bullets I shot at him.

"Don't shoot, man!" he yelled. "What the fuck?"

Lowering the gun, I looked around for witnesses, but the parking lot was empty.

"What the hell's wrong with you?" I said.

"With me?" he said. "What about you? What you did to my sister. That shit's whack, yo."

"Now what did I do?"

"You hit her, that's what. Nobody hits my sister."

"Have you *seen* your sister?"

"Course I ... why?"

I laughed. "Johnny, what your sister and I ... Whatever she's been telling you, you shouldn't believe it."

"She said you punched her where it wouldn't leave a bruise."

"Come on, Johnny. She's bigger than me." I pulled back my shirtsleeve to show my upper arm. "I mean look at me."

To emphasize the point, I flexed one of Scott's flimsy psychologist muscles.

"See that?" I said. "Like a little white soda straw, with freckles."

Shaking his head, Johnny said, "You could have threatened her with that gun."

He loved his sister. It wasn't his fault she was a woman scorned.

"I didn't start carrying it," I said, "until you and your buddy George jumped me. I'm a psychologist, not a gangster—we don't carry guns. All I did was break up with her. Just a guess, but how many men have broken up with Melody that you know about? I bet you can't name one." I could see him thinking about it. "Now, how many men have stalked her over the years?"

Johnny glanced at me, then he looked away, then back at me, then away again, then at his bat, then up in the air, then back at me again. He started to say something, but then he stopped. Then he opened his mouth again and said, "Shit."

He stood up.

"She did it *again*," he said. "Like high school all over again. Dude, I'm sorry. This one's my bad, not yours."

Despite the loaded weapon in my hand, he walked over like everything was okay now and took me in a crushing bro-to-bro hug. Then the strange brotherly moment was over and he stepped back.

"Sorry again, man," he said, laughing ruefully.

I needed to get to my appointment.

"No worries," I said. "Take care, Johnny. I'm in a hurry, so..."

"Go ahead, man, it's cool. Thanks for not shooting me."

I threw him a thumbs-up and jumped in the car.

* * *

Jane was coming out of the clinic entrance when I got there.

"Hey, hold up," I said. "You'll never believe it, but I got held up by a crazy guy with a bat. Then we hugged."

Jane blinked at me and smiled. Then she laughed. It was her fake laugh, the one she used with all her friends when they were pretending to be grownups. Her friends almost universally hated me, except for one of them—a pretty brunette named Darcy, who was never nice to me in public.

"I was about to call and suggest a reschedule," she said. A soft rebuke.

"No need," I said. "Let's go."

I held the door like a gentleman, and she went in first.

Melody glared at me from across the room, her face pinched and angry. Pam pretended to read her book.

Jane said, "I really appreciate you seeing me on such short notice."

"Happy to help," I said, and casually flipped Melody the bird behind my back.

Behind the desk, Pam gasped.

When we were both inside, I escorted Jane over to the cushy chairs and said, "One second."

From Scott's desk, I grabbed a straight-backed chair, a pen, and the sign-in sheet. I set the chair outside the door and put the clipboard and pen there in an unmistakable gesture of trust. Then I shut the door.

"Is it always this muggy in here?" Jane said, rubbing her arms.

Same old critical Jane, getting everyone defensive and worrying about her.

"Only in the morning," I said. "Would you like some tea? I was about to pour myself some coffee."

Jane threw me a curious look. "What makes you think I don't drink coffee?"

"Jane, please," I said, smiling enigmatically. "I *am* a psychologist, after all. Let me guess ... no sugar, right? Two bags?"

"That's right..."

"Give me a minute."

I unlocked the door and left the room, then skirted the desk with Pam and Melody, both pointedly ignoring me. I poured coffee for myself and brought back a cup of hot water and two tea bags for Jane.

"So, Jane," I said, after the caffeine drinks were arranged to our mutually professional satisfaction. "Did you grow up here in Toledo?"

Jane glanced quickly at her watch like she didn't want me to notice, except she really did. She was a busy real estate agent. Places to go, people to sell places to.

"No," she said. "Just outside of Allentown. Mom's still there, same house I grew up in. She's actually why I'm here, so…"

"She's why you're here in Toledo? Or why you're here in my office?"

Jane laughed her trendy laugh again.

"I'm sorry," she said. "I mean here in Toledo. After Daddy died, Mom got even more messed up than before. My boyfriend's from here and … it sounds bad, I know, but I had to get away from her." She shrugged. "So I moved."

Jane folded her arms briefly and then lowered them. She'd done everything she could to look like someone else, even dying her hair thirty different shades. But in the ways that mattered—how she paused for breath, where her eyes roamed when she talked, the speed she moved her head, the things she did with her hands—all of these were classic Jane.

I said, "Why did you have to get away from your mom?"

"After my brother killed himself—sorry to just spring that on you—she was a broken woman. Weak. She cried all night long and slept all day. Nothing Daddy said helped. That's when the calls started coming."

Jane studied my face for a reaction, but I kept it as blank of emotion as possible. I felt my heart thumping in my chest, and my breathing came quick and shallow. As casually as I could, I slipped my hands under my legs to keep them from trembling.

"What calls?" I said.

"That's the part that actually weirds me out a little," she said. "It goes back to when my brother committed suicide—it's sort of embarrassing."

I smiled thinly. "No worries. You were saying?"

"So the calls—it seemed like every week for a while, then every month, we'd get these calls from people saying they were looking for Suzie, Pete, Mike, Louie, Alex ... you know, just random names, right?"

I nodded.

"The thing is, they all said the same thing: the numbers were so similar. They hit seven when they meant to hit eight."

"It's plausible, right?"

"Maybe," Jane said, biting her lip. "But they were always for different people—and *from* different people. Different voices, anyway. And we got so many calls, at least for the first few years..."

"Maybe it was a prankster," I said. "Faking a different voice every time. Something like that."

She shook her head. "In the end, it doesn't matter who they were—Mom wouldn't change the number. Dad and I gave her hell about it because it was really sort of creepy, coming on the heels of my brother's selfishness and all."

"*What?*" I said, sharply.

Jane flinched. "What?"

"Sorry, you said your brother's selfishness—didn't mean to shout. I was just surprised."

"What do you mean?"

"Your brother. Most people ... that is, you know, when someone commits suicide, you don't..."

Jane laughed. "Don't speak ill of the dead? That kind of thing?"

I nodded.

"Please," she said. "He was a weirdo, and yeah, he was selfish. Killing himself—over a girl." She laughed again. "She wasn't all that, trust me."

Yes, she was.

"Let's go back to your mom," I said. "You said something happened recently?"

Jane nodded. "She got another phone call. Same M.O. Called and said he hit seven instead of eight. Only now Mom's saying he called from up here, in Toledo."

"Probably just a normal wrong number."

"That's what I said! What's it been, like eight years since

the last time?"

Five years, ten months, eleven days...

"So what's the problem?" I said, trying to hide my impatience. "Moms are funny sometimes. That's why they have loving daughters, right? To be there for them."

"*I* was there for her," she said, a trifle haughtily. "Never mind that. Here's the problem: Mom thinks all this has to do with Dan. Sorry, Dan's my—*was*—my brother. She thinks it's his spirit reaching out and messing up everyone's dialing. Can you believe it?"

I grinned and shook my head like it was harmless. No big deal. Moms and their funny ways. One day we'll all look back and laugh.

"It'll pass," I said.

"Nope," Jane said. "She's been like this forever. That's why I finally left—couldn't take the craziness. I needed my own life again after my second divorce—long story, don't ask. Now I have a career, a wonderful new boyfriend, and I'm making good money. We're planning on moving to L.A. to sell houses at an agency I contacted. *Better* money."

I spread my hands wide—crazy mom, second divorce, better money.

"How do I snap her out of this? Medication? You must have seen this kind of stuff before. It's embarrassing, if you ask me. The way she talks about it."

I couldn't help it—I dropped my head in my hands, right there in front of my sister, and a sob burst out of me like a bomb.

Jane said, "What the...?"

My shoulders shook as I cried—for what I'd done to my poor mom and dad with all those stupid, stupid, *stupid* calls. I'd just wanted to hear their voices. Every time, hoping they'd pick up sounding happy. Maybe with a lingering trace of laughter from one of Dad's lame-o jokes.

"Uh, Mr. Schaefer? Is this a part of your therapy, because that's not why..."

I said, "What do you care about?"

"What?" Jane said, shifting uncomfortably. "Pardon?"

With tears streaking down my face, I repeated: "What do you care about?"

"Um, I'm just gonna go now, okay?"

Jane moved to get up but I got there first and pushed her back in the chair. She opened her mouth to scream and I covered it.

I pulled my gun, held it pointed up, and said, "If you scream I'll blow your head off. You got that?"

Jane nodded frantically.

"What do you care about?"

She made a noise and I moved my hand out of the way.

"What?" she said, panting for breath. Crying now, shuddering in fear.

Good.

"I asked what you cared about: your stupid life in L.A or your mother. Which is it?"

Blubbering now, red-faced and splotchy and crying a mewling sound I'd never heard from her before, Jane said, "W-what are you going to do to me? Please don't hurt me. Please, I'll do anything you want. Just don't shoot me. Please!"

She was starting to get loud again, so I shook the gun—being very careful to keep my finger off the trigger and the barrel still pointed up.

"Your mother needs you," I said. "She's all alone in that damn house and you're out here because she had the temerity to *embarrass* you? Because she misses her son? Her husband's dead and now her daughter's gone and she's alone. And you sit there calling her crazy? What the hell happened to you?"

Through her fear, a glimmer of confusion poked through. "Please just let me go. *Please!*"

No, I wasn't about to shoot my sister. The gun had a single round in it, in case I decided to shoot myself. It would fire on the third pull.

I looked down at her and ... and just looked at her. Sitting there crying and sniffling, messing up her makeup and staring at me in terror. To my own sister, I'd done this.

The madness was starting to recede.

"If I let you live," I said, "you gotta promise me something. Think you can do that?"

Desperately, she nodded.

"I'm leaving town in a couple days," I said. "You're gonna call the cops, and—"

Shaking her head, Jane said, "No! I'd never call them, I swear, I wouldn't, I—"

"I *know* you'd never do that," I said, smiling like the friendly guy I was. "But I want you to. Tell them I went to Canada. Don't tell them I'm still here in the city."

Jane nodded. Canada, absolutely.

"Stay where you are for thirty minutes before calling. Got it?"

She nodded again—she'd stay there forever if that's what it took.

"And call your mom after," I said. "You're all she's got left."

Sermon completed, I pocketed the gun and walked out.

THIRTY-EIGHT

The name of Scott's bank was conveniently written down on his credit card.

"Can I get a balance?" I said to the nice lady behind the bulletproof glass.

The Schaefers were sitting on more than eleven thousand in checking and over forty thousand in savings. Scott had turned scamming the government and abusing mentally challenged young girls into a lucrative business.

I didn't want to leave Tara penniless. She was doing the best she could with a real bastard of a husband, so I took out two thousand in a mix of fifties, twenties, and hundreds. Then I got on Route 23 South out of Toledo heading toward Upper Sandusky.

I called the minister at the number he'd put in his email.

"Hello?" he said.

"It's me."

"Yes."

"Don't get all mushy," I said. "Slight change of plans."

I told him what happened at the clinic between me and my sister and left nothing out. Kind of like a confession.

"You've been busy," he said.

"I don't think Jane will sell Scott and Tara's house now. So if you could be there for Tara, after … you know, I'd really appreciate it."

"What do you mean *you know*?" he said. "I warned you—you're forbidden to hurt Scott Schaefer!"

I laughed. Cackled, even. All that anger at my sister, my worry for Mom—all of it spilled out in a string of giddy laughter at this man who thought he knew the mind of God when all he had to do was ask *me*. I'd tell him God was out of his gourd.

"Keep it together, Dan," he said. "Where are you?"

"Just take care of Tara for me. I'd like to get that right."

The minister said, "Tell me where you are. I'll bring you in, we'll figure it out."

I thought about it for a moment.

"I don't know," I said, and hung up.

I didn't want my cell phone pinging off towers and revealing my location, so I shut it off. Also, I didn't want to talk to the minister again, and definitely not Tara.

The minister was a decent guy, beneath all the grumpiness. He wasn't like those bad-apple priests the media gleefully held up as examples of clergy everywhere. He'd use the recordings to save Beth—and it'd kill Tara, the idea she'd married Scott, a sexual predator, a thief, and an all around bad person.

I pounded the steering wheel in rage.

"And you want me to keep coming back here?" I said.

I got off the interstate and filled up the tank. I also bought sodas, water, cookies, chips, and several packages of beef jerky. The less stops to eat the better. But I couldn't drive forever. I knew of a motel chain that used to take people without a credit or debit card, but it had been a long time. Maybe they didn't do that anymore.

I hadn't killed anyone, so the police wouldn't necessarily turn the state upside down looking for me. The interstates were the fastest route to safety, but I couldn't risk a possible APB on Scott's car.

At times like this it's good to know your back roads, and I knew *all* the back roads.

I stayed on 23 until I got to 30, then took that east through farmland, more farmland, and after that more farmland. Between the farmland and the farmland were places like Canton, Wooster, Mansfield, East Rochester, and East Liverpool. I didn't pass through them. Instead, I gassed up when I could and skirted around them on spaghetti-like roads that twisted deeper into the country, ever wary of encroaching suburbs and radar traps and good Samaritans. Not that country folk weren't good Samaritans. They simply had fewer Samaritans per square mile to worry about.

The biggest reason I'd chosen the scenic route had less to do with the police and more to do with me. I needed a break. Never in my wildest imaginings would I have pulled a gun on my sister, nor said such terrible things to her. Sure, her attitude was awful, but her abandonment of our mother was nothing compared to the way I'd abandoned everyone in that little dorm in college. So when I was yelling at her, I was really yelling at myself.

The other thing I needed was a break from Tara, Melody, and her dumb brother Johnny. Having a job, mingling with people—it had sucked me right in. I was like one of those undercover FBI agents who goes so deep he can't tell the good guys from the bad guys anymore. I'd broken one of my biggest rules and had sex with Melody—twice. Then I'd publicly dumped her and insulted her.

In some ways, what I'd done to Tara was the worst. I hadn't just abandoned her—I'd assaulted our real estate agent for no reason and then driven off. And pretty soon I'd be adding *never to be seen again* to the end of that. If I was here to help her fix their marriage I was messing up utterly with every mile I put behind me.

I'd all but consigned myself to killing Scott. Wonder of all, I felt a tiny bit bad about that. He hadn't killed anyone. He'd done a lot of awful things, and I'd probably only scratched the surface. But I wanted him severed from Tara's life completely. It was a selfish decision with an unfair outcome, one I didn't have the right to make, but I was beyond caring about fairness anymore. Killing Scott wasn't eye for an eye—it was more like heart for an eye. Or maybe both lungs for an eye. Something critical to live, certainly...

My mind wandered for a while, pondering the various organs needed to keep someone alive. Then I wondered if

I'd keep coming back long enough for humans to create robots they could transplant their brains into. Would such beings have super strength? Implants in their brains for speaking vast distances, that kind of thing?

After a while, I turned on the radio and hunted for anything old and good and didn't think about much except junk food, heartburn, and what I could see through my windshield. I crossed into Pennsylvania just after 9 p.m., way later than if I'd taken the interstate. The whole time, I hadn't seen a single police cruiser.

There was a motel outside of Pittsburg that used to be fine with cash, and I decided to try my luck.

Scott pulling a gun on someone shouldn't have been big news, but the media might find it interesting. Crazy redheaded psychologist attacking his patients could make for a lively story. He'd be easy to recognize if the authorities circulated a picture. So it was with a distinct feeling of unease that I walked into the motel lobby, trying to act normal while scouring the ceiling for those little black security domes.

They didn't have any domes—they had cameras out in the open behind the desk, pointing at the entrance when I walked in. Unable to avoid them, I didn't bother. It'd just make me look more suspicious walking around covering my face.

A young lady with a tight half shirt was working the desk. She had curly brown hair and dark eyeliner and a silver bracelet with dangling clovers circling one wrist. No name tag.

"I'd like a room," I said.

She clicked around on the computer. "If I can just get a credit card."

"Don't have one," I said. "Don't believe in credit."

"You believe in debit?" she said.

"Debit's even worse. How about cash?"

She clicked some more and made me pay a cash deposit in case I stole the towels, then gave me my room key. She treated me like girls with half-shirts and clover bracelets had treated me my entire pre-suicide life: like I wasn't even there.

For once, I didn't mind.

In the morning, I rolled out and continued my drive, staying on Route 30. With Ohio behind me, I stopped at family-owned restaurants and diners whenever I thought about food, which was often. I made sure not to talk to anyone, and nobody wanted to talk to me.

Again, I didn't mind.

Four hours later, I switched over to PA-222 toward Allentown. Though I should have expected changes, I wasn't prepared for the shock of seeing the area I'd grown up in. Every road sign had familiar names like Dorney Park & Wildwater Kingdom, and the Allentown Art Museum. Signs I'd seen hundreds of times coming and going on family trips. I wondered what Coca-Cola Park was, and marveled how so many trees had been swapped out for buildings.

But when I pulled into our old neighborhood, except for new fences and a marquis with the neighborhood name spelled out in fancy writing, the place looked pretty much the same.

After finding our street, I parked the car in the roundabout next to the same field I used to build forts in and got out.

Home again.

THIRTY-NINE

Ours was a small townhouse in a row of three, and when I lived there we had dense shrubbery under the windows, neatly trimmed. The shrubs were still there, but they weren't neatly trimmed anymore. The powder blue paint didn't look half as bright as it had when I'd lived there, and the gutter up near the right side was sagging down and pulling away from the roof.

If I'd known things were in such disrepair I would have sent money. Except for the occasional wrong number, I'd been too afraid to look in on them. Too ashamed.

"Just leave," I said to myself for the hundredth time since fleeing Toledo.

I didn't leave. I stood in the yard looking first at my old house and then at my friend Miles's house. The Horners had probably moved on long ago. And Miles ... where was he now? Where was anyone I'd ever known?

I glanced at the spot beneath the window and saw the built-in flower holders had been taken out. Back then, all the houses had them, but looking around the courtyard I saw they were all gone. They'd been little more than boxes turned upside down so you could put flowerpots on them, but they'd added a nice aesthetic.

Behind me, a door opened.

In the summer, large wasps' nests grew underneath the

boxes, tucked into the corners, which made it scary getting in and out the front door. Everyone in the neighborhood came and went through the back to get to the communal garages, so most folks probably didn't even notice the wasps. Just us kids, coming out to play.

"Are you looking for someone?" a voice said.

If I turned around I'd start crying and freak her out, so I kept looking at Miles's house.

I nodded, afraid to speak.

"I know everyone around here," she said. "Who are you looking for?"

I'd thought about this moment countless times over the years. Always with me walking in and telling my parents and sister stuff only the real Dan Jenkins would know: long dead pet's names, teacher's names, favorite movies and songs, the food we ate on different days of the week, how the kid next door used to stand in the window pressed against the screen, and how one day he fell out and landed in a lawn chair. I'd tell them how Dad worked part time as a handyman in the neighborhood and was always on someone's roof after a big storm. So many stories, so incredibly specific they'd have to believe me.

I folded my arms so she wouldn't see my shaking hands, then turned around.

Mom's face was more deeply lined than I remembered, but still her in all the ways that mattered. Her hair was light brown and glossy with blond highlights, and no gray. She didn't look like an old woman, hadn't crossed that indefinable line. I liked that she'd styled it and kept it colored. Her eyes were intelligent and alert, and she was standing in the front yard talking to me, a man she didn't know.

"I used to live in this neighborhood," I said. "A long time ago. There was a kid who lived in that house over there." I pointed at it. "Miles Horner."

An almost imperceptible tenseness in her bearing seemed to fade. She smiled comfortably.

"The Horners moved away a long time ago," she said. "How old are you?"

Back then, everyone played with everyone, and she'd

wonder why she never saw Scott playing with Miles and her son.

"Thirty-five," I said. "I didn't usually play with the big kids, but I remember them all."

Mom nodded. "So you must remember my son, Daniel."

I didn't want her asking lots of questions about me, so I scratched my head and paused in reflection.

"He was sort of my hero," I said, fondly. "Everyone called him 'Dan the Man.' "

Mom laughed and said, "I don't remember that part, but he liked being called Dan, yes. What school did you go to?"

"St. Thomas More," I said. Because no way would Dan the Man have associated with a preppy private school kid.

"You still have family here?"

"No," I said. "They're all gone. Dad took a job somewhere, so..."

The wind seemed to pick up. Mom rubbed her arms, though it wasn't cold.

"Uh, I suppose I better go now," I said.

Mom smiled like it was okay I needed to go and said, "It's nice you came back to see the neighborhood. It's too quiet around here. Smaller families now, and everyone stays inside."

I nodded, mouth shut, and turned to leave.

"Would you like to come in for coffee? Tea?"

I should have smiled, thanked her, and left. But I made the mistake of looking into her eyes. Then, just like with my sister back at Tara and Scott's house, something familiar seemed to pass between us. A subliminal, resonating thought, connecting us and yet eluding comprehension.

Mom's eyes were wise and her half smile inscrutable. Waiting.

I went to say no thank you and take my leave, but messed up and blurted, "That sounds great."

She nodded like that made perfect sense—a stranger coming into her house for a tea or coffee—and headed to the house.

Though my common sense screamed *leave*, I followed her through the same front door I'd banged out of at high speeds so many times before.

The living room, with the stairs going up on the left, looked very different. I recognized two photos on the walls, and one of the lamps. The furniture was different, and she had a newer model television. Hardwood floors had replaced beige carpeting, and she'd painted the kitchen a pleasant sunflower yellow. New cabinets, too. And there were way more plants than I remembered as a kid.

"Nice plants," I said, following her into the living room.

"Thank you, I like them too. Having something to take care of is good for a person. Would you prefer tea? Coffee? Something else?"

"Don't be put out," I said. "Whatever you're having is fine."

"Coffee it is."

While she was in the kitchen, I sat on the couch and quietly freaked out.

This was absolute madness. I needed to get up and apologize and say I was late for something, be real nice about it *but get out of there*. Nothing good could come from this. She'd say something, I'd say something, she'd say something back, and then I'd pull a gun on her.

No, I'd never do that—I'd left the gun in the car.

Mom popped in and said, "Do you take cream? Sugar?"

"No cream, no sugar, and thanks."

The Harrises used to live on the other side of the parking garage. One time, Mom and Mrs. Harris were out there talking. Acting like an adult, I'd come up to them drinking a cup of coffee I'd made without permission—my first cup ever. Mrs. Harris told Mom what I was drinking, and Mom took it and dumped it down the sink. It wasn't for kids, she'd said.

When Mom came out, she placed my coffee on a small table and sat down across from me in a red wingback chair.

"I noticed your gutter's sagging," I said, ever helpful.

Mom laughed. "Paul was supposed to fix that. I just … I'll get to it eventually. Maybe when it falls off."

"That makes sense," I auto-responded.

"Don't you want to know who Paul is?"

"Yes," I said. "Please."

She took a sip of her coffee and then said, "He's my husband. He died four years ago."

"I'm sorry," I said.

I also took a sip. Instant coffee. It tasted exactly the same way it had that day with Mrs. Harris.

"Paul took care of the plumbing and electricity and anything involving tools. I took care of the kids, paid the bills, cooked the dinners. We were old-fashioned, but we didn't know it."

For a while, neither of us talked. She'd glance at me, I'd smile and take a sip. Uncomfortable for me, but she seemed at ease. Nothing much perturbed her in the old days, either.

"Miles Horner," she said. "That was a long time ago."

I nodded.

"So where do you live now?" she said. "I'm sorry, I don't even know your name. I'm Cheryl Jenkins."

She held out her hand.

I shook my mother's hand, and I didn't want to let it go ever again.

"Frank," I said, letting it go.

"Where you from, Frank?"

"These days I'm from everywhere. I'm a salesman. Where I lay my hat is my home."

"I don't see your hat."

I smiled. "Left it at home."

"You're joking with me," she said. "My son used to say stuff like that. All the time. And if I could go back and change things, I would have laughed at every joke. Now it's too late."

We were quiet, and then I realized I hadn't asked why it was too late. I opened my mouth to say something—

"So you know about my son, then," she said. "That he died."

I could have denied it, but I didn't. I sat there with my cup of coffee staring at her—my grieving mother—after all this time. Her eyes welled with tears, her hands shook, and her face reddened with emotion.

"I had the strangest phone call the other day," she said, "from a man in Toledo, where my twice divorced daughter moved to sell houses to people who can't afford them. You know what happened then?"

I shook my head.

"That man came to my house. He's sitting here *right now*."

I didn't ask what she was talking about. I couldn't. All I could do was stare into her eyes, imploring her to forgive me.

"What is this about?" she said. "I deserve to know!"

And because I wanted to help but didn't know how, I said, "Your husband's dead, but his soul lives on."

She blinked at me. "What?"

"Your son too."

I put my cup down and stood.

"Where do you get off saying that?" she said, standing up too. "Why are you here? What's this really about? Did Jane put you up to this?"

And just like that, as deep as I'd dug myself and as low as I'd dragged my mother down with me, I saw a light in the distance, the promised land, the perfect turnkey solution for the worry I'd caused her.

I hung my head down, shook it guiltily like I'd been found out, and said, "I'm sorry. I tried, ma'am, but I can't lie to a nice lady like you. I'm Jane's psychologist. She told me about your situation and I felt bad about it. I thought maybe if I visited you, I could help. Clearly I've made things worse." I sighed—a sad, weary sigh. "All these years, Jane's felt guilty about Dan's death. She always blamed herself. Told me if she'd only treated him with more respect, maybe he wouldn't have done it." I sighed a very sad, very weary sigh again. "Grief does terrible things to a person."

Mom blinked in surprise and then barked a laugh. "She said all that?"

"I'm afraid so."

"My Jane is seeing a psychologist? She wouldn't even go to marriage counseling. I never would have imagined ... not in a million years. But wait a minute—what was all that stuff about the Horners?"

I shrugged. "Jane talks about them all the time.

Apparently she had a crush on Miles and never got over it." She'd hated Miles, totally didn't have a crush on him, but whatever. "I was caught off guard. Felt I needed to say something."

Mom frowned. "You could have tried the truth, you know. You could have told me all this over the phone." She seemed a little angry, though not yet upset—which for Mom was an actual distinction. Not quite in the doghouse, but maybe sleeping on the floor.

"She told me to say it was a wrong number," I said. "That it would mean something to you."

Mom's mouth tightened and then she nodded, once.

I got out Scott's wallet, took out a thousand in hundreds and handed it to her.

"Jane paid me to come out here and talk to you about your husband. Grief counseling. But I didn't actually help, did I? I don't feel right taking her money, and you have those gutters that need fixing, so..."

Mom pushed the money away and smiled. "It's lovely that she cared enough to send you." She shook her head. "Wow, she must be doing better up there than I thought. Well good. But I'm doing fine, really." She patted me on the hand. "You keep the money. I'll get those old gutters fixed soon, on my own, don't you worry about it."

"If you're sure..."

She folded her hands over mine and closed them over the cash. I sat there with my head bowed, unable to look her in the eyes, willing myself not to cry.

I put the money away and went to the door. I opened it, crossed the threshold, and turned around.

Mom laughed and said, "You know, it's funny. Your eyes ... when you thought I was mad at you. For a moment there, I..."

"A moment what?"

"I thought ... Oh, but you'll laugh."

"I love to laugh," I said.

She gazed into my eyes as if searching for something.

"Yes?" I said.

Mom smiled and said, "It was very nice to meet you, Frank."

"You too," I said, and reached to shake her hand.

Ignoring my hand, Mom leaned over and kissed me on my left cheek.

"What was that for?" I said, blinking in surprise.

"That was for *Frank*, the psychologist," she said. Then she kissed my other cheek. "And that's for who you might have been."

Then Mom stepped back and slowly shut the door.

FORTY

I took the corner and passed a man walking his dog. I wished him a happy day and continued to the roundabout where I'd parked.

It was sort of funny how Mom thought Jane was in therapy. Sweet revenge, served cold. I'd finally gotten Jane back for all those times Dad put me in charge and she'd pretended like I wasn't.

"Not too bad," I said, trying to force myself to feel good about what I'd done.

I could still feel my mother's kiss on my cheek—the one for who I might have been. Now all I wanted to do was cry like a son who missed his mom. And when I got in the car, that's exactly what I did.

It didn't matter if she learned I was Scott Schaefer—not Frank—and that Scott was a monster who preyed on his patients. Mortal monsters she could deal with. Odd as it sounded, a crazy, gun-toting psychologist driving hundreds of miles to comfort a grieving widow was just the thing to take her mind off Dad.

When Jane called the cops and said I'd pulled a gun on her, she'd have to relate my rambling about abandoning people and selfishness and all that. Tara might think Scott, wracked with remorse, had gone off the deep end. For her, a *crazy* cheating husband had to be way better than a smart, successful cheating husband who didn't think she was good enough. Didn't it?

Of course, there was always the chance Mom would go on for the rest of her life never learning the truth about Scott. For all I knew, Jane hadn't even called the cops. Maybe she'd left Scott's office in fear and hadn't said anything to anyone.

The sky was the limit, and the skies were clear everywhere I looked.

* * *

The next day, I returned to Ohio using the interstates. Having done what I'd set out to do, I was no longer afraid of getting caught by the fuzz.

The more I thought about it, the more I doubted Jane had reported me at all. From her perspective, she couldn't prove what I'd done in Scott's office. She would have wanted to win, to be right, to not have a crazy guy with a gun get off for lack of evidence. Likely she was already packed and trying to get out of town with her dumb boyfriend as fast as she could.

Testing the theory, I stayed in Columbus for two days and used Scott's credit card. I saw the sights and thought about my dad. I thought about Mom and how strong she was, and how she deserved better children than what she'd gotten.

Mom's parting words followed me wherever I went.

And that's for who you might have been.

What was I supposed to make of that? Jane said Mom thought all those wrong numbers I'd made were a sign, like I was contacting my family from beyond.

I remembered the day after my great grandmother's funeral. We were walking down a switchback road in the mountains where Granny Jenkins lived, enjoying the walk down to the river one last time, when a sparrow came down and landed five feet away. We were in the country, not the city, but that little bird hopped around and pecked like it was a bread-eating city bird. It got closer and closer, and nobody moved for fear of scaring it. When I looked at Mom to see what she thought of the strange little bird, her cheeks were wet with tears.

"It's Granny, it's Granny," she said, over and over.

At the time, I couldn't understand how Granny could be a bird now. Mom was too upset to ask, and nobody else was saying anything, so I stayed quiet and forgot about it for a long time. But yeah, Mom had a superstitious streak. And where it concerned me, at least, she was right.

From Columbus, I drove to Sandusky—to the greatest amusement park of all time. After waiting thirty minutes in a maddeningly long line at Cedar Point, I finally got to the ticketing booth.

"Can I get a Fast Lane pass?" I said.

Some kids behind me had been talking about the intriguing things nonstop since getting in line. Apparently, if you had one, you could get on rides quicker.

"Fast Lane passes are limited to availability," the girl behind the inch-thick safety glass said.

As an experienced amusement park veteran, I knew never to lose patience with the staff. They didn't get paid much. They dealt with pushy people all day, and their only joy in life was tormenting the masses by being as useless as they could possibly be—all with a scientifically calibrated passive aggressiveness. You could never actually pinpoint where the line was and whether they'd crossed it. It was almost art. But I was tired of being in line, art confused me, and I wanted to play Whack-a-Mole.

"Let me put it this way," I said, weighing my words carefully. "Are there any Fast Lane passes available?"

Her eyes narrowed fractionally. "Go to the Fast Lane kiosk when you enter the park. Thank you, sir. Just the one ticket, sir?" This last with a possibly judgmental glance at the empty space behind me.

"Just the one," I said, and handed her Scott's credit card. "Where is the Fast Lane kiosk?"

Blandly, without inflection, she played her trump card: "The Fast Lane kiosk is on the left-hand side when you enter the park ... sir."

I paid her over sixty dollars, after the taxes and fees, and entered the park. When I got to the kiosk, it was closed. Taped to the window was a sign saying they were out of Fast Lane passes.

My usual strategy at amusement parks is to do all the so-called boring stuff early, while everyone else waits forever in the lines for the cool stuff. Then at the end of the day, after all the corporate picnics and tour groups have left, I ride the roller coasters as many times as I want—at night, with everything lit up, flying through the darkness in my clickity-clanking chariot in the sky.

Keeping to the strategy, I tried a few of the tamer rides at first, marveling that even *those* lines were long. So I made the most of it and eavesdropped on the conversations around me, sometimes even joining them. It was easy—being in an amusement park line was like this great communal consciousness. As one, we hated the park for being greedy and letting too many people in. We hated the signs saying not to sit on the rails, the heat, and the kids who rushed around and switched spots with their friends when they got to the front. We hated getting to the top of a tall, twisty, scaffolding only to look across to a different ride and seeing *that* line was short.

After an hour and a half, with only bumper cars and this spinning octopus thing to show for my time, I abandoned the long lines and simply walked around.

Being at an amusement park is a great place to witness the best and worst of humanity at leisure: children begging, parents sitting on benches by ride exits or dragging crying children behind them from place to place. Everyone eating. Good, bad, and *really* bad tattoos everywhere I looked. Young men carrying around oversized stuffed animals. Girls with too much makeup. Bare chubby bellies with bellybutton rings. Teenagers racing through the crowds. Security everywhere. Cameras everywhere. The mingled smell of fried food and cotton candy. *Amazing* ice cream cones. Every color of flip-flops and sandals, and smoking in the designated areas.

At one point I saw a fistfight between two women in bikinis. They were grabbing and pulling each other's hair out and screaming at each other.

Watching the fight with the grinning crowd, it seemed we'd reached the pinnacle of our collective tension, bursting through to something as close to nirvana on Earth as a group could come.

When I got tired of walking, I passed the afternoon playing carney games. I spent two hundred dollars flipping pennies onto plates, dropping tiny hoops onto bottle-tops, dropping softballs into vertically tilted boxes, and climbing ladders over this bouncy airbag to push a button at the far side before flipping over. At one point I won an enormous stuffed gorilla, which I gave to a little girl. It was funny watching how happy she was under the withering glares of her parents, who had to carry the thing around the park for the rest of the day. Other than that, I passed on all the prizes.

With dusk approaching, I quit the carney games for what I really cared about—the roller coasters. Because that's what Cedar Point is best known for. They had sixteen of them, and I got on as many as I could, starting with the big ones: the Blue Streak, the Corkscrew, the Gatekeeper, the Magnum XL-200, the Mantis, and the Iron Dragon. I rode them all and I had a blast.

But I'd saved one very special roller coaster for last.

A half-hour before the park closed, I walked quickly through the vacant maze of guide ropes to the front of the line. When I got there, a cartoon character with the measuring stick said I had to be *at least* fifty-two inches tall to ride it, which I most definitely was.

The Top Thrill Dragster is a seventeen second ride. It zooms from zero to a hundred and twenty miles an hour in four seconds, sending the rider over a four hundred foot-high hump before returning back to the launch platform.

There was a kid about sixteen or seventeen years old who got in beside me, in the last cars, despite plenty of open seats at the front. I respected him for it. Anyone who knows anything about roller coasters knows the back is the best because of all the extra bumping and whipping around. Also, you're guaranteed to have a consistently fast ride from the very highest point of a hump down to the bottom. Basic physics.

"You ever ride this before?" I said to him as we waited for the staff to come by and check the safety arms and seatbelts.

"Tons," he said, making it sound like he was bored.

"You're not scared at all?" I said. "Not even a little?"

He laughed. "Nope. I even raise my hands in the air."

I'd seen this kid raise his hands in the air five times in a row before I decided to get on.

"You actually do that?" I said. "Put your hands up?"

"All the time. You should try it."

"Is it safe?"

"Totally," he said, with a superior smirk. "But don't do it right out the gate—wait for it. Your hands fly back faster."

"Okay," I said. "If you're sure..."

When the visibly tired and overworked staff finished testing the restraints, one of them gave a halfhearted thumbs-up to the guy in the control booth. The control guy did something and we pulled slowly out of the station in pursuit of the perfect ride—then we *blasted* down the track and into the sky.

My head snapped back against the headrest. Against all common sense, I raised my hands in the air and thought they'd fly off from the force of the wind and the acceleration—it was awesome.

Earlier, from down on the ground, I'd noticed it took five seconds for the coaster to traverse the hump completely. That one section at the top was the slowest part of the otherwise speedy ride.

When those employees had checked the safety bar, I'd been propping it back an extra four inches with my knee while leaning forward with my chest puffed out. Very painful, when they'd tugged it, but nobody noticed the extra inches of space I'd stolen.

The coaster slowed down and we crested the top. This was where I'd planned to leap to my death. With the lingering momentum from the ride up, it would have been so easy to slip out from under the bar and push off yelling, *Why did I listen to you...?*

Instead, I curled up around the safety bar and held on for the terrifying ride back to the station, cursing myself for a fool.

* * *

On the way out of the park, I saw that employee from

earlier today—the ticket booth Nazi. She was walking hand-in-hand with a boy her age, over to a table with about ten other employees, all laughing and talking and having fun.

I took a folded piece of paper from my pocket and reread the suicide note I'd penned:

Dear Tara,

I wasn't a good husband. I was a cheat and a liar, and I didn't deserve you. Deep down, I was very unhappy. I knew what I did was wrong, but I couldn't stop and I hated myself.

You're a beautiful, special person. I'll always love you, and I hope that one day you can forgive me.

Scott was a bastard, and no doubt about it. But he deserved his natural fate, and Tara did too.

I crumpled up the note and disposed of it in the proper container, to be recycled for later.

EPILOGUE

The rest of my ride as Scott Schaefer passed uneventfully. I stopped using my credit card and stayed in cheap hotels that still took cash. I watched TV, read some fun books, and eventually found a lemon filled doughnut.

When my third kick came, I called the minister and found out he'd given the laptop and camera to the police. Beth's mom and boyfriend had been arrested, and the cops were actively looking for Scott.

I was happily surprised to learn Nate had come to Toledo. He'd donated a hefty amount to the church to help both Tara and Beth with any financial difficulties they'd have in the days ahead. What a great guy.

My next ride came fairly quickly. About a week later, in fact.

I was in Arizona, in the body of a man who liked to smuggle people into the country. Only, when they got here, he'd raise the fee on them and make examples of the ones who couldn't pay.

I'd shown up right when my ride's partner was about to shoot an old man, but I killed the gunman instead.

After dropping off my load of smuggled people, I took the money they paid me and got a hotel. The next day, I contacted a tour company and flew for several hours in an actual hot air balloon. Later that week, I signed up for a motorized tour through the desert, and then visited a Frank Lloyd Wright house called Taliesin West.

Talk about easy rides.

Near the end, about three weeks later, I dialed my mother's house in Allentown. When she picked up, I quickly apologized. Wrong number, I told her. Off by a single digit.

She said that was quite all right.

I thanked her for being so understanding.

She said it was an easy mistake. It could happen to anyone.

ABOUT THE AUTHOR

John L. Monk lives in Virginia, USA, with his wife, Dorothy. A writer with a degree in cultural anthropology, he moonlights as a systems administrator by day and Honey-do consultant on the weekends.

Made in the USA
Middletown, DE
09 September 2021